HANNAFORD PREP

Just Drop Out

Also by J Bree

The Mounts Bay Saga

The Butcher Duet

The Butcher of the Bay: Part I

The Butcher of the Bay: Part II

Hannaford Prep

Just Drop Out: Hannaford Prep Year One

Make Your Move: Hannaford Prep Year Two

Play the Game: Hannaford Prep Year Three

To the End: Hannaford Prep Year Four

Make My Move: Alternate POV of Year Two

The Queen Crow Trilogy

All Hail

The Ruthless

Queen Crow

The Unseen MC

Angel Unseen

HANNAFORD PREP

J BREE

Just Drop Out
Hannaford Prep #1

Cover Design by Cover It! Designs
Edited & Proofread by Samantha Whitney
Interior Formatting by Wild Elegance Formatting

Just Drop Out/J Bree – 2nd ed.
ISBN-13 - 978-1-923072-06-0

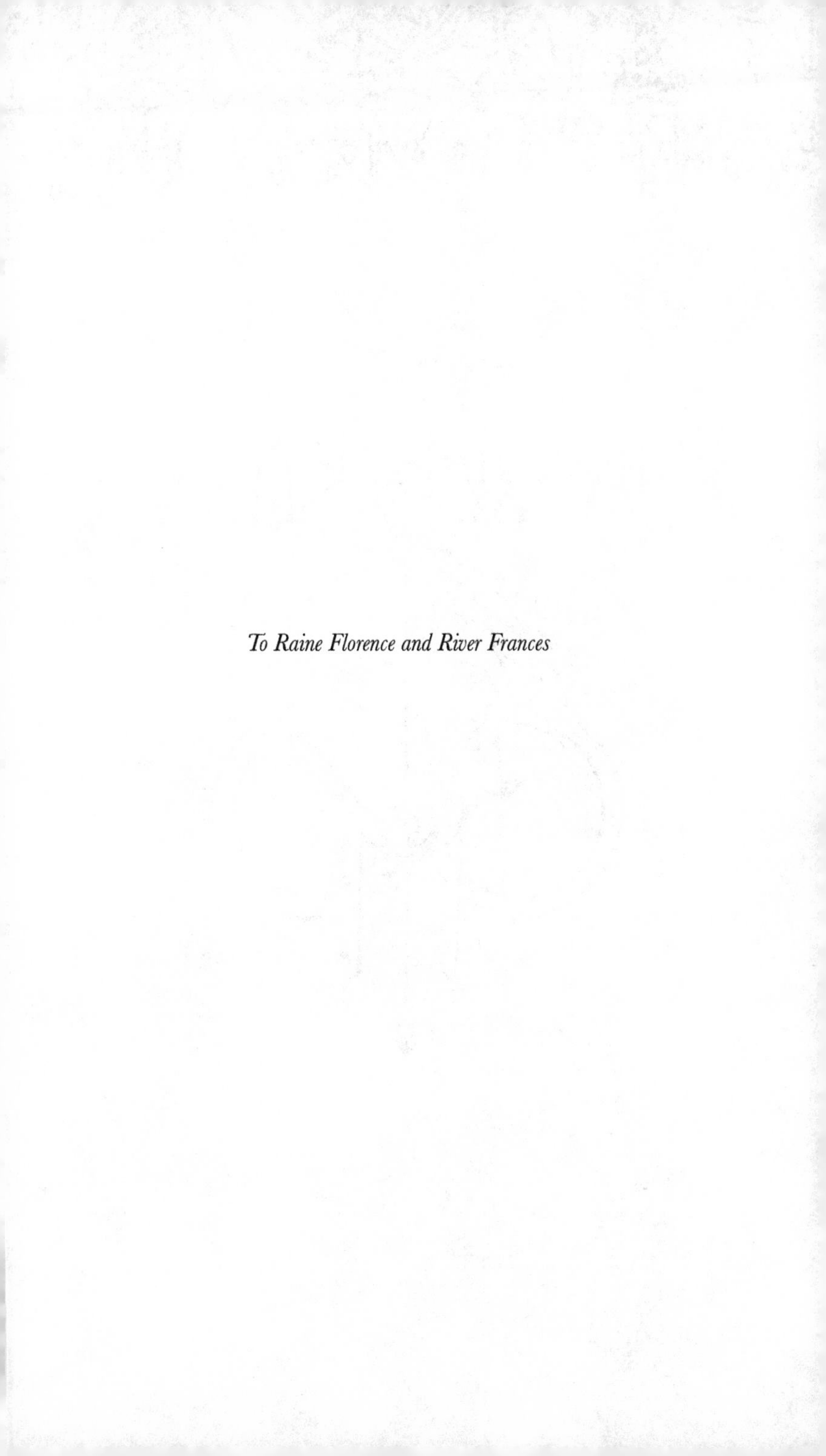

To Raine Florence and River Frances

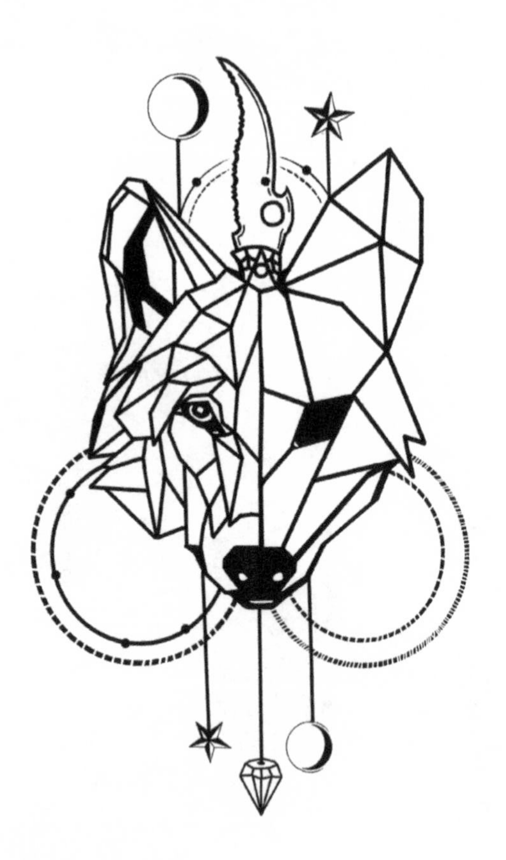

Prologue

The forest at the edge of Mounts Bay, California, city limits are well known for being haunted.

The kids at the local high school have spent generations whispering about the bodies buried in shallow graves, waiting for the wolves to scent them and dig them up for food. There're even more legends about the souls that walk amongst the towering redwoods. It's quiet, not silent, but compared to the ever-present sounds of traffic and human experience, it's eerie and adds to the haunted feel.

While I don't believe in ghosts, I can feel the souls that linger here.

It's probably just my guilty conscious giving me the heebie-jeebies as I look over the corpse of my opponent. His blood is still fresh on my hands, cold and congealed, and I wipe them uselessly down my jeans. My clothes are just as stained as my hands, even my face is spattered with the red stains of his life ending. I look like something out of a horror movie, which is about right considering I've just bashed a man's skull in with a rock while a whole crowd of people looked on in sick fascination. There isn't a person watching that dares to make a noise. The vise-like grip of the Club holds their tongues.

I'm not afraid of being caught.

I'm small for my age. Years of food insecurity have taken their toll, and I was the youngest contender in the Game this season. None of that matters though; I've won. I've beaten thirty men and teenage boys to take the victory and the spoils of this war.

I stumble toward the men at the perimeter of the fighting ring. They're all cloaked in black, hard looks on their faces and black ink etched over their cheeks. My hands tremble at the thought of wearing those same marks. The marks of the Twelve. But I've earned them. I've earned the right to stand with them and be one of them.

To be free.

"Congratulations, you've won the Game," the Jackal speaks, and I shiver at the cold tone of his voice, so unlike the warmth he usually extends to me.

I nod my head. I want this over with. I want a hot meal and an even hotter shower.

"Welcome to the Twelve. You're replacing the Hawk. Who do you choose to be?"

Free. I guess a hawk is a good embodiment of freedom, but it feels strange to take a dead man's name, like climbing into his bed with the sheets still warm. I look around at the other men that make up the Twelve. Their names are what they're known as on the streets, what their gangs cover themselves with as protection and a warning. I could have that too. I could make myself a queen of my own empire. I could rule the streets and never go hungry again.

I could escape the cycle of poverty my mother has left me in.

My eyes land back on the Jackal, and I lift my chin until I no longer feel like I'm looking up at him.

"I am the Wolf."

One

The boy on the stand is so gorgeous, it's hard to look directly at his face.

Instead, I look at his hands as they clench tightly where they rest on his lap. There are dozens of other teenagers in the room, but I can't look away from him for long before I am drawn back to him, a moth to a stunning flame. He has broad shoulders and big arms, like he works out more than regularly. His hands are big and strong. I like the look of those hands. The more I look at them, the more I imagine what they would feel like on my skin. I imagine them stroking over my arms, my neck, cupping my face and pulling me in against his chest, tilting my head back. A flush settles over my skin. Who is this guy? How has the mere sight of him turned me into a babbling mess?

I can look as far as his neck without breaking out in a sweat, and as the trial drags on, I manage to make out the script tattoo on his neck. The words '*honor before blood*' are tucked under his chin, the black ink stark against his pale skin. He has to be a gangster, but that doesn't suit his fair looks at all. He looks as though he has never done a hard day's work in his life. His sandy hair is messed artfully, and his nose is straight and unmarred. The tattoo tucked under his jaw is the only suggestion that he's not a pampered model. When the judge reads out his case, he says the guy is my age, and no boy of fifteen gets ink like that unless they're already out on the streets.

When I spot the Rolex on his wrist, I realize he must be a drug dealer. It's like a cold bucket of ice over my lustful body. Drug dealers are scum, and I do not want to admire him anymore. I am doing everything in my power to get away from drugs and the people that peddle them. It doesn't matter how drawn I feel to this guy. I look away and resist the pull of his stunning looks.

The courthouse we are trapped in is a converted historic building that had been built by convicts. The district of Mounts Bay is small enough that court proceedings are held twice a week. All children's cases are held here in the morning, and then the adults are brought through in the afternoon. My case was supposed to start half an hour ago, but the beautiful dealer is arguing belligerently with the judge and taking up more than his allocated time slot.

What a dick.

His rap sheet isn't great, but it also isn't violent, which makes me feel slightly better about ogling him.

Car theft. Breaking and entering. Violating a work order.

Clearly it isn't his first time in this building. I glance up at him again, I can't help myself, and I can see how bored and unaffected his eyes are, like this is all such an inconvenience to him and his time. I want to roll my eyes, but once again I'm transfixed.

"You ready, kid?" My social worker interrupts my staring and I startle. She's looking at me like I'm fragile again, and I don't know how to tell her that I'm easily the strongest person in this room. You don't survive what I have without becoming bulletproof. I have five pins holding one of my legs together to prove it.

I'm the Wolf of Mounts Bay, and I can survive anything.

The gangster kid steps down from the stand, and it's my turn.

As he walks down the stairs, we cross paths. I force myself to look up at him. His face is a mask of disinterest and apathy, but my breath catches in my throat when I see his eyes. The icy blue depths pull me in, and I feel like I'm drowning. He's angry. He's hiding it well, but he looks at me and I can see the burning pits of hell in his eyes. This guy is one step away from being a killer. I shiver. I should not find that attractive or exciting. But, fuck me, I do. It's my curse for being a loyal supporter of the Jackal.

He doesn't seem to notice me the way I notice him,

and it makes sense. I'm not stunning. I'm not the most gorgeous girl in the room. I'm just trying to get by, skate under the radar and make it through to adulthood. I take the stand.

Unlike him I'm not here to defend myself from my own mistakes.

If I were, I'd probably be locked up. The things I've done to get here, to have a chance at freedom, they will follow me for the rest of my life. But that doesn't matter. Act by act, brick by brick, I've built my way here and now I'll get what I've sacrificed so much for.

I'm claiming my freedom.

It's time to put away the empty, cold shell I had to become to survive. I don't know who the new version of myself will be, but I'm ready to find out.

TWO MONTHS LATER

"This is your last chance to make any requests of the state before you are officially emancipated and on your own."

Heather has her eyebrow cocked at me like I'm being dense for not having anything to say, but honestly, I'm torn between being afraid of saying goodbye to her and wanting her to leave so I can start my new life.

We're standing outside Hannaford Preparatory

Academy, and the building looms over us like a ghoul. It looks more like a castle than a school, and there are honest-to-god turrets and an incomplete moat surrounding the building. There's a bronzed statue of a light-horseman in the gardens. The school was built in the 1800s and boasts many presidents and political savants as alumni. The extracurricular roster includes an equestrian program and an Olympic-level swim team. It has a near perfect college acceptance rate from the students who have walked these halls, and the waiting list to get in is the stuff of legends. Looking at the building alone makes me feel so intimidated that I consider getting back in the car.

A tingle runs down my spine at the thought of going back to my old school, and I turn back to my social worker. Huh, ex-social worker now. The tingle turns into a shiver and takes over me, despite the warmth still in the air.

"I'm fine. I understand all of my rights, I've done the mandatory counseling, and I'm ready to be a big girl out in the world."

She snorts, then hands me my case files and the enrollment forms for the head office. She's a brusque sort of woman, not maternal at all, and I think that's why we get along so well. It's weird to think I won't see her again. I've gotten used to listening to the comforting Southern tones of her voice.

"You ain't ready for shit, kid. I've left your emergency

line on a card in your files if you get into trouble, but you're off my roster now. Try to do well at your fancy school and stay off the streets."

What a glowing statement of confidence. I think about giving her a hug but decide against it, and instead I give her a small wave. She gets back in the car and I watch as she drives away. For a second I feel a flare of panic in my chest, but I quickly push that away. It doesn't matter that I'm alone now. I don't need anyone but myself. If my life so far has proven anything to me, it is that I am strong enough to survive anything.

Once the car is no longer in view, I grab the small satchel that holds all my belongings and head up the cobblestone path toward the main building. It's like a fairy tale here, and if I believed in such things, it probably would have felt like a good omen.

There are students everywhere. The entire grounds are teeming with teenagers, and I'm getting a ton of curious looks. I try not to let it get to me as I walk up to the office. When I make it, huffing and puffing under the weight of my bag, the door is being held open by a group of teenagers and it's clear they're closely related. They're all dark-haired, blue-eyed, and their facial features look as though they were carved from marble by a master artist. The older boy is smirking at the front desk, and the other two, a boy and a girl, are looking at him despondently, glassy-eyed and utterly bored. None of them spare me so much as a glance.

"Yvette, I really don't care what your policies are, I'm not sharing with Ash. Put Avery in with him. They're attached at the hip anyway."

The receptionist, a lush woman who is at the very least in her forties, gives him a firm look, but he clearly doesn't care. His shoulders are broad and tight under his blazer. He looks like he's poised and ready to strike. I press my back against the wall out of habit, a lesson learned years ago. When there's danger in the room, you don't leave your back unguarded.

"Mr. Beaumont, as you well know, it is against school policy for there to be co-ed rooms, even amongst siblings."

He sneers at her and spits out, "I am not sharing. Who do I have to write the cheque out to? You will give me a single room."

I scoff at that, but then Yvette is pulling out a ledger and he's handing over a shiny black credit card. This is my first clue at how truly messed up this school's moral code is.

"And who, exactly, are you?" the girl, Avery, says and I startle when I realize she's talking to me.

"Lips. Lips Anderson. I'm a freshman."

A smile dances around the edge of her painted lips, but her eyes aren't amused.

"What sort of degenerate names their child *Lips*?" the boy drawls and, weirdly, it makes me feel kind of boneless. He turns to face me, and I'm struck dumb by the sight of him. That is until I see the disgust on his face. He looks at me like I'm a venereal disease. I choose not to answer him and push away from the wall. I brush past the group to pile all my paperwork up on the desk, feigning confidence, even though I'm kind of shaky. Is the whole school full of gorgeous, rich assholes? The older sibling looks down his nose at me as well before he turns on his heel and stalks out, presumably to go find his new single room. The receptionist ignores me and turns soft eyes onto the remaining boy.

"I'm so sorry. I assumed you would want to share with your brother, Ash. Do you want a single too? I have a spare in the boys' dorms."

He smiles, and his whole face changes. My breath catches in my chest and I take note. This boy can use his looks as a weapon, and he very clearly knows it.

"Actually, I'd rather share with Mr. Arbour and Mr. Morrison, if that's possible? I know there's some triple rooms, and we're probably the best candidates in our year to bunk together."

Yvette blushes and stumbles over her words. She's quick to take his bait, and it's hard not to roll my eyes.

"Oh, the triple rooms aren't for boys of your breeding

or stature. They're for the lower families."

Lower families? Sweet lord, here we go. I assume with just how low my family is, I'll be in the damn basement. That suits me just fine.

"I insist. I need to keep a close eye on them both and make sure there isn't a repeat of last year." He winks, and Yvette nearly swoons.

I glance over and see Avery watching the entire exchange with molten fury in her eyes. I think for a minute that she's pissed at her brother, and then she reaches out gently and clasps his hand. He doesn't look back at his sister, but he gives her hand a quick squeeze. She doesn't like that he's being forced to flirt with this woman; she's protective of him.

"Are there singles available in the girls' dorms?" His voice is back to the drawl. Yvette checks some papers in front of her and smiles.

"Avery is already in one of the singles. There's two available, and I popped her straight in it. Your twin called me earlier and…expressed her desires."

Her hesitation seems totally out of place, and when she looks at Avery there's fear in her eyes. I make a note of that too and file the information away.

"Lovely. Thank you, Yvette."

The twins leave with another look my way, and then Yvette turns to give me a once-over.

“I’m assuming you’re the scholarship student?” Jeez, if only I looked like Ash, I might have gotten a better welcome. I smile despite her tone and offer her my hand to shake.

“Eclipse Anderson. I prefer Lips, though.”

She ignores my hand, gives me a hard look, and takes my paperwork.

“Scholarship students are a handful already, and now we have an emancipated student? I’ll warn you that this school is held to the highest standard of morals, and you will be expected to behave in an exemplary manner,” she says, like she wasn’t just getting hot and heavy over a teenage boy.

I make sure my face is a mask of polite obedience and nod along with her. You don’t survive foster care as well as I have without being able to lie a little.

“You are also being put in a single. There was some upset about your lodging amongst the other students.”

“Upset?” I raise my eyebrows at her tone.

“These are girls of very prestigious families, and they have some serious concerns about sharing with a girl with your…reputation.”

What the hell? “What exactly is my reputation?”

“We’ve had a few run-ins with Mounts Bay High girls before, which has led to strict rules about how our students spend their time outside of Hannaford. There are concerns for the safety of the students and their property."

I flush scarlet and clench my teeth together so hard I might crack them. I'm about to tell this woman where to shove her opinions when the door to the principal's office opens and Mr. Trevelen steps out. His eyes light up when he spots me, and he lets out a long exhale.

Mr. Trevelen was responsible for awarding scholarships, and he personally interviewed me at the end of my last school year. He had sat in the care house I was stuck in, and listened to my entire life story like he actually gave a damn about helping me. Even with my great marks, I had been turned down for other scholarships because of my living situation and family history, so I knew he had gone out on a limb for me.

"Miss Anderson, what a relief you've made it here safely! I had some concerns after the Academy car was declined by your guardian."

I smile and readjust the bag strap on my shoulder.

"I think she just wanted to be nosey and see the school up close."

The entire school property is surrounded by an extravagant fence, and the ornate gate is electric. I'd been given a keycard to get in, which I now hand back to Mr. Trevelen.

"I won't hold it against her," he says with a wink, "I have cleared some time from my schedule this morning to walk you to your dorm, and then show you around a little. Most of your peers will already know where to go, as they have completed an orientation week here during the spring. I wouldn't want you to get lost."

Yvette gives me another look, but I smile at her sweetly and grab my bags to follow the principal out the door.

At least I have someone on my side.

My room is tiny.

It's at the end of the hall in the girls' dorm. I had to walk past all the other large and luxurious suites to get to it, so I know it must be a converted closet. Some of the other girls are lounging around the common areas and sniggering behind their hands as I walk past, like it's so funny I've got this room.

It's the first time in my life I've got a room to myself.

These spoiled brats have no clue what I've survived and having a room that barely fits my bed in it is not hard. The bed is a double, which is another first, and there's a small closet that would still fit ten times the clothes I own. I can feel a silly smile tugging at my lips, and I fight the urge to squeal.

I have my own room at the best school in the country.

I am going to nail this year, and then every other year until I graduate. I'm going to go to an Ivy League college on another scholarship, and then I'm going to become… actually, I haven't figured that out yet. I'm still researching what the highest paid industry is and whether I could work there for forty years without wanting to kill myself.

I unpack and stash my bags away. I get down on my hands and knees and tap away quietly until I find a suitable wooden board to pull up. It's easy enough work with my knife, and once it's out, I slide the tiny safe I've brought with me into the gap. I use some old shirts to stuff the space and hide the hollow crevice from others who would think to tap around, then I slide the wood back over it. What the safe holds is worth more than my life.

I've got a text waiting on my phone, and I don't have to look at it to see it's Matteo. He's the only person who has my number and, really, he's the last piece of my old life I have left. The the same icy fingers of fear up my spine as I read his text.

This town doesn't feel the same without you. Come home soon.

I snort, but there isn't much I can say to him without some sort of consequences.

Matteo D'Ardo was another foster kid, and four years older than me. We met at school, and he had taken me under his wing even before my mom died and I wound up in the system. He was dangerous. More dangerous than any of these rich kids could ever be. They play pretend in their safe little bubble, but Matteo was the Jackal. He owned more than my home city; he owned the entire state. In a lot of ways, he owned me too.

Keep me in the loop. I'll be back for the party and trials next summer.

When the scholarship offer had arrived at the care home I was living in, I had made the decision to put aside my life in Mounts Bay, California, and to take a chance on a better life. The public school I had left behind had a reputation for churning out drug dealers, gangsters, and single mothers. If I didn't make it at Hannaford Prep, my options were limited. I didn't want to follow Matteo. I didn't want to settle for a desperate life.

I shove the phone into my back pocket and head down to the dining hall. The whispers follow me and it's creepy as fuck. It's pretty clear that not only am I not welcome but the other students actively resent me being here. I wonder what exactly the other Mounts Bay students have done to leave this kind of impression.

The dining hall is a long room that resembles a wide corridor. It's in the center of the building, so there're no windows and the room is lit only by massive chandeliers. There's only room for a single, stretched wooden table that could easily seat two hundred people. Hannaford is very exclusive, but I know there must be more students attending than that. At the far end there are teachers already eating, but there's gaps everywhere. I only spare the logistics of mealtimes a moment's thought before I go to stand in line. I get to hear more of the crap that's being said about me. One girl even says I slept with Mr. Trevelen to get the scholarship, and I turn to give her a proper glare. The arrogance in this room is astounding. I need to build up a shield to it all. I need to become immune, so I can make it through my time here.

The food looks incredible, and I heap it onto my plate. I'm way too skinny, the type of skinny that only happens after years of food scarcity, and I'm licking my lips at the thought of eating three big meals a day.

Once my tray is full, I start to look for a seat that isn't surrounded by glaring students. I end up at the far end, close to the teachers, with no other students within ten chairs of me. It's actually perfect.

Until the far door opens and they walk in.

The twins are flanked by a guy so gorgeous I'm stunned, and it takes me a second to realize it's the guy from the courthouse last month. He looks absolutely devastating in his uniform, and there are girls frothing left, right and center over both him and Ash. Avery is looking down her nose at them all. I notice again that the teachers all eye her like she's a ticking time bomb with their name on it. *Interesting.*

I watch them discreetly as I eat, the subtle art of

surveillance being something I picked up from my time with the Jackal. Ash is holding two plates, and as Avery picks out food, he's filling one up for her. It's kind of sweet how close they are, how effortlessly they're taking care of each other. The other boy is laughing and joking with them both, but his laugh is dark and twisted, like he's making fun of everything around him.

When they're done, they head to the table and a hush falls over the room. I can practically see students praying they decide to sit with them, like it'll somehow boost their social status. This school is so weird.

Avery leads the boys to sit across the table and a few seats down from me. The stunning guy pulls out a chair for her. I know they have no intention of speaking to me, so it makes it easier to duck my head and eat, listening to the scraps of conversations around me.

"Morrison is going to start mid-semester; he's still in Europe doing his thing."

"Lucky us, we get a reprieve from all of the little shit's revelers. If I have to find one more pair of lacy panties stuffed in his door frame, I will retire on the spot."

The explicit language from a teacher makes me smile, but I don't look to see which one said it. What kind of a school is this? I shake my head and try to focus on my dinner. I've never eaten such delicious food in my life, and I'm looking forward to the next four years for that alone.

"I can see the hole from across the table. I'm ordering you a new one, so swallow your useless pride," Avery says, and even with the harshness of the words, her voice is much nicer when it's not directed at me.

"I don't fucking need a new one. It's a design statement. Leave it be, Floss," the other boy says, and even though he's swearing at her I can hear the affection. I can also *feel* Avery seething.

"Don't call me that here. And the only statement you're making is 'too poor to care'. Do you want a repeat of last year?"

That's the second reference to something happening last year I've heard, and now I'm interested to find out what they're going on about. I glance up and make eye contact with the hot boy by accident. I hold it for a second, and then glance away because I don't want to look like I'm scared of his attention, even though I'm beginning to sweat in his general proximity. *Get ahold of yourself.*

"Who's the new kid?"

"Lips." Avery stretches my name out, and it sounds so juvenile coming from her. Both boys snigger, and I roll my eyes where they can't see. Ash sums up the opinion of me that the whole room has already come to.

"Who gives a fuck, she's Mounty trash."

If only that were true.

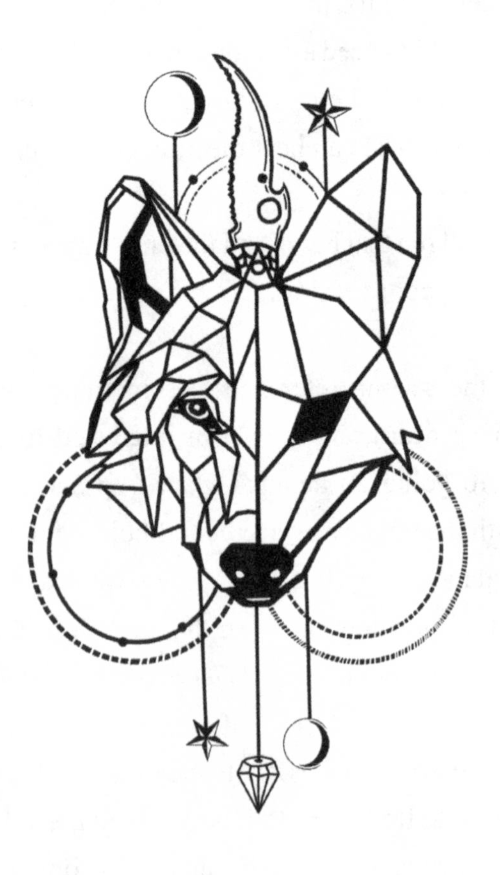

Two

If you're in the top classes at Hannaford, they start at 7 a.m., which seems to be cruel and unusual torture to me. Why punish the high achievers?

I sleep like the dead, and still I want to pitch my alarm at the wall.

I manage to get up and look human in my crisp uniform. I even squeeze in the time to put on a little makeup to try and hide the dark marks under my eyes. I don't need to give the other kids any more ammo.

My scholarship pays for exactly three daily uniforms, two sets of sporting tracksuits, and a formal uniform for representing the school at social functions. This means I have to be very mindful of what happens to these clothes, because the school skirt alone costs more than a month's worth of groceries.

The dining hall is basically empty, so I get to sit close to the door and stuff my breakfast into my mouth. I wish I had the time to savor the fluffy scrambled eggs and crispy bacon, but I'm on a serious time crunch. I hoover it down, and then grab an apple on the way out.

My first class is history, and I'm relieved to see a seating plan posted on the door. I'm at the back and sharing with a male student, Harley Arbour. Avery is at the desk in front of us, and Ash isn't in the class, which is great because I don't want to be called trash this early in the morning. It's harder to rein my temper in.

It's like a gut punch when I realize the super hot guy's name is Harley, and I now have to share a desk with him three times a week. He smells incredible, like bergamot and cloves, and I find myself angry at him for it. I have never really taken much notice of guys. I'm not interested in being knocked up and abandoned like my mom was. It was easy enough in Mounts Bay. All the guys in my grade had that air of desperation that comes with teenage hormones and poverty. Everyone at that school was living below the poverty line, and everyone was going hungry. I couldn't look at any guy without getting the distinct feeling they just wanted an escape from the bleak hole that was their life. Plus, they all knew I was associated with Matteo. They all steered clear of me.

None of the boys at Hannaford are desperate. They all have the means to be here, they've never struggled for anything, and I quickly learned that with money comes looks. I'm not saying that only rich people are attractive, I know that's not the case, but they can all afford to take care of themselves and show their best side every day. There isn't a single girl I've seen yet that doesn't look plucked, primped, and plumped to within an inch of their life, and all the guys are sporting Rolexes, coiffed hair, and expensive cologne.

Harley winces when he sees me at the desk, but he sits and methodically empties his bag. His handwriting is much neater than mine, and he already has notes from the textbook we were assigned. All of this conflicts with the gangster image I had in my head, and my eyebrows are raised as I take it all in. He might just be the person to beat in the class.

"Your name is Eclipse?" His voice drips with venom. Fucking rich boys.

"What can I say, my parents were hippies." That's not even close to true, but it's an easy lie I've told a hundred times. It's much easier than saying my mom had a conversation with the moon one night and decided to dedicate her unborn child's name to it. That kind of story comes with blank stares, or worse, they figure out she must have been high. I wonder how many kids can say they spent the first three weeks of their lives detoxing from heroin in a NICU? Lucky me.

"Whatever, Mounty. Don't cheat off my notes. I can see you eyeing them. I don't share, I don't want to work as a team, I'm not fucking helping you."

A laugh rips out of my chest in shock. He doesn't look at me; his eyes stay glued to the front of the classroom.

"I don't need your help. Why would I need help from some gangster kid? Steal any cars recently? What the hell are you doing at this school?" I say, and the words come out harsher than I intended.

Shock flits across his face, but it's gone as quickly as it was there. He turns and looks at me with such intense loathing, I swallow. My survival instincts have clearly been misplaced since I arrived here. Who would have thought a school full of rich assholes could be just as volatile as Mounts Bay High? I have to remember I'm not the Wolf here. I'm at the bottom of the ladder with no friends, no allies, no hope.

"What the fuck are you talking about?" Of course, he didn't recognize me, why would he remember seeing me there? I only remember him because he's, well, utterly drool-worthy.

"I was at the courthouse getting my emancipation last month. I had to sit and hear all about your summer activities."

He shoves away from the desk roughly and turns on me. I notice immediately that he's much bigger than me. His shoulders are wide and filled out, like he knows his way around a gym. The words tattooed under his jaw flick as his muscles clench tightly in rage.

"Listen here, you little bitch—"

"Harley. I will deal with it. Focus on your schoolwork." My head snaps around at Avery's voice, but she hasn't even bothered to look at us. What the hell? Deal with *it*, like I'm not even a person?

Harley hesitates, like he'd rather rip my head off himself, but then the teacher is stepping into the room and he gets situated back at the desk. I glance around to see wide eyes in every direction.

Great.

I'd just pissed off one of the alpha males at the school.

Ms. Aurelia introduces herself, and then hands out a pop quiz to each student.

"I like to start out the year knowing what my students already know, so we don't accidentally cover old subjects. Anyone who does not get 80 percent or higher will be moved into the lower classes, as we won't have the time to cover older subjects."

At least a half-dozen students groan. I glance through the pages and I'm relieved to find I know all the answers. My biggest concern with coming to Hannaford was that I'd be behind thanks to my public school education. I'd spent the entire summer break reading all of my textbooks.

I have all three pages filled out in under three minutes. Harley glares at me as I put down my pen, but he finishes up less than a minute later.

Ms. Aurelia collects our papers and grades them while we wait on the rest of the class. Harley flicks through his notes like he's grading himself from memory, and I'm forced to stare around the classroom in silence. It's pretty clear that at least four of the students are going to be lucky to stay in the class, the panic easy to read in their posture as they slouch over their work.

"Oh dear, Mr. Arbour," says Ms. Aurelia, and Harley's head snaps up to look at her. His eyes are wide.

"You got 99 percent, with only one question wrong. A very good score."

He exhales, and then his eyes narrow. "What's wrong with that?"

"I know you enjoy being the top of the class. Miss Anderson got 100 percent. I don't think you've ever been beaten in my class before, so I hope you're up for a challenge."

If I thought he had looked angry when I'd called him a gangster, it was nothing compared to his face now. Avery turns to smile at me, but it's the smile of a predator who has identified their prey. Dread leaves a trail of ice down my spine.

Maybe I have made a mistake coming to Hannaford.

Lunch is a hellish experience, and I desperately wish I could eat out in the sunshine on the grass.

My stomach rumbles loudly at all the delicious smells coming from the buffet tables, and once again I fill my plate to the brim. The long table is bustling and overflowing with students, and I have no choice but to take the first empty seat I can find. The girl to my left gives me a hard look and turns her back on me. The boy on my right leers at me and tries to peer down my shirt. I elbow him, hard, and then start in on my food. The noise in the room is raucous and deafening, so when it suddenly dies down to whispers, I look up.

The guy from the office, the older Beaumont kid, is standing in front of a group of freshmen kids seated at the end of the table, not too far away from where I'm sitting. He's flanked by four other students who are all smirking.

"Move."

The freshmen look at each other, and then one of them, a guy I haven't seen before, says, "We haven't finished yet. You have to wait."

All of the whispers stop.

You could hear a pin drop in the room; even the kitchen staff are silent.

"Get. Up," he says again, but the guy stares at him blankly. The flush on his face betrays him.

"Let me explain to you how this works. I'm a Beaumont.

My family is old money, so old it will never run dry. In fact, I wipe my ass with more money than your pathetic little family has ever made, and I have the connections to not only ruin your life, but to end it. If I tell you to move, *you move*."

All the freshmen stand at once and move. The guy who spoke grabs his tray and manages one step away before Beaumont slaps the tray and covers him in his lunch. He hisses as the hot soup splashes on his face and down his uniform.

"There is a clear hierarchy in this school, and you are at the bottom. Don't fucking forget it."

No one moves to help the guy, and I can see angry tears welling up in his eyes. The kitchen staff starts motioning for the kids in the line to move along, ignoring the situation happening before them.

Fucking rich kids.

I focus on my food again, except now I can hear the older kids talking because they're sitting so close to me.

"How are the twins settling in? I'm thinking about fucking your brother, by the way. I like the scowl on his face. It'll be like fucking an angry, miniature you."

"You're such a slut, Harlow. Make sure he pays you well."

The girl just laughs, like she enjoys this pompous dick speaking about her like she's nothing.

"Maybe I'll do him right after I do you, just to see who fucks better."

The group laughs again, and they start a terrible game of comparing their conquests, loudly and in detail. I chew faster to get out of the room. I don't want to attract their attention. I can't help but listen to them, though.

"I want to fuck Morrison, just to say I've had him. Joey, get your sister to get me in with him. I've heard she's the gatekeeper to all three of those boys."

Joey, who is the older Beaumont sibling, scoffs.

"She's a little cunt, just like Mom was. You have no chance there; I've always assumed she's fucking them all. I'm expecting her to get knocked up by Ash and them to have a three-headed, incestuous baby. Father would be so proud."

They cackle again and I get up with my plate, too sick to keep eating. What a great guy to have as a brother. I mean, the twins didn't exactly seem like upstanding human beings, but no one deserves a sibling who speaks so badly of them, and in such a public way.

I leave the dining hall to walk to my next class, and I try to ignore the looks and whispers.

The girls' dorms don't have individual private bathrooms, so you have to use a giant communal bathroom.

It's worse than being in the group home.

I manage to get in and out of the shower before any of the other girls come into the bathroom, and I tuck my toiletries bag under my arm as I walk back to my room. I'm dressed in old boxer shorts and an old band tee that I love.

Every girl in my dorm stops and watches me walk past.

I don't get what their problems are with me. Surely being on a scholarship doesn't mean I'm the enemy, and yet I haven't had a single student try and talk nicely to me. It's exhausting.

As I open my door, I hear Avery's voice, and I pause for a second.

"Fucking pathetic."

I whip my head around to stare at her. She's leaning against her own door frame across the hall from my room. I can see her room is at least four times bigger than mine and furnished luxuriously. I can't help but feel jealous, even as her eyes are fixed on my shirt. I glance down, but there are no holes or stains in it. What does she have against band tees?

"If you think that will get his attention, you're an even more stupid Mounty slut than I thought."

"Whose attention? These are my pajamas; I don't want to show them to a guy."

She stares at me for a second before smirking. She is

strikingly beautiful, but with her lips twisted into a sneer, I think she looks older than fifteen.

"You're totally clueless. Even better."

I see a flash and blink owlishly. She's taken a photo of me on her phone and then retreated into her room, locking the door behind her.

These rich kids are going to do me in.

After I'm safely behind my own locked door, I collapse onto my bed and groan. I had better end up with an amazing career for putting up with this school.

I check my phone and see Matteo has texted me again.

Are you raising hell yet?

I bite my lip. While I've always been academically driven, and always the top of my classes, I had a reputation for being a bitch at my last school. Not that I was a bully, I just had a lot of anger because of my home life.

My mom was addicted to drugs and, because of that, neglected me.

It's hard to admit that out loud. It makes me feel like she mustn't have loved me very much if she was willing to spend all our food money on heroin, coke, meth, pills, whatever she could get her hands on really. I didn't ever want to admit how much easier my life had become after she died. I must be the worst child in the world to think that, and yet it's true. In foster care, I never had to worry about if there was going to be food on the table at night.

Granted, the food was shit and never quite enough.

My mom told me that my dad had been sent to prison in a different state for drug trafficking, which meant I had basically been left to raise myself. I think I'd done a great job of not turning into a hopeless asshole, and someday I would be a doctor or an engineer or some other career that paid ridiculous money. Then I would never have to worry about food ever again.

So, I was known for having a smart mouth and being angry all the time. It had worked out in my favor with Matteo.

I'm definitely not in Kansas anymore, Toto.

I smile as I hit send. Matteo had sent the same message to me the day after he had moved out of the group care home. Back then, I'd wished so hard that I could move out of there with him. He was like a security blanket to me in the group home. Something safe to go home to. He'd told me when I'd accepted the scholarship that I would have to go back to him when I was done with school, that I wasn't allowed to grow apart from him. It made me feel wanted, in a dark, twisted way.

I've never felt that before.

Come home then, kid. I'll take good care of you.

I smiled and rubbed my thumb over the screen. How I wished life was that simple. How I wished he hadn't become a monster.

I have to make a life for myself, we can't all be the Jackal.

The Jackal. His name on the streets. I knew he was involved in all sorts of trouble, and I tried not to think too hard about it.

This Jackal just wants his Wolf safe and by his side. Don't forget that while you're at this big posh school.

A shudder ran down my spine. Why did that always sound more like a threat than a promise?

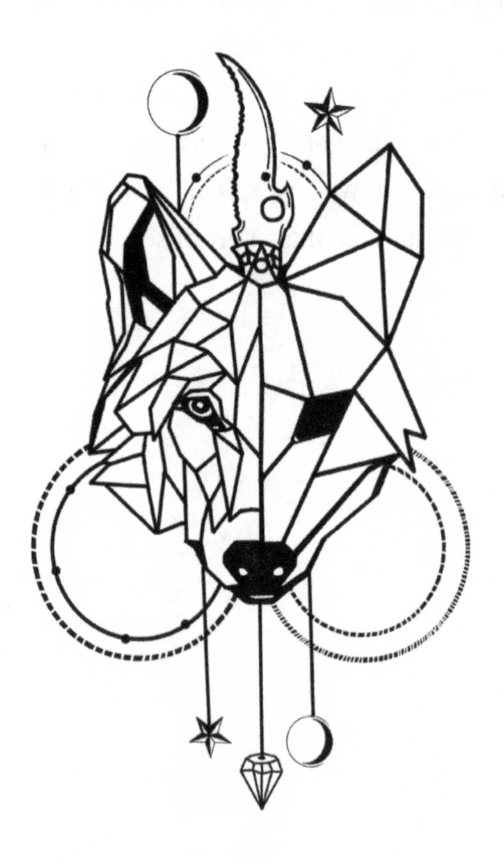

Three

The first time I get a real break from Avery and Harley is during study hall. It is the one required unit that's flexible about the location, and I choose to go to the library.

The library is huge and looks vaguely Victorian. The fiction section is a third of the size of the non-fiction and referencing sections, and the librarians are all matronly women with tight gray buns perched on their heads. I feel most out of place at this school in this room. It makes me feel like a grubby child to walk through the doors, and I still cringe after weeks of doing it.

I don't have a laptop to use quietly in my room, and the library has a selection of computers to use, the only modern luxury. I get there early and choose a desk toward the back of the room. One of the librarian's nods at me in acknowledgment but doesn't offer any help as I struggle with the technology. My last school only had one computer in the library, and it was a glorified typewriter. Internet access was limited, and students generally didn't bother using it. The computers here are high-tech, complicated, and in my opinion, high maintenance. I guess they fit in well with the student population.

The bell tolls, and the room begins to fill with students. A girl I recognize from my biology class approaches my desk and smiles sweetly before taking a seat across from me. Once the rest of the seats at the other tables are taken by students, a group of freshmen reluctantly fill the remaining seats at my table. I don't even spare them a glance and instead focus on my assignment.

I'm focusing on my research at the computer when a piece of paper slides toward me.

I saw your argument with Harley in history. You shouldn't piss Avery and the boys off. The rest of us learned that lesson in middle school.

I look up at her, and then at the rest of the table, but no one is paying us any attention. I scribble a reply and slide it back.

If I always did what I was supposed to do, I wouldn't be at this school.

She smiles and scrabbles back. The library isn't exactly quiet, students are talking all around us, so I'm not sure why we're doing this with notes, but I'll play along for now.

My name is Lauren. If they hadn't put a ban on the rest of us speaking to you, I would've already approached you.

I know what it's like to be the new girl at school.

How the hell do they ban other students from talking to people? Who the hell do they think they are? I'm angry enough that I grip my pencil so hard my hand shakes.

What happens to you if you speak to me?

She bites her lip before sliding the paper back.

Then they add me to the list, and they will do to me what they're going to do to you. I'm sorry, I'm terrified of Avery.

The list? Was that metaphorical, or did that psycho Avery actually organize her reign of terror that methodically? I let out a deep sigh and nod my head at Lauren. I guess I didn't blame her, or any of the others in our class. I'd seen what Joseph had done to the other freshmen. I was fine on my own, but sometimes it was hard to see the other students walking around, chatting and laughing together, and not wish I had someone to talk to.

I give her a nod and scrunch the note up in my hand, a clear sign of conversation over. She gives me a sad smile and gets back to work on her own homework.

I try to focus back on my own work, but I'm all hot and cranky. I hate this sort of bullying. I'd rather they just come at me with fists so I could fight back properly. Whispers and intrigue are annoying, but then I think about life back home and Matteo. Maybe learning this political shit isn't such a terrible idea.

It might help me survive the Jackal someday.

As the first few weeks pass, I learn something very important.

Harley and Avery are in every single one of my classes except choir, and they, along with Ash, have a lot of influence on our classmates.

News had spread quickly of my argument with Harley, and it has made me even more of a pariah than my scholarship status ever has. No one tries to speak to me, not during classes or meals. I think they are trying to make me feel shitty enough to leave, but little do they know I am enjoying the quiet.

At the beginning of the year, I had signed up for a bunch of extracurricular duties to get class credits and plump up my applications for college. The one I am looking forward to the least is tutoring especially now that I've pissed off Harley. It takes three weeks before I get an email from the school's admin to let me know I have had someone sign up and to meet the student in the library during three of my study halls. I groan but go along to it. When I see who the student is, I begin to think it's a trap.

Ash Beaumont.

Clearly, I've pissed someone off in a past life.

He's waiting at the assigned desk in the library, his books

and supplies spread out around him. He's so classically good looking, like he's a Grecian fantasy, and I have to remind myself that he is a dick before I sit down with him. The sneer he gives me helps to calm my hormones down. I can admire him from a distance, but the vitriol he spits at me on a daily basis, proves just how badly I need to keep him at arm's length.

"Oh, goody. I get to spend three hours a week with trash," he drawls, and I grit my teeth.

"If you want the help with your assignments, then yeah, you're stuck with the trash."

He grins at me, and it's not a nice thing.

I pull out my own schoolwork and get the utter joy of his criticism on what seems like every aspect of my life. I do my best to ignore it, but I'm not the most patient person.

"Your handwriting is atrocious. Why do you bite your nails? They make you look like a boy? You shouldn't slouch; you might actually have a decent rack, and no one will notice it if you're all hunched over— "

"Can you shut the fuck up and tell me what you need help with?" I hiss at him. He smirks like he knows he's got a direct hit. Fuck, I wish I'd met him at Mounts Bay. I'd have destroyed him with calculated calm and a grin on my face. I would have Matteo at my back and be able to end him in creative and devious ways. We could have made a real game of it. But instead I'm at Hannaford, and I've already pissed one of Avery's boys off so far. I can't push it until I know the lay of the land. I need to hold my cards close to my chest until I know the best way to play them.

He shows me his math homework, and then starts to work through the problems quietly. I watch him while he works, and I realize straightaway that something is off. I can't quite put my finger on it, but the way he looks at the paper, he's not really trying to work out the answers. It's infuriating.

"Can you at least do a better job of pretending to try? If you're not going to take this seriously, I'll use the time to study instead."

He gives me a look. His eyes are penetrating, like he's trying to get a good look at what's happening under my skin. I'm used to being looked at like this, but it's disconcerting getting it from a rich kid at Hannaford. Why would he need to know anything about me? In four years, I'll cease to exist in his life, and he'll take over his family's billion-dollar empire. Yeah, I looked up the Beaumonts. Billionaires. It made me queasy to think about that sort of money.

"You only get the credit if you do it properly. I'll let the office staff know how little you care about helping other students."

"Why should I help you if you won't try?"

He leans back in his chair and folds his arms. He's

leaner than Harley but he's still much bigger than me. I shiver. God, I'm broken.

"Because you're Mounty trash and you need the credits. I could never work a day in my life and I'll still out-earn you exponentially."

I clench my teeth. I hate him. Even if he is gorgeous.

We continue to bicker and fight our way through all his homework. He tells me he needs help with every subject, and as the hour dwindles down, I can taste my freedom. The library door swings open and Avery walks in, making a beeline for our table.

Great.

I brace myself, assuming she's here for me, but she doesn't even glance my way. Her eyes are glued on Ash.

"What's this about you starting fights with Joey?"

She's softer with Ash than anyone else, like he's some precious thing that needs to be handled with care. He doesn't look that way to me, especially as he looks at her with a glare. It's clearly not aimed at her. He treats her with the same unflinching care.

"Fuck Joey. He knows Harley is off-limits, and yet, he still keeps coming for him. I'll fucking end him, Floss."

Her eyes flick at me when he calls her that, but she doesn't pull him up. She has her hands on her hips and she's looking at him like he's a naughty child she needs to discipline.

"Can you please contain yourself? It's a lot harder to minimize damage here than it was in the lower grades. I have a lot on my plate as it is."

"He's the one being a dick. I couldn't exactly sit around with my thumb up my ass while they started in on Harley, could I? I don't know why they seem to think that they'll be able to beat us. We've been handing them their own asses since middle school."

He goes back to his homework, but if he thinks she's going to let it go, he is sorely disappointed.

"I wasn't saying you should! Next time, call me." She tucks a perfect black curl behind her ear with long, slender fingers. She makes me feel so damn unrefined and clumsy. I stop looking at her altogether.

"So, I should just make you fight all our battles, then? I should hide behind your skirt when our big, bad brother zeros in on us? That's not how this works." Some of his cool demeanor slips, and I see the rage burning in his eyes.

"No, let me deal with it so I have less to do. Once you let him get to you, it turns into a bigger problem, and then I spend weeks cleaning it up. Do you really want to put more on my plate, Ash?" she pleads.

"Fuck him. Don't clean it up, I'll burn him and everyone who decides they're on his side." He starts packing up, and I follow his lead. Family politics are not my thing, and I want to get out of here before Avery remembers I'm sitting here listening to them.

"I can't wait for Morrison to get back. I need a sane ally in this place," Avery moans, and Ash scoffs at her, stepping around the table to sling an arm over her shoulders.

"If you think he's sane, then you're not as smart as you think you are, Floss."

They walk out together. He doesn't even bother to thank me for helping him.

Fucking rich dicks.

My first clue that something isn't right is the hush that falls all around me as I walk to my room.

I've just finished up with Ash in the library, and I need to change before dinner. The hallway that leads to my room is so quiet I can hear my stomach rumble. I try to ignore it, to walk in carefully measured steps like none of this is bothering me, but I just want to snarl something snarky at the lot of them.

I make it to my door and find Avery standing in her doorway, smirking over at me, her entire body screaming with smugness.

The second I crack the door open I can smell it. The eye-watering stench of piss.

There is urine on everything in my room.

Every. Single. Thing.

I gag as the door swings fully open, and that's when I hear the laughter start. It isn't just Avery. All the girls on our floor are laughing. They have all been in on this disgusting prank. I take a deep breath, through my mouth so I don't pass out from the stink, and then close myself inside my room.

I find gloves stashed in my first-aid kit and then I get to work stripping my bedding off and piling all the clothing I can salvage. My sneakers can be saved, but the three books I brought with me are ruined. Luckily, I had taken all my textbooks with me to my tutoring, just in case I needed them, because they were easily more expensive than everything else in the room combined.

I drag all the piss-soaked linens to the small laundry room and completely ignore the gaping looks from the girls.

It's clear they thought this would rattle me, maybe even break me. No chance of that.

After all five washing machines are running, I sit on the floor in the laundry room to start on my own homework. There's no way I'm going to leave my things out in the open, and now I need to invest in some serious hardware for my door.

Fuck these little rich kids, throwing tantrums and acting like animals. Never in all my time in foster care did anyone play with their own piss. I try hard not to think about which diseases are transmitted through urine and try to remember these kids have access to care, so they should be clean.

Should be.

I've finished two classes' worth of homework when Avery walks in, carrying a single sheet of paper. She stands over me with contempt in her eyes and a sneer on her painted lips.

"Finished yet?"

I know she's not talking about my sheets swirling in the washing machine. I turn back to my homework.

"Nope." I pop the 'p' obnoxiously and don't even look at her. She drops the paper, and it lands at my feet. I read the title and scoff at her.

"I'm not leaving. You think your little prank can run me out of here? All it shows is that you're disgusting and desperate."

She laughs like tinkling bells, but all I hear are the shards of glass she'll wield to stab me with.

"I've never been desperate in my life, Mounty. I don't have to be. You are, though. And if you don't leave, I'll see just how desperate I can make you."

What the hell was this girl's problem? What had I done to her that would make her act like this? Did rich people really hate the poor that much?

I pick up the paper, and then I maintain icy eye contact

with her as I tear it in half.

"Feel free to fuck off, Beaumont."

The smirk doesn't leave her face as she prances out of the room, her kitten heels clicking on the hardwood floors. I can feel the creeping fingers of a migraine at the corners of my brain. How was it that I made it through a drug addict mom, absent dad, foster care, public school in a bad district, and now I'm rewarded for my efforts with Avery Beaumont?

A deep, dark voice whispers to me: *it's punishment for the Wolf.* I give myself a little shake and get back to work.

It takes two hours to get my room back to normal. The piss had soaked through the floorboards, and I had to scrub my little safe clean as well. I have to go ask the cleaning staff for bleach and air purifiers, because the smell lingers, but eventually I can't smell it anymore and I manage to fall asleep around midnight.

Four

I'm cranky as hell the next day from lack of sleep. I'd kill for a hot coffee.

The boys all hear about the piss prank, and the whispering that follows me makes me grit my teeth. I'm so distracted by it all that I don't notice the extra attention the juniors have begun to give me.

Turns out I've caught all three sets of Beaumont eyes.

Lucky. Fucking. Me.

I'm at my locker swapping over textbooks—why does this school love hardbacks that weigh more than I do?—when I get approached by one of Joseph's flunkies. I recognize him from the dining hall, and I eye him warily.

"Hey there, Mounty. Do you have a name? Everyone just calls you Mounty or trash, so I wasn't sure your family could afford a name."

Kill me now and just put me out of my misery. I level him with my most deadly glare. I don't like the feel of his eyes on my skin, it makes me feel as though I need to scrub myself raw.

"Do you need something? Your winning personality isn't exactly doing anything for me, and I have a class to get to."

He smirks at me, and then makes a big show of working his eyes over my body lasciviously. I fight the urge to either cross my arms over my chest or smack him in the nose.

"So, I've always wanted to fuck a Mounty. I hear you poor folk are wild in bed, and I'm willing to give it a go. When are you free this week for a quick fuck?"

I see red, and then my vision whites out, and then I think I'm having a full rage blackout. I'm a little concerned that when I come to, this dickhead will be dead. I hear his laugh and then, without meaning to, my hand shoots out and jabs him in the throat. The noise he makes is magnificent, and he sprawls back into the lockers like I've shot him. Sometimes my survival instincts are a goddamned blessing.

The hallway goes quiet, and I grin down at him maliciously. I speak quietly, but I know everyone can hear me. All eyes are on us.

"I wouldn't fuck you if you were the only rich dick left in this building. I wouldn't touch your disgusting cock for a million dollars."

He manages to straighten himself, and then throws me a haughty look.

"We'll see about that," he rasps, and then turns on his

heel to stride off.

I glance around as the whispers start up again, then roll my eyes. This place is exhausting. Surviving four years here may be harder than I thought. I start walking to my next class and try not to let the dread creep in.

Hannaford requires either a sport or some form of music as subjects and picking between them was like choosing a method to die. I physically could not do anything that required strenuous use of my legs. I have five pins and two plates holding one of my legs together, which is a violent and dark story for another time, which means unless I could've done basketball sitting down, I couldn't pick gym. Music was a very different beast. I can't play any instruments, but I can sing. Actually, I can fucking *sing.* But I haven't been able to hear the sound of my own singing for years without my PTSD kicking my ass all over the shop.

I've managed to only open my mouth during group numbers and warm-ups so far, but I have a copy of the class syllabus, and I know my project is a solo. I need to ace this class to keep my score up, but it feels impossible to me right now. My past is royally screwing me over.

I have one last class before choir, and I round the corner to get to chemistry when everything changes.

My entire world view changes.

The door in front of me opens, and out walks Blaise *fucking* Morrison.

Blaise. Fucking. Morrison.

Never in my wildest dreams did I ever think I would be at school with Blaise Morrison. I knew that he went to an ultra-exclusive private school and that he had dozens of privacy orders in place to make sure he could go to school like any other teenager, but I couldn't have ever hoped that I would see him in the flesh, let alone breathe the same air as him.

I should probably explain why my entire existence is melting at this boy's appearance.

Blaise Morrison, Blaise *fucking* Morrison, is the lead singer and guitarist for Vanth Falling, which is my favorite band and, not to be too dramatic, is also my entire reason for existence. I first heard of Morrison when he was still solo and uploading covers of his favorite songs. I was completely struck by the fact he was my age and doing what I could only dream of doing. I have every song he has ever sung, even his earlier less-great stuff, and I sleep in one of the band's shirts every night. I have followed his entire career—of two years, but that is irrelevant—and I'm basically a walking encyclopedia on all Vanth Falling knowledge.

He is perfection. A living god.

My obsession for him is for his lyricism and his range. He is so talented, and a modern poet, and I respect him so much as an artist. Now, seeing him up close, I can also say with absolute confidence that he is panty-dropping hot.

His hair is spiked up like he's run his hand through it a hundred times already today, and his glowing green eyes are dancing. He's tall and leanly muscled, he fills out his uniform in a mouth-watering way, and I want to rip it off him.

My knees are weak just looking at him, and I'm sure I look like a deer in the headlights. My brain finally catches up with my body, and I move out of his way.

He doesn't notice my meltdown, thank god, and he swaggers down the hall with an air of confidence that would be so obnoxious on any of these other rich dicks, but on him I am swooning.

Swooning.

Lord save me, because I may die from the very presence of this guy.

I duck behind something random, a potted plant, to stay out of his sight line because honestly, I'm making a complete fool of myself and my heart stutters just a little when I see him grin. Sweet lord, there's his dimples.

Then he throws his arms around Ash *fucking* Beaumont's neck, and they grin at each other like they're in love. Then Harley pops around the corner and joins in on the group hug and then, fuck me, Avery squeals and piles on too.

This school is ruining every aspect of my life.

Why couldn't I keep Blaise? It is so unfair, and I feel like this might be the thing that breaks me.

Why! Ugh.

Suddenly I remember all the conversations I've been listening to about 'the Morrison kid'. The teachers had talked about his door being stuffed with panties, and Avery had told Ash she couldn't wait for him to get here. Fuck.

Because the world hasn't actually finished shitting on me, I have to sit next to Harley in chemistry, and Avery is sitting in front of us once again. The whole seat assignment by surname is really a pain in my ass, and I consider a name change to get away from him.

I'm sweating and shaking like mad when I sit down, but Blaise isn't in this class, so maybe my brain will kick in at some point. I can feel Harley's eyes on me as I empty out my bag with trembling hands.

"What's your problem?" he says in a haughty tone.

I give a shrug because, well, we're not friends and I don't owe him an answer. He grunts at me, and then grabs my wrist to turn my hand over. My knuckles are red and a little puffy. I must have hit that dickhead harder than I thought.

"Fighting isn't tolerated on campus," he drawls.

I give him a look, and he surprises me by grinning. The teacher walks in and starts to take attendance. Harley leans over to whisper in my ear.

"I would have paid good money to watch you punch that asshole."

The corners of my mouth tug up into a grin. Who would have thought the way to civility with Avery's boys was by acts of violence toward Joey's group?

The positive of sitting next to Harley is that he doesn't speak at all during classes. He just sits and soaks in information, like the hottest sponge you've ever laid eyes on. Watching him helps distract me from the throbbing pain in my knuckles. I'm going to have to start packing instant ice packs into my school bag.

I watch as Harley writes neatly spaced notes flawlessly. Unlike every other rich boy, I've ever had to sit next to, he doesn't spread out obnoxiously onto my side of the desk. If he wasn't tied to the devil that is Avery Beaumont, I might fall for him.

But I only have to remember the stink of urine on all of my belongings to shudder and swear off him.

When we are dismissed from chemistry, I have to take a minute before I can get up and head to choir. Harley looks at me curiously, and then falls into step with me. I shoot him a look of my own, but I don't say anything. Avery ignores me completely and tucks her arm into Harley's.

I make it three steps out of the room before another random junior I've never seen asks me out. He words it better than the last guy, but it's still pretty obvious he's after sex. Avery's giggle is infuriating, but I manage not to hit this guy. I just tell him I'm not interested. Four more steps, and I see another junior make a beeline towards me.

"Fuck, am I going to have to elbow my way to class?" I mutter, and Harley grins at me.

"Such popularity! Maybe you should try and move up to the junior class instead of slumming it with us, Mounty," says Avery as she breezes forward, tugging Harley with her. He grumbles at her. "If she flattens another guy, I want to see it. If she does it to Joey, I will wank over it for the rest of my life."

I blush, and then I curse myself for it.

"If she hits Joey, she'll be dead before the week is out." Avery's tone is no-nonsense, monotone, and dark. I shiver.

The Beaumonts are not the type of people to fuck with without serious consideration. I need a plan.

Blaise Morrison is in my choir and voice development class.

I avoid him like the plague. It's easy because he stays attached to Avery, and I was already trying to stay as far away from that girl as possible. They're such close friends, it's easy to see in the way they banter with each other and their casual touches.

I had been planning on speaking to Miss Umber about doing my solo privately but, embarrassingly, I find I can't even speak in Blaise's presence. It's humiliating and humbling, and I consider leaving the school for the very first time since arriving in the hellhole.

How can he affect me so much?

But I know the answer to that already. He's every single one of my fantasies come to life and walking the halls of Hannaford with me. I can't look at him without thinking about all the times I've listened to his crooning or sung along at the top of my voice. I used to listen to him and imagine what my life would be like if I were brave enough to start a band and run away from all my troubles. But I'm not brave. Not that type of brave, anyway.

We make it through warm-ups without a hitch, and then Miss Umber breaks us up into groups to work through the vocal exercises. I'm with Lauren, who smiles at me shyly, and two other girls I don't really know. It's easy enough to distract the other girls and not actually do any singing myself. Lauren is good, but not as good as I am, and the other two can harmonize well. I'm kind of shocked to realize how much fun I'm having. I wish so badly that I could sing, but the loss hurts less when I can laugh with the other girls.

"Oh god, he's about to sing!" Dahlia says. Well, squeals is more accurate.

I glance over, and Avery is grinning up at Blaise as he starts with his vocal work. I try not to show on my face what his voice is doing to me because honestly, I've never been so turned on in my life. It's wildly unfair and cruel.

All the other groups have stopped to listen to him as well, and Miss Umber is *blushing* at Blaise as she watches him over her glasses. She's looking at him like she'd eat him right up. Are all the teachers at this school predatory, or is that just the intense allure of Avery's guys?

Speaking of Avery, she is enjoying being in the thick of it. Her hand is curled around his arm possessively. I roll my eyes at her, and Lauren giggles next to me. She's a sweet kid. I wish she were a bit braver, and we could actually be friends.

"Any other songs you'd like, Claire?" he says to Miss Umber with a flirty wink.

I could just die.

If he ever does that in my direction, I *will* expire.

"O-oh, no, that's quite alright! How was your touring during the break? Did you get to spend some time at home with your family?" She blushes her way through her questions, and then sits down with his group. The room stays quiet. He's the focus of everyone's attention, and he grins easily.

"It was great! I did a lot of Europe and a little bit of Asia. We focused on smaller, more intimate venues, so I could look into the crowd and see people rather than just a giant, writhing mass. My parents came out to me, so I did get to see them. It's hard being young and still going to school. I have to try and fit a lot into my year."

Miss Umber nods along with him, her eyes affectionate.

"I'm ready to be here, though. I missed my friends and I need a rest."

"Only you would see school as a rest," Avery scolds him, smiling like a Cheshire cat.

"Well, I'm expecting to sleep at least ten hours a night, and my liver is going to have a chance to empty out a bit, so yeah, it's a break. You never realize how precious sleeping on a stationary bed is until you're trapped on a bus for months," he says with another wink at Miss Umber. I'm starting to worry the poor woman's heart wouldn't be able to cope with all the blushing she's doing.

"Trapped, like you don't love every second of it! Last year you were the worst to be around because you'd been home for too long. I give it a week and you'll be planning your next move."

He laughs, and his whole face lights up when he looks at Avery. I've never been so jealous in all my life.

"I'd kill for a boy to look at me like that," whispers

Lauren, and I smile at her. Dahlia nods frantically, and Jessie hums in agreement. At least I'm not the only girl feeling this way.

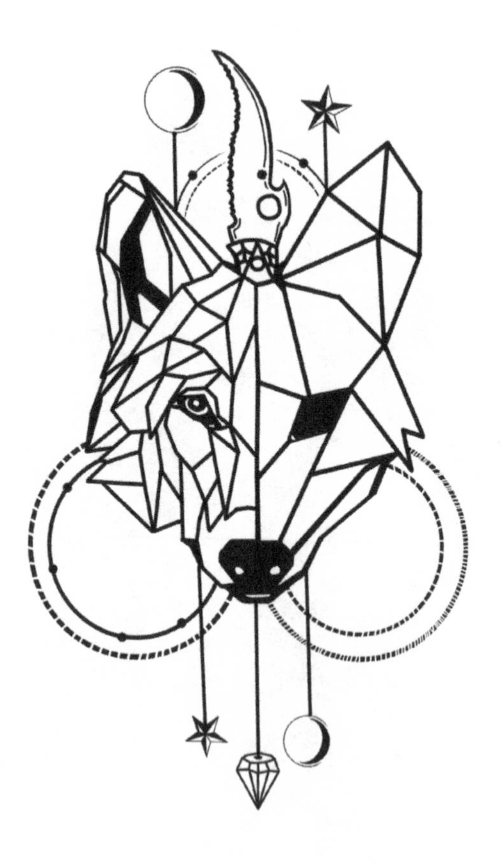

Five

I've decided I'm going to try every breakfast option at least once, so I'm sure I'm eating the best while I'm here. I'm sitting in the dining hall enjoying a giant stack of pancakes when Joseph Beaumont sits down beside me. I stiffen up, but I try not to make it obvious. I fail.

"Relax, Mounty. I'm here to chat," he says, and his voice is like dark malt liquor. Rich, seductive, dangerous.

"Is there something I can help you with?" I put down my cutlery and stare across the table at him. He's attractive like his brother, but his features are sharper, like you could cut yourself on him and bleed out in seconds.

"I've heard that you've been getting some unwanted attention."

Right. I'd been propositioned by eleven juniors this week, and it was only Wednesday.

Eleven.

So far, I've only had to punch that one guy, but I'd had a few more close calls. It was beginning to make the short walks between classes unbearable.

My eyes narrow at him. “Do you know why this is happening to me?”

He laughs and leans back in his chair, crossing his arms. He’s so similar to his brother that it’s jarring. I had been tutoring Ash for long enough that I could pick out his mannerisms, his little ticks, so seeing them on Joseph was weird. I glance over his head to see the twins and the other two boys walk into the room. Avery frowns deeply when she sees Joseph sitting with me, and Harley looks like he wants to come over and interrupt. The students around us are quickly finishing up their breakfast and moving away.

“I know that it’s going to stop. I’ve made it clear to the boys that if you were interested in a quick fuck, you would have taken one of them up on the offer by now. You won’t be bothered by them again.” It’s a nice thing to do, and so I’m instantly wary. He’s sitting there casually, like he owns the school. Fuck, maybe his family does own it.

“What do I owe you for that favor?”

His smile is all teeth. I’m sure he thinks he’s terrifying, but I’ve befriended the Jackal. I’m sure Joey is a kitten by comparison. “I’d like you to come to a party next week. I’m hosting. It’s unusual for anyone to miss my parties, and yet you haven’t been to any of them yet.”

I have no interest in getting drunk with spoiled brats and bullies. Still, if it takes one night of hanging around these idiots so I can walk to class alone, it's worth it, right? I hope so.

"Okay, sure. Why not."

"Great. Do let me know if you have any more troubles with students. I know my sister can be a little cunt when she's forced to share her toys."

I glance over at Avery and find the whole lot of them are watching our every move. This sibling rivalry was dangerous; best to steer clear of it. "I'm fine. It takes a lot to bother me."

Joseph smiles again and stands up.

"Oh, I'm counting on it," he says with a wink, then leaves me alone.

What a dramatic asshole, I think as I tuck back into my food.

He's true to his word. I can feel the eyes of the other students on me, but no one approaches me for the rest of the day.

I'm not looking forward to my tutoring session with Ash after my conversation with his brother. I still meet with him three times a week for an hour, though I have no idea how much I'm actually helping him. He's an infuriating student. We go around and around in circles, and when I'm ready to strangle the life from him, he writes out the answers perfectly, as if he's known all along.

I arrive early to set up, like I always do, but this time Ash has beaten me there. He's brooding, all dark and frowning, and when he sees me coming, he crosses his arms and glares at me.

"If you're going to be like this the whole hour, I'm just going to go study in my room."

"If you think my brother wants to be your friend, then you are a dense Mounty slut," he snaps at me.

Oh, the ways I would break this boy if I didn't desperately need my scholarship. I sit, because I also need the credits I get for these sessions, and then I fold my own arms to mirror him.

"It is such a joy to spend this time with you. Rest assured that I don't trust a single hair on the heads of any human bearing the name Beaumont."

His eyes narrow, and he leans in toward me. "Then why did you agree to go to his party?"

I roll my eyes at him and start setting up my books. I have assignments due in every damn class, so I don't have the time to explain myself to this ass. "What do you need help with today? I know you must have the same economics stuff due, so let's work on that."

"Fuck economics, why did you agree?"

He is the single most infuriating human I have ever met. Even Avery is easier to deal with, all smiles and knives in the back. How do you inform the privileged that you're just trying to survive when they can't see the danger from their vantage point? I want to kick him under the table.

"Maybe I don't enjoy having guys follow me around all day begging me for sex. Maybe I'm starting to get worried I'll have to fight one of them off who won't take no for an answer. Maybe it's easier to go to a party than be on my guard all the fucking time. Now, do you want to do the assignment or not?"

We were starting to attract the attention of the other students around us. I'd rather not be at the center of another Hannaford scandal, but Ash is oblivious. "Go to the school staff, then. Go tell your student advisor. Do anything else."

"Why do you care? Your sister has been my biggest torturer, so why are you telling me to stay away from Joseph and not Avery?" I hiss at him, all my patience gone.

The glare he levels at me is his best yet. A shiver runs down my spine, but I refuse to back down. "Don't *ever* compare them."

"Why not? She's just as cruel as he is."

He snaps forward in his chair and grabs my tie to yank me forward. Our faces are so close together, I can feel his breath on my lips, and I fight the urge to lick them. Or lick his lips. God, I need some serious therapy. I wonder if my scholarship covers that.

"My sister is perfect. She is selfless, smart, and the

kindest person I know. Joey is a sociopath. Don't you ever forget it," he whispers, and I feel the words on my skin.

He doesn't let me go. If anything, he pulls me closer, and I can feel the heat of his lips on my own. My face flushes. My legs are trembling, and he smells unbelievably good. Maybe all my time spent with the Jackal has damaged me permanently, because lusting after a guy who despises me so deeply must mean I'm irreparably broken.

"Don't go to the party, Mounty."

I roll my eyes, and he lets me go suddenly. I slump back into my seat like a rag doll and try not to think about how hard my nipples are underneath my thin blouse. I straighten up and roll my shoulders. I glance over to see the librarians eyeing us both, but they don't approach. How easy life must be with Beaumont as your last name.

Ash looks completely unaffected and just opens his textbooks. He's starting with history, because he's a pompous brat, who won't do anything I ask him to. He's pulling out his notes when I finally snap. "You know he tells people you're fucking Avery. He's told half the school that you four are having some big orgy every night, and someday he'll be an uncle to a deformed, incestuous child."

Ash stops and grins. I think it's the first true smile I've ever seen on him. Clearly, he has a twisted sense of humor if he finds that funny.

"And you believe him? Are you asking me if I'm

fucking my own sister?" His voice is sultry and seductive and promises dark things. I swear he can see how hard my nipples are, and he's messing with me.

"No. I just thought you should know."

Ash doesn't look up from his notes. "I'm well aware of the depths of Joey's depravity. I do have to live with him occasionally."

It's hard to choose between the Beaumont boys. Which devil should I trust? Neither of them is the obvious answer, but I have to make a decision on whether or not to go to the party. What's the worst that can happen to me there? A lot of things, but how many of those could actually break me? Very little.

I feel like no matter what I choose, I'm going to get burned.

The rest of the week is so blissfully quiet that I should have known something was up.

Harley doesn't speak to me in class, Ash is quiet and studious during our library sessions, I barely see Avery, and I manage to completely avoid seeing Blaise altogether. If I could keep this up, I would have a great year.

I eat dinner by myself, reading the *Iliad* for Lit while I chew. I can zone the entire room out that way and get ahead with my homework for the weekend. I might even be able to take a day off and sleep for the whole day.

That would be incredible.

I make it to my room with no interruptions, and I grab my pajamas to head in to have a shower before bed. The group bathroom is empty, and I feel as though I've won the lottery. I take my time, washing my hair and shaving every inch of unwanted hair until I'm feeling like a smooth goddess. When I still lived with my mom, we never had hot water, so showers were rare and quick. During winter I'd only really shower at school after gym. It was gross to think about now, but it was all I could do at the time. Once I got moved to the group house, showers were hot but on timers, so the water would shut off after two minutes. Still, it felt like a luxury to me to have those two minutes every day.

Most of the girls in my dorm shower twice a day and can easily spend twenty minutes under the hot spray. I find it shocking and wasteful, but none of them even realize the small luxuries they have.

After the fourth passover with the soap, I know I'm just lingering to enjoy the warmth soaking through my skin into my bones. I'm as clean as I'm ever going to get. I reach for my towel and find it's not in the stall with me. I frown because I'm pretty sure I brought it in with me, but I open the door anyway.

My bag is gone.

I have no towel, no clothes, absolutely nothing to dry myself with or to cover my naked body.

Fucking Avery, I think, but there's nothing I can do about it. I start to shiver now that I'm out of the heat of the water. This is bad.

I can feel tears prickling at the corners of my eyes, but I refuse to cry. Losing my clothes and having to walk back to my room naked isn't great, but I've survived worse. I can feel the panic start in my chest, and I count backwards from a hundred. In French, just to really keep my mind busy.

This isn't so bad. Foster care meant I was forced to shower around other girls all the time. It's practically the same thing, except the other girls will probably be standing around laughing. Oh god.

Cent, quatre-vingt-dix-neuf, quatre-vingt-dix-huit...

I'm not ashamed or embarrassed by my body. I used to be scrawny, too thin and lanky for my frame, but the months here at Hannaford have put some meat on my bones. I have boobs for the first time in my life too, nice ones and big enough that they hide the scars on the left side. I didn't need Avery seeing that and digging around in my past. I am more than a little shy about how many scars I have. My leg is mottled with red and white raised skin after all the operations to put it back together. I have a burn on my hip that I can't think about without triggering my PTSD, and then there's the two perfect circles on my shoulder. Bullet in, bullet out. Would these girls know what a healed bullet wound looks like? Would they question me about it?

Could I handle them asking without lashing out?

When I'm sure I won't cry or scream at these rich bitches, I open the bathroom door and start walking back to my room. It's maybe thirty steps, and I force myself not to run.

The giggling starts the second the door opens.

I don't look down at myself, I don't look over at the giggling to see which girls are watching, don't cross my arms over my boobs.

Head held high, looking straight ahead, fuck the lot of them.

The giggles sputter out. I'm not doing what they expect me too . I'm not crying or breaking down. I'm not screaming at them.

I make it to my door and find my bag sitting on the floor. I bend down to pick it up, and then I catch Avery's eye as I straighten. She's not laughing or smiling. She's just watching me. Her eyes are cold on mine, and I think about how Ash described her.

She doesn't seem very kind to me.

I lock my door behind me and throw my clothes on with trembling hands. It takes me a minute to realize Avery must have had the opportunity to case my room while I was in the shower, if she had my bag and my key, and I rip the loose board up to check my safe is still there untouched. Once I'm sure it hasn't been tampered with, I spend two hours pulling everything else apart in my room until I'm sure there isn't anything missing, or a hidden camera planted. That's all I need, that girl having video of me drooling in my sleep. Or dancing around with my headphones in, listening to Blaise's crooning. I shudder at the thought.

When I finally put my room back together, I climb between my sheets and text Matteo. I need something, anything, from someone who cares about me and, in his own twisted way, Matteo does.

Do you remember when I drank for the first time and you told me I was too good for that kind of thing? I think I'm going to go out next week, and I think I may end up in a fight.

If I see Avery while I'm drinking, she may not walk out of it alive.

You could call in a favor. There are many people that would take care of your problems for you.

I could.

But I won't.

Six

By the time I make it to breakfast on Monday, the photos—yes, *photos*—of my naked walk have been seen by the entire school.

The first guy to approach me about it gets ignored, but the second guy gets a bloody nose. He made the mistake of telling me how much he wanted to watch my tits bounce while he fucked me, and I take note of his name when his friend calls out to him while he slinks away. Spencer Hillsong is a dick.

I don't get approached after that. I eat breakfast in my usual spot, and there's a three-chair buffer on every side of me, like no one is willing to risk my violence.

That is until Joseph Beaumont sits across from me again.

"I hope you're not embarrassed, Mounty. I'm actually impressed with what you've got going on under the uniform. I didn't realize your rack was so big."

I don't even glance up at him. I'm reading the last

book I need to for Lit for the year, having spent the entire weekend studying like a fiend to keep myself distracted. I hadn't gone to the dining hall to eat, so I'm starving, and my plate is overflowing with eggs and bacon.

"Aww, don't be like that, Mounty. Nudes are an everyday thing here at Hannaford. I can show you mine, if you want. I'm quite the photographer."

I would rather gouge my eyeballs out than see Joey's dick. I think about telling him that, but it's more appealing to ignore him until he fucks off.

"Cold shoulder, and I'm trying so hard. You're a hard girl to befriend. I could deal with Avery for you, you know. Would that win me your trust?" he coos at me.

"No." I look up at his cold, blue eyes. The color and shape are identical to his siblings, but they don't feel the same. Looking into Joseph Beaumont's eyes was like staring into a void.

I get the impression that this boy tortures his siblings for the simple pleasure of it, and I have no interest in being dragged into it. Besides, I was starting to get ideas of what I would do to Avery senior year when graduation came closer and my chances of being expelled were drastically reduced.

I'd destroy that girl.

But I'd do it myself. I wouldn't hide behind her evil brother.

"She speaks! Are we talking now, or are you insisting on freezing me out?"

"What exactly would you like to talk about, Joseph?" I put down my book and fold my arms. His eyes trace over my chest, and I clench my jaw because I know he's thinking about the damned photos.

"Call me Joey; my father is Joseph. Let's talk about my party. We're going to the edge of the school boundaries, there's a small woodland area that I've made my own. I'll pick you up after curfew and personally walk you down there, so you don't run into any trouble."

I didn't want to go to the damned party at all. How many of the guys would proposition me there? Would Avery and the boys be there, and would I get drunk and confront her? It was a recipe for disaster. I open my mouth to say so when Harley sits down next to me.

I glance around, but he's alone.

"What the fuck do you want, degenerate?" Joey sneers at him. Harley looks at him the same way you would look at dog shit you've just stepped in. His uniform is crisp and new, so I guess Avery finally wore him down enough for him to replace his older one. He looks hot, but then he always does.

"Lips and I have a chemistry assignment to discuss." True, but we had already finished the assignment. Neither of us leave things to the last minute.

"Well, fuck off and talk to her about it later. We're busy."

A slow smile works its way across Harley's face, and he starts to eat his eggs. His plate is even bigger than mine. He's a solid guy, but I get the impression it's all muscle, so he must spend serious time in the gym. The image of him in a tank and gym shorts flits into my head, and I lock the image down fast. I do not need to get turned on surrounded by these assholes.

"I'm good here. Lips and I are regular desk buddies. She enjoys my company, you know. I don't have to taunt her to get her to speak to me."

Joey scowls at him, but I refuse to speak to either of them. Instead I pick my book back up and zone their bullshit out. Joey finally gets up and storms off. Harley doesn't say a word, just eats his eggs and smells delicious.

"I don't need rescuing." I say as I turn the page.

He snorts at me.

"Everyone needs rescuing from Joey Beaumont. You shouldn't be speaking to him. If he sits here again, get up and walk away."

"Oh yeah, and what should I do if Avery sits here?"

Harley pauses and then puts his fork down. I watch as his face does a complicated dance before settling into what I think is an attempt at a sincere look.

"I know you won't believe me, but Avery didn't set

you up, and she definitely didn't take the photos."

It's my turn to snort. I give up on my eggs and start in on my apple instead. I kind of want to vomit thinking about how many people were looking and laughing at the photos. It's bad enough that I have to put down the apple too.

"Think about it. Plus, I haven't looked at them. If Joey actually gave a shit about your feelings, he wouldn't have looked at them either. He's a snake in the grass."

No, he's not in the grass. He's a snake that's wrapped around your throat. "You expect me to believe you care about my feelings?"

He pauses shoveling his food into his mouth and says, "Nah. I just don't find naked photos all that great without consent. I have enough sent to me from willing partners that I don't feel the need to look at yours."

That's…really decent. Like, a really human and empathetic thing to say. I have to fight back tears. This place is making me soft.

I sniff and say, "You're not missing much. I'm just a scrawny Mounty."

He laughs, but it's not as cruel as it usually sounds.

My go-to reaction to the gossip and whispers from other students is to stare at them like they're stupid until they get uncomfortable and leave me alone.

It works well, and by the time I get to the library for my tutoring, I've used this against a decent enough amount of people that now everywhere I walk, the other students clear a path. I think they're waiting for me to snap. I kind of am too.

I sit at my usual table and get started on my assignments. I'm now five weeks ahead of schedule in every class except choir.

Ash walks in ten minutes later and joins me, sitting at his usual seat across from me. He doesn't speak while he gets out his textbooks and notes.

"Do you need help today?" I say without looking up.

"I'll ask if I do," he replies, and I give him a curt nod.

We work in silence, and I enjoy the time to just focus on what I need to get done. For once it doesn't feel hostile; more companionable. When the bell goes, I stay put, since I'm only halfway through a math worksheet—and to my surprise, Ash does too. The rest of the library starts to empty and a girl from our year comes to lean against the table, twirling a strand of her long russet hair around her finger. She's gorgeous, but she was also present for my walk, so I throw her a filthy look before turning back to my work.

"Hey. You didn't come out last night, I was waiting for you," the girl—no idea what her name is—says in a seductive tone. I try not to gag. Ash doesn't look very impressed. I try not to feel pleased about that, but I fail miserably.

"I'm sure you found an adequate replacement."

Oooh, *burn*. I smile down at my equations so the girl doesn't notice. Ash's eyes flick to my face, before he zeros back in on the girl.

She tosses her hair over her shoulder and pouts at him. "That's a bit harsh. I was forced to when you didn't show. What, am I supposed to just wait around at your beck and call? Your dick isn't that great."

The smile he gives her is dangerous. It's the type he would give me, not a potential fuck.

"We both know that isn't true. You're gagging for it."

Sweet lord. He doesn't sound like he's flirting, but maybe I'm just bad at reading the signs. I have no experience to fall back on, so it's entirely possible. "If you two are going to fuck right here at my study table, please tell me so I can make other arrangements," I say as I tap formulas into my calculator. I don't look up, because I don't want to see if Ash is into her and they're just gearing up for a hate-fuck.

"Fuck off, then, Mounty," she says, and I sigh as I go to grab my books. Ash puts his hand over mine and stops me. It's the first time he's ever touched me, and I feel flutters in my stomach.

"Allow me to paraphrase for you, Mounty, I wouldn't fuck Harlow if she were the last piece of pussy left at this school. Stay. I need help with my equations when you've finished yours."

The girl, Harlow, glares down at us both. She snaps, "I thought you and Avery hated the Mounty bitch."

"I hate my brother more. Tell me, how did his dick feel up your ass last night?"

"Sweet lord," I murmur and try not to laugh. This just gets worse and worse. Maybe I should just leave and study in my room?

"At least he isn't a frigid little bitch like you. It's your own fault you lost me to him," she hisses back at him.

Ash throws his head back and laughs.

The chair next to me pulls back, and I look up to see Blaise *fucking* Morrison slinging his bag down. He drapes himself into the chair so casually and gracefully, like the god he is. Ugh, one look at him and I'm a dripping mess.

"Is this seat taken?" Lord help me, his voice even sounds amazing when he's just talking.

How the hell do I get out of this?

I've been preparing myself for weeks for this moment.

I knew at some point I'd be faced with Blaise, and I'd have to speak to him. We share a class, I'm kind of on speaking terms with two of his best friends, and from what I'd observed from a safe distance, he's a pretty social guy. Too social for my liking.

I gesture vaguely in his general direction, and then start to move my textbooks so he has somewhere to put his stuff. He grins at me, oh *god*, and then opens his bag.

Ash and Harlow are still hissing jabs at each other, but I can't find it in myself to care now that Blaise is here. It's taking all my energy not to pass out.

"I've signed up for your tutoring. I haven't been given a time slot yet, but I'm hoping to just tag into Ash's. Do you think you could do us both at once?"

I nearly faint.

He must be doing this on purpose.

"That's fine. I can—I can do that. What do you need help with?"

He grins, and I decide that the only way to get through this is to just avoid looking at him until I'm desensitized, like I did with Harley. I barely notice he's the epitome of panty-dropping gorgeousness anymore. Okay, I do notice, but I can look past it.

"Great! Are you guys working on math right now? Because I may fail math, and if I do my old man will have a stroke."

I try to smile reassuringly, but I'm sure it looks like *I'm* having a stroke. He gets out his worksheets, and I see he's in the lower math class, so I learned this stuff two years ago. I focus on the sums and walk him through the first set. Harlow finally stomps off, and Ash now looks like he wants to bathe in her blood.

"I need a drink," he says as he loosens his tie with a sharp yank.

"Oh, have you two finished arguing over which brother has the biggest dick?" Blaise grins at Ash wickedly, and I keep my eyes firmly on the page in front of me.

"We both know I win that one. She's a lousy, backstabbing whore. She sold herself to him in the hopes it'll give her a leg up in the social hierarchy."

I move back to my own worksheet while they gossip. It's not like I can tell them to get back to work. The tutoring session has ended, and I can't even look Blaise in the eye yet.

"What were you expecting, loyalty and devotion? She's a Roqueford. They're widely known to be double-dealing sluts. Her father has more bastards than legitimate children, and he has six of those."

"I wasn't expecting her to be so open about it. Floss woke me up this morning with the picture, so forgive me if I'm not in the greatest mood."

So Avery was sharing around more than just my photo? Great. *What a kind girl*, I think with no small amount of sarcasm. Ash glances over at me like he's forgotten I was here. His face is flushed, and he looks less like the perfect Grecian statue than I've ever seen him. He looks approachable and hot. Why did I hate him so much?

"Are you enjoying your infamy?" There it is. He always knows just what to say to make me feel like an insignificant fleck of dirt. I clench my teeth.

"Fuck you, Beaumont." There's no heat behind my words, but I still mean them. I snatch his worksheet up and start marking it. He's gotten most of the equations right, but I enjoy the small amount of red ink I get to use. When I shove the page back at him, he's still watching me, his eyes unreadable.

"I told you not to trust Joey." He shrugs at me like this is all justified.

I snort at him. Blaise watches us both with captive interest, twirling his pen between his long fingers. I wonder how they became friends.

"Your sister did this to me. Now the entire fucking school has photos of me naked, and I get to enjoy the *privilege* of being looked at by you lot, like I'm a piece of meat. Like I actually want your rich dicks, when really I'd rather fucking die."

Ash rolls his eyes at me. "Avery doesn't use naked photos against people. She does have a line, you know."

"Sure. Piss on all my belongings, but she draws the line at naked photos. I definitely believe you."

Blaise's nose wrinkles, and it's goddamn adorable. I turn away from him, so I don't humiliate myself by blushing at him or drooling.

I am in real danger of drooling.

"You don't mean actual piss, do you? I cannot imagine Floss ever handling piss."

"Yeah, actual urine. It took me hours to fucking clean, all because I'm a scholarship student and I pissed Harley off by accident."

Ash groans and runs his hands through his hair. He shares a look with Blaise, and then turns to me again. "Avery is very protective, and you managed to get on the bad side of one of the three humans she gives a shit about. She won't let that go, and sometimes she goes to great lengths to keep us safe."

"Right. Which is why I don't believe you about the photos. Doesn't matter anyway, a few pictures of my tits aren't going to break me."

Ash's eyes dip down to my chest and then back to my face. It doesn't feel lecherous at all, nothing like Joey's looks. More curious. "There isn't a whole lot to see though, right? I've been sent the photos eight times and deleted them without looking."

I raise my eyebrow at him. Blaise knocks my elbow gently with his, and I flinch away from him hard. "Whoa, sorry! I was just going to say that we are pretty anti-revenge porn in our group. There was… an incident. No one has looked at it. I'm not saying we're friends, and Avery still wants you taken out, but you have at least four people who haven't seen your nudes."

"Three. Avery was there when the photos were taken," I grumble, and start to pack my bag. I'm so done with this for the night. I don't want to think about the weird, twisted triangle that is the Beaumont siblings and their friends.

Blaise scratches the back of his neck and grabs his papers.

"So, tomorrow we can meet up, right? I really do need help with my math."

I sigh and sling my bag over my shoulder. I brace myself, and then look right at his gorgeous and alluring face. Damn, his eyes are such a beautiful, clear green that I could just lose myself in them.

"Sure. I meet with Ash during the study period. If you're here, I'll help you too."

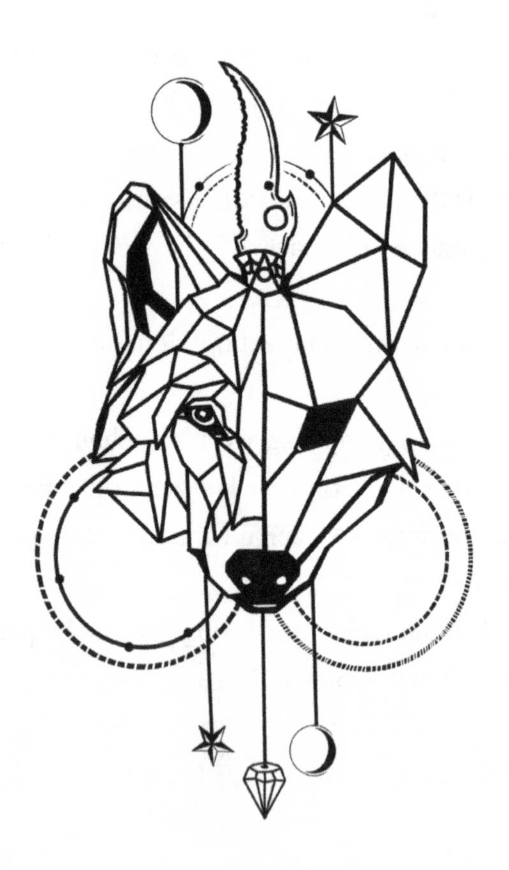

Seven

The one free study hall I have for the week without tutoring the boys is my haven.

Seeing Joey sitting at my desk is enough to piss me off. Seeing him sitting there with his boots on the table makes my blood boil. Of all the pompous, dickhead things to do, this guy just takes the cake.

His uniform is hanging on his frame a little loosely, like he's lost some weight in the last few months. His eyes are as manic and calculating as ever.

He smirks and waves an arm at me, like a king entertaining the petty whims of a peasant. I want to punch him. In the dick.

I manage to contain myself, but it's a close call.

"Mounty! I thought I'd find you here. I'm starting to think you're a bit of a nerd." His smile would be called flirty by lesser folk. I saw it for what it was: a baring of teeth, like a lion would do to its prey.

"What can I do for you, Beaumont? I have homework

to get to."

He drops his feet back to the floor and then leans forward towards me as I empty out my bag. He doesn't have any of his own class work with him, so I'm hoping he'll disappear once he has what he wants. "What's your poison? I'm having some supplies sent in, and I don't know what you like to drink. Any party favors you like? I can get whatever you'd like, on me as my guest."

Party favors.

He's asking me if I want him to buy me drugs. I give him what I hope is a bored look. His smile doesn't falter.

"I don't need anything. I'll drink whatever, I'm not a rich dick with fussy taste," I say in an airy tone.

Joey grabs one of my pens and twirls it in his fingers. I wonder how many girls he's done this with, this casual dance to lure in a victim. He's attractive, but all I see when I look at him is the evil in his eyes when he looks at his siblings. All I can see is the guy who talks down to everyone around him, the guy who calls girls he's slept with sluts.

He's waiting me out. He wants to see if I'll tell him to leave or try to get him to talk to me. I choose to ignore him instead. I've spent years learning to study no matter where I am or who is around me. I focus on the Lit assignment in front of me, and I'm jolted out of my study by another voice.

"Chatting up the Mounty? I thought she was off limits." I look up and see a familiar senior. It takes me a minute, and then I realize it's the dickhead I punched in the throat, the one who told me he would schedule me in for a fuck. Guys like this are the type to rape a woman and then tell his friends she was gagging for it. The type of guy who thinks he's a gift to the world and everyone should get on their knees for him.

I fucking hate him.

Joey is watching me with this sly look on his face, like he knows what I'm thinking. The other guy doesn't notice at all. "I don't really think that's fair-"

"Fuck fair. If you don't leave now, I'll have to make an example of you, Devon."

A single bead of sweat appears on Devon's brow and rolls down his face. It's not that warm in the library. I can see the tremble on his lip. The tiny flick of the muscle in his cheek.

Joseph Beaumont Jr. doesn't have friends.

He has victims, plebs, and pawns.

Better to be a pleb, out of his eye line and safe, than to be a pawn in his game. I don't think I have that option anymore. I think he's toying with me, testing me, until he knows whether I will have any use to him.

I fucking hate him, too.

Devon leaves without another word, and I get back to

my studying, intent on just blocking him out. I can study under any circumstances, so it's nothing for me to shut him out and get back to work. "What if I want to buy you something? I've invited you there as my guest, it would be rude not to."

I grit my teeth. I don't want him to think I owe him anything. "I'm not interested, thanks. If there's not going to be some sort of drinks table, I'll just go and dance. Not a big deal."

He blows out a breath like he's frustrated. I don't think he's ever really known that emotion. "Suit yourself. You sure do make it hard to impress you, Mounty. I've had girls start Fight Clubs over who got to have me for the night. I'm a little put out."

"No, you're not. You'll forget I exist the second you leave this room."

He laughs, and then finally he does leave. I try to ignore the sinking feeling in my stomach. I don't like the way Joey speaks about me, like I'm a thing to possess. It takes me a minute to realize why it feels so wrong, but so familiar.

That's exactly how Matteo talks about me.

One of the perks, or drawbacks depending on how you look at it, of sitting next to Harley, in the majority of my classes is that we are always paired up for assignments.

Hannaford is big on joint assignments, as they like to foster working relationships. I know this is because the other students all come from their own dynasties, and they'll all be dealing with one another once they take over the family businesses. I'll never have to worry about that shit. The best I can hope for is to be accepted into a pre-med college course.

Harley is an exemplary student, we are neck-and-neck for the top of every class but working with him can be a major pain in my ass. He likes things done his way, to the point that compromise is a dirty word to him. He will look at the syllabus and just cut the assessment down the middle, the exact middle, and in the same way every time. I'll be handed one half, and he will do the other half.

After my first experience with him, I'd made the decision to just roll with his shitty attitude, but that means that it is difficult to get ahead in my classes without knowing how he is going to split the assignment up. So I do what only an insane person would do.

I do the entire assignment, and then give him whichever half he deems to be mine.

This has become a truly joyful experience for me.

The highlight of my week, even.

Every time he tells me what I need to do, I open my bag and hand him the half I am required to do. The first time, he had scoffed at me but took the papers anyway. After reading my work, he was incredulous and pissed off. After I've done this to him in five different classes, he is now used to lagging behind me, eating my academic dust.

"How far ahead are you, really?" He's holding my half of our French Revolution assignment. I am particularly proud of this one and tempted to give Harley the other half. If I thought he would take it, I totally would, just to know how highly the teacher would mark it.

We're sitting in our history class, and we're supposed to be plotting out how we plan to do the assignment. Harley is reading through my half with raised eyebrows and a little frown on his face. I'm reveling in that look. I'm gloating. I'm feeling fan-fucking-tastic.

"I could catch a plague and be out for three months and still be the top of the class." I'm so damn smug. I can't help but be.

He shakes his head at me, but he drops my work into his binder and snaps it shut. Avery is whispering furiously at the girl she's partnered with, and I feel sorry for the poor soul. Dealing with the devil is never pleasant.

"I heard you're going to Joey's party tomorrow night." A statement, not a question. I give him a look.

"I promised I would, so I am. If I say I'm going to do something, I always follow through."

He blows out a breath, and then leans forward on his

elbows toward me. I can see his brain working, the cogs moving and mice running on the wheel. He's not happy about something.

"Look, I get that I've been a dick to you. I get that Avery has been full-on, and you have no reason to trust me, but you should not go tomorrow night. Joey is up to something, and when he's scheming, it never turns out good. Things have gone really bad in the past before, like *permanent-damage-and-death* bad. You should just pretend you've gotten sick."

How do I explain to this gorgeous, infuriating rich prick that there is no way Joey Beaumont could break me? That I'm friends with the Jackal and I survived becoming the Wolf? He wouldn't even understand what any of that means, that I'd been put to the test by the most dangerous underground criminal organization, and I hadn't just survived. I'd won.

There is no way to say it without risking more questions, so I shrug at him vaguely.

"Seriously. What do you hope to gain by going to the party with him? He's not going to date you."

I snort and give Harley an incredulous look. "You think I want to date anyone at this pompous school? None of you lot know a damn thing about real life. None of you will ever have to live in it! You'll all graduate and then live in the perfect little worlds your parents have already carved out for you, and then you'll go on to have kids and set them up into your billion-dollar empires, while I scrape to make sure I can afford to eat and keep the lights on each month. Fuck you and fuck your assumptions. I'm just here to graduate and get scholarships for college."

He looks at me like I'm a piece of shit, which is so damn confusing.

"Yeah, well, fuck you and your assumptions about me."

Because my week hasn't been bad enough, I have to sit through another choir class watching Ms. Umber fawn over Blaise.

Choir and voice development is the only class I hate going to, and I sometimes fantasize about faking a recurring head cold to get out of it. I tell myself I hate it so much because she's a teacher and at least thirty years older than him, but I think I might be a little jealous that he smiles at her and jokes along with her. It's fucking pathetic of me. We break up into our groups to run through our warm-ups, and Avery slips into the class. Her lips look pouty and bruised, like she's been making out for hours and only just come up for breath, and she smirks at Blaise. He gives her a look in return, and if I had to guess, I'd say he was pissed off. Ugh, he is probably in love with her, and I'll have to deal with them getting together and running off into the sunset and having beautiful, talented, rich babies.

I need a drink.

Maybe going to this party won't be the worst idea I've ever had.

Lauren is nice enough to take the lead in the warm-up, and I can fake my way through. Dahlia is too busy watching Blaise to contribute much, but I don't blame her. The second I hear his voice, my skin prickles with goose bumps and I mentally weep over my misfortune at going to school with him.

"Ash is going to murder Rory. Well, if Rory is lucky it'll be Ash. Otherwise Harley will do it, and Rory will *actually* die," Lauren whispers to Dahlia, and they giggle together.

"Who the hell is Rory?" I ask. Ms. Umber is busy teaching one of Avery's flunkies proper breathing techniques, so I'm not worried about my class marks.

"He's Avery's new boyfriend. He's in our grade, but he's—well, not as bright as you, so you wouldn't have any classes with him. He plays football."

A jock. Of course, she would date a football player. I glance over at Avery and find Blaise frowning at her and talking in quiet tones. I can clearly read the disapproval in the tense lines of his shoulders.

"Why will they kill her boyfriend? That's pretty

misogynistic; they all date too."

Dahlia and Lauren share a look, and then lean in toward me.

"First of all, the guys don't date, they sleep around. And Avery is the center of her brother's life. He does not cope with any sort of sharing unless it's Harley and Blaise. Last year she kissed one of the upperclassmen at the end-of-year party, and Ash broke the poor fool's jaw. *Broke it.*"

He did not seem like the type to rule over his sister. It was jarring to think of him like that. My face must give my thoughts away, because Lauren gives me a half-smile. "Cillian is a dickhead. He told his friends he would bag her and her fortune, and it got back to Ash. He was already pissed about the kiss, and when he heard that, he took Cillian out. When Cillian came back to school this year, Harley had a… chat with him, and then Cillian changed schools."

Fucking rich people.

I shake my head at them in disbelief. Imagine the arrogance, to be able to affect another kid's whole life just because they hurt your sister's feelings. The things that had happened to me without any sort of justice were staggering. My mom's neglect. Her death, beatings in foster care, seeing the Game as the only way out. I look over at the perfect princess Avery, and I've never hated the girl more.

"Don't look at her like that unless you want to die, Lips!" Lauren whispers urgently. I school my features into something more placid, and we start taking notes from Ms. Umber again.

When the class finally wraps up and I'm packing up, I hear a gasp behind me right as another body slams into my own.

My bag spills out onto the floor. I glance behind me to see who the hell knocked me and find Harlow, the girl who stood up to Ash.

"Get out of the way, Mounty trash! Bottom-feeding scum like you should bow at the feet of the elite students who actually matter."

It takes every ounce of willpower, but I don't react to her at all. After a full minute of me just staring at her, like she's the piece of shit she is, Harlow makes a noise low in her throat and flounces off. The room empties out while I pick up my books and move on to my next class.

Nothing seems amiss, right up until I get back to my room to change out for dinner.

My stomach hollows out when I see my keys sitting in the lock on my door. I know I didn't leave them there. Someone has once again had access to my room.

It takes until the early hours of the morning before I'm confident nothing has been taken or left in my room.

I hate this fucking school.

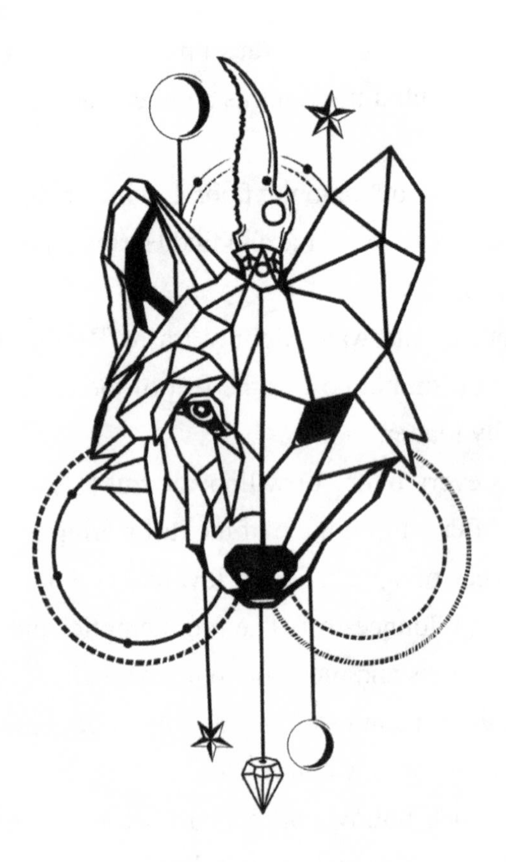

Eight

Picking an outfit for a party I don't want to go to with rich kids I hate to be around is its own special form of torture. I'm not going to wear a dress on a cold night in the woods, though I'm sure I'll be the only girl who doesn't, and my selection of jeans is tiny. Finally, I go with a dark, distressed denim, and I pair them with a lacy top, Doc Martens, and I throw my hair into a high ponytail. I do a smokey eye and nude lip color because despite my Mounty status at the school, I can make myself look great if I need to. I give myself a once-over in my mirror and try not to let the dread creep in. Going to Joey's party is a dangerous idea. I have no real friends, or even allies. I don't have Matteo there to keep an eye on me, which is a first. I've never gone out drinking without him. He'd bought me my first-ever bottle of vodka when I'd moved into the group home, and then he'd held my hair while I'd puked my guts up for hours after finishing it. One thing was certain—I would not be getting drunk tonight. As a final precaution, I slip my Matriarch serrated knife into my pocket. It's easily the most expensive thing I own, and it's gotten me out of trouble more than once.

Joey arrives at my door a little after our 10 p.m. curfew, dressed in a crisp white shirt and pressed black slacks. I try not to flinch away from his eyes as he slowly inspects every inch of my body, like I belong to him.

"Wow. I thought after seeing your nudes I'd seen everything you had on offer, but you clean up good, Mounty."

"Gee, thanks." I make sure my tone is dry as fuck, and he laughs.

"Come on now, I didn't mean anything by it! I'm just giving you a compliment, jeez. Let's head down, the underclassmen should have it all set up by now."

He holds out his arm, and I reluctantly slip my own into it. He smells like something expensive and sinful, but it does nothing for me. I can't be in his presence without seeing him slapping that kid's tray and covering him in scalding soup.

We walk out of the girls' dorms and even though I know he practically owns the school; it still shocks me that the teachers we bump into just turn on their heels and walk away without a word. It should be an instant expulsion for him setting foot up here, but he's untouchable.

There's a crowd already forming, flowing down and

out of the building, a mass exodus into the woodlands and toward the free booze. I'm sure I'm the only one who really cares about the free part. It's colder than I thought it would be, and I curse myself for not throwing on a jacket. I don't recognize any of the faces around me because there aren't a whole lot of freshmen here. I do see quite a few of the junior boys that have approached me for sex, and my face sets like concrete into an icy look.

"Don't worry about them, Mounty, let's get you a drink to loosen you up a bit. You can't dance if you're that pissed off." Joey's tone is thick and smooth, and I'm sure it did wonders on that bitch Harlow. He tugs me over to the small clearing and begins to pour drinks from a loaded table. He does a pathetic job at it. Truly terrible. I could have wiped the floor with him at any bar in the state. I glance around and see a sound system pumping out shitty pop music that makes me grit my teeth, but there's already drunk girls dancing in tiny skirts. I was right about the dress code. Joey hands me a cocktail that's some godforsaken mashup of a daiquiri and a mojito, and I down the whole thing in two gulps.

"Atta' girl! Another?"

"Fuck no. You may be rich, but you're shit at this." I push him out of the way as he roars with laughter. I swipe a bottle of tequila and drink it straight. I hear the tinkling of laughter that says Joey's friends have arrived and they're enjoying watching the poor girl drink. He steps away to greet them, and I feel the sinking sensation of unease pooling in my stomach, but I drown it with another swig straight from the bottle. I need to have enough of a buzz to survive this, but I'll have to ride the line carefully. I can't lose my head, or I might lose something else.

Joey walks back over to me and says, "Dance with me." It's not a request. He holds out his hand expectantly.

I'd rather choke, but I take it anyway and let him lead me to where the other students are grinding on each other in time with the beat. I take the tequila with me, and Joey grabs the bottle to have a swig of his own. I don't want to drink from the same bottle as him, but when he lifts the rim to my lips, I have no choice but to take it. His arms drop to my waist and he pulls me in tight against him. I hate every single thing about this, but I go along with it.

I can feel the haze of alcohol start to dig in and my limbs grow warm and loose. Joey twirls me in his arms, and as I turn, I see the girls around us staring, glaring at me. They all want to be where I am. They all want Joseph Beaumont.

Rich kids have nothing on the parties at Mounts Bay.

There's music and dancing, I've seen two blowjobs and one girl bent over a fallen tree with a guy pumping away behind her, but overall, it's pretty tame. I'm enjoying my buzz, and I'm surprised to find I'm enjoying the eyes that follow me around the party. Being here with Joey means no other guys approach me, but that doesn't mean they don't watch me dance. I've always loved jumping around and swaying and gyrating to music, and it's even better with tequila coursing through my veins.

When the bottle has been passed between us and is finally empty, Joey pulls away and whispers in my ear, "I need something a bit stronger."

I hate the feeling of his breath on my neck, but I smile and nod like a good guest. He leaves, bumping shoulders with his friends, and they take off into the denser section of the woods. I twirl and spin until the song finishes, and then I stumble over to a lawn chair set up near the drinks table.

I can't see where Joey has disappeared to and I'm starting to get suspicious that his 'something stronger' is drugs. I need to find a discreet way of leaving this party before he gets back, because there is no way in hell I'm going to be around drugs. My mother was a hard lesson to learn, but boy, did I learn it.

I'm pooling the energy to get up and leave when Harlow and three other girls sit down around me. They're all in tiny dresses, high shoes, and shivering like crazy. I groan and level her with a look. "Well, you're clearly better at this than we originally gave you credit! Bagging

Joey as your first Hannaford fuck."

Harlow is a tall girl, she has a good foot on me, and I know she enjoys playing basketball, but I'm sure that even with half a bottle of spirits under my belt I could beat her in a fight.

"I'm not fucking him."

The tinkling sounds of their giggles makes me clench my jaw. It's so fake and grates on me something wicked. "We all know he brought you here. He wouldn't do that unless he wanted something in return."

"He can want all he likes. That doesn't mean I'm going to sleep with him."

One of the girls, a platinum blonde with fire-engine red lips, leans in toward me, and I can smell the whiskey on her breath. "His family is richer than god. Why wouldn't you fuck him? Maybe your Mounty cunt will bewitch him, and you'll never have to worry about who's paying for your clothes and shoes again."

Clothes and shoes. Yep, that's my biggest concern. I roll my eyes at her and stand up. Harlow's hand shoots out, and she grabs my wrist hard. I freeze and look down my nose at her.

"Don't fall for him, Mounty. Don't you even try and get your claws into him." Her voice is dark as she stakes her claim on him. I shake her off, and then walk off in the direction of the school to the sounds of their tittering. I don't see Joey, but that suits me just fine. I'd be able to tell him I got cold and bailed tomorrow.

I can hear the sounds of students having sex as I stumble out of the clearing. It's such a cliché, these kids could sneak into each other's rooms, but instead they're out here freezing their asses off to get laid instead. I try not to look at any of them closely, since I have no interest in anyone's sex life, but as I get to the edge of the woods, I look up… and make eye contact with Harley.

He's leaning against a tree.

There's a girl kneeling at his feet, her head bobbing as she sucks his dick.

I freeze. I can't look away, and Harley doesn't break eye contact either. He doesn't look shocked to see me or embarrassed. He looks blissed out and smug as the girl goes to town on him. I can't see who it is, and I'm glad. My skin feels all hot and prickly. I'm jealous.

I guess I really am broken.

Harley quirks an eyebrow at me, but he doesn't call out to me or wave me off. He just stares at me. I can feel my face heating up and beads of sweat forming on my forehead despite the brisk breeze. Why can't I leave? I shouldn't be standing here watching this! But my traitorous body won't move. I begin to pant as a loud moan rips out of Harley's chest, and then he shudders as he starts to come. His hand digs into the girl's hair and he pulls her head back. I can see the thick white streams of his come as it coats her face. He finally shuts his eyes, and I can move away.

I bolt for the school.

I get as far as the light-horseman statue at the front of the school before I hear Joey call out to me. I curse under my breath as I turn around, and I'm still shaking from watching Harley…finish. *Jesus fucking wept.*

"Hey! The party has barely started. Don't bail on me now, Mounty!" Joey's voice is strange, hyper and excited like I've never heard it before. His sleeves are pushed up around his elbows so I can check for track marks, and I'm relieved to see none. It doesn't mean he's not smoking something, but at least he wasn't injecting heroin. I feel relieved for a second before I remember that my mom used to inject between her toes so her boss wouldn't find out, and then I'm looking at his shoes to see if they look messed with. I don't care about him at all, I just hate drugs so much that I need to know if he's using. If he is, I'm going to stop playing this little game of ours and freeze him out completely.

He catches up to me and throws his arm around my waist, pulling me into his body, and I smell it.

Cocaine.

The good shit too, all sweet and floral and none of the

chemical scent that comes with poor product. I'm sure anyone else smelling him would brush it off, but my mom spent a summer dating a cocaine dealer and he would pack his little Ziplock baggies in our living room in the morning before I would head off to school. The second I smell it on Joey, I'm back in that tiny goddamned living room getting yelled at by my mom. I freeze and Joey pulls me into his body tightly. "Come back to my room, we can party there instead," he murmurs.

I'm going to scrub my neck when I get back to my room, because he just keeps breathing on me. I can feel the tremble in his arms, and I know he's high. I'd never been hugged by my mom without feeling that vibration under her skin. I should leave him, walk off and enjoy my buzz in my room by myself, but stupidly, I feel like I should see him to the safety of his room. I know he would never do the same for me, but that didn't mean I had to stoop to his level, right? One last kind deed for this dickhead, and then I'll never speak to him again.

"Lead the way."

I feel him chuckle as the wind drowns out any sound of it. He begins to babble incessantly, but I ignore him.

My mom's addiction made some sort of sense. She had been a foster kid after my grandparents died in a house fire. She herself had only made it out of the blaze in the nick of time, and half her body was covered in thick scars. She had never been smart or motivated like I am, and she dropped out of school at fourteen. She had worked as a waitress, a dock worker, in the factories, anything she could do to eat and keep some sort of roof over her head. Then she got knocked up and found drugs. I'd never known her sober. The woman I knew was a shaking, cackling, retching, screaming banshee that would beat you if the demons in her head told her to.

Joey's addiction stemmed from boredom, and that made me so angry. All the privilege in the world, and he decides to snort cocaine instead of making something of himself. I wonder if the twins know what their brother is getting himself into. Is this why they're so afraid of him? Cocaine usually made people ecstatic and happy, not the deep and cruel violence of other narcotics, but that didn't mean he was a good person to be around.

We arrive at the boys' dorms and climb to the juniors' floor. I wonder if Ash is downstairs or if he, too, was in the woods getting off with some girl. I shake my head at myself. Pathetic. It doesn't matter what any of those boys are doing. I don't let myself think about Blaise. Seeing Harley was bad enough.

We stop outside the end room, and Joey shoves the door open. No lock. I'm guessing the other guys know exactly what will happen to them if they dare to enter this room. I push Joey's arm off my waist, and his hand latches over my wrist.

"Come in, little Mounty girl."

I pull against his grip, but his fingers tighten like a vice. He's easily twice the size of me.

He shuts the door behind us, closing me into his room.

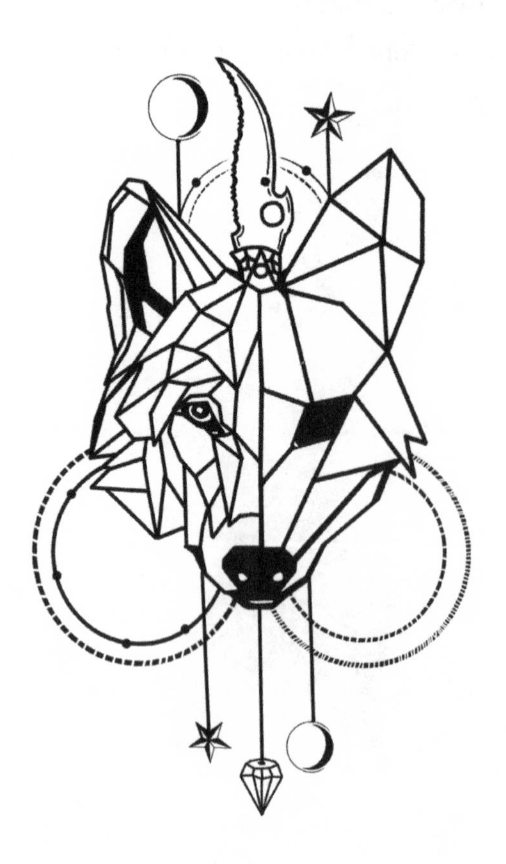

Nine

Joseph Beaumont's room is easily the size of the house I used to share with my mom.

It has a kitchen, a sitting area, a giant Cal King bed, and he has a private bathroom, which is the only thing I'm truly jealous of. Joey drags me toward the bed, and I go with him begrudgingly. I'm waiting for him to let my wrist go, and then I'll make a run for the door. I size Joey up and I know, without a doubt in my mind, that he would have no problem sexually assaulting me. His drug use makes him a bit of a wild card, so I don't know how hard he would fight me if I tried to shake him off. I could scream, but I don't think that would work all that well. The walls in the dorms are pretty thick, the other boys are probably at the party, and even if someone heard me, it's likely they wouldn't want to take on the psychotic Beaumont sibling for a poor scholarship student.

I'm on my own.

Joey sits and pulls me down next to him. His eyes

are still dancing wildly around the room, bouncing off everything they touch. "Have you ever been fucked on a mattress that costs more than a Bentley?"

I jerk away from him when his lips touch my ear. What a dumb question. I'd never tell him I am a virgin. I won't hazard a guess about what he'd do if he found out. I decide to just be honest with him, and if he attacks me, I'll have to take my chances with my knife.

"I'm not fucking you."

He chuckles and kisses my neck. I cringe away from the feeling. His fingers are still tight on my wrist, tight enough that I can feel the bones grinding together and I know it's pretty close to snapping. My fingers start tingling. Writing assignments will be a bitch if he breaks it. I slip my fingers into my pocket and grip my knife, but I don't pull it out just yet. I give it one last try.

"Joey. I'm not having sex with you. Let me go."

He grunts and rips my arm until I sprawl backwards onto the bed and covers me with his own body. The hand I have wrapped around the handle of my knife is trapped between our bodies, and I can feel his erection digging into my thigh. Instinct tells me to scream, but I choke it back. I put the scared fifteen-year-old girl into a box, and I let the Wolf take over. The Wolf is calm and patient and can wait for the right moment to go for his throat.

"Just lay still. You might find you have less trouble at

this school once you've been fucked by me." His lips crush into mine, and I can feel his tongue come out and force its way into my mouth.

I've never been kissed before.

It's disgusting.

I might never kiss a guy again, if it's always like this.

I arch my back deliberately and he purrs at me, obviously thinking I'm melting for him. It gives me just enough room to pull the knife out of my pocket and press it against his groin. I'm aiming for his femoral artery, but I know he's more worried about his dick when he pulls away and gapes down at me. There's a comical look on his face, and I know it's only there because the cocaine has taken hold.

"Get off me." I say softly. The vein in his neck is flicking, his blood pumping like crazy. He's frozen for a second, just staring down at the knife pressed against the hard line of his dick.

He finally releases my wrist and stumbles back. I can see the high is really setting in, and for once in my life I'm glad he's taken cocaine. I don't want to think about how he would fight back if he were lucid. He runs a hand over his face and laughs.

"Fuck it. It's not like I need the money, I was just hoping for the bragging rights."

Money? Bragging rights? What the hell was he going

on about? I shoot him a glare and raise the knife toward him as I edge around him toward the door. Maybe Ash had been right, maybe I should have taken his warnings a little more seriously. Clearly, Joey is more than a psychopath. He's also deranged. "What the hell are you going on about? I wasn't going to give you money."

He laughs again, and I flinch at the cruel edge to it. "My family earns more money in a minute than your worthless bloodline ever has, so clearly I didn't mean your money. If you fuck me, I'll win the sweep."

"What fucking sweep?"

He smirks and stands up. His pants have a clean cut in them from my knife, and I can clearly see the outline of his erection in his dark boxers. A dark thrill of panic shoots through my blood, and I look back up at his face quickly.

"First to fuck you gets the sweep. There's currently a hundred and forty grand on the line, and it's climbing daily. I thought it would be worth a quick fuck even if you are Mounty trash."

A hundred and forty grand?! That's more than four times the amount my mom used to earn in an entire year at the docks, and these pompous dicks are throwing it around on a stupid bet? I see red. I see so much red that I think about slapping his handsome, cruel face. I think about stabbing him too, but then I count down slowly from five until my vision clears. This boy is way too dangerous for a scholarship girl to mess with without a plan. If I want to end him, I'll have to be more subtle about it.

And now.

Now I want to end him.

The walk back to the girls' dorm is much more tense now that I don't have a rich dickhead to clear the path from teachers. I have to duck and weave, and I find myself thankful that Hannaford is a big, old, castle-like building with lots of alcoves and statues to hide behind. I sigh with relief when I make it and sneaking past the other freshman's rooms is easy. I get to the sitting area across from my room when I see Avery straddling some guy and making out with him like she's starving for oxygen, and he's the best option she's got.

I don't have the problem I did with Harley, and I sprint to my room. Once I'm safely locked inside, I give myself a minute to freak out about Joey and how close I came to something terrible happening. When the minute is up, I change into my pajamas and climb into my bed.

I don't sleep.

I think about skipping classes the day after the party because it's the last day before fall break, but I don't want to ruin my perfect attendance record. I spend double my usual time on my makeup, because you can see every sleepless minute carved into my face. I finally give up and head straight to class, skipping breakfast. My stomach is rolling with the memories of the tequila last night, and I'm sure if I touch food, I'll hurl. I'm early enough that I've even beaten the teacher to history, so I enjoy the quiet.

I collapse into my desk and rest my head against my textbooks. I'm sure I look hungover, but I can't summon enough energy to care. I hear the teacher arrive and I give her a little wave without looking up. She doesn't seem to be concerned that I'm expiring at my desk. Then I feel the chair next to mine pull out and Harley drops into his seat. I glance up at him and he looks too healthy, too happy, just too much, and I give him a glare.

"Did someone have a big night?" he says, too loud and far too cheery. I want to hurt him.

"Feel free to choke," I reply, and he grins at me. Avery is already at her spot in front of us and she looks down her nose at me with a smirk. The class starts, and she flips her hair at me. I spare her a second of my time, just long enough to wonder if she has anything else planned for me, before I push her out of my mind.

I manage to pull myself together enough to get through the class. My stomach gurgles toward the end, and Harley keeps slipping me these looks until I'm squirming in my chair.

"Enjoy the show?" He doesn't look at me when he says

this, and I know it's on purpose. He's taking notes for the homework we're supposed to get done over the break. It takes me a second to remember what I saw last night in the woods. I can't think about any of it without thinking about Joey's dick pressing into me and his body pressing me into the bed. My wrist is still aching, and I'm a little worried he's sprained it.

"Not particularly. Though if you need my opinion, I'd suggest you start using protection. The girls at this school get around even more than Mountys do, and you don't want to catch something that makes your dick fall off."

He smirks at me, and then leans in toward me. He smells amazing, and usually I'd secretly love feeling the heat from his torso against mine, but I'm just not in the mood for his shit today.

"That's why she was sucking me off."

I lean away from him and shoot him a glare. I don't find his banter amusing. I don't want to high-five him, except maybe slapping him would be cathartic. I decide to change tactics instead.

"Did you know there's a price on me? Did you know that's why I'm being stalked by guys at this shitty school?"

Harley's smirk falters on his lips for a second, and then it's as strong as ever.

"Everyone knows about it. They all know Joey staked his claim on you as well."

Staked his claim, like I'm a slab of fucking meat. I feel the grips of that white-hot rage taking me again. Harley must see it too, because his face splits into a grin. "Like I said, Mounty, if you hit Joey, I will take that memory to bed for the rest of my life."

"Fuck hitting him," I whisper back, and Avery turns to glare at us both. It must kill her that I'm next to Harley in nearly all our classes. She can't contain him or control him if she's not right beside him.

The bell tolls. I shove my books away and pull out the required homework for the fall break. I enjoy the feeling of all the students' eyes on me as I hand it over to the teacher. She takes it with a shocked look, and then scans over the page.

"Well done, Miss Anderson. Enjoy your fall break."

Harley is the only student who knows how far ahead I am, so he's the only student not gaping at me when I arrive at every class for the day with all the assignments already complete. Even Avery is hissing at me by the end. I'm smug as fuck, knowing they'll all be at home with their families and slaving over classwork, and I'll be running around Hannaford doing whatever the hell I want to do.

I refuse to go down to the dining hall for dinner. I don't want to see Joey or be approached by any of his raucous group. I don't know if he's now lifted his ban and I'll be propositioned in the halls again, so I settle into my bed and try to ignore the rumbling of my stomach. By tomorrow afternoon I'll have the building to myself, and I'll be able to eat all I want.

Fall break is the best week of my life so far.

I sleep in. I shower at odd times of the day. I eat whenever I feel even the slightest bit peckish. I watch movies on my phone and dance around my room in my underwear while listening to good music. I do whatever the hell I want, and I do it in my own time. I feel free.

I should know by now that nothing good in my life lasts.

I'm enjoying my last day of quiet in the sitting area when I hear my phone ping. I very rarely get texts, and there's only one person with my contact details. My heart sinks as I pick it up and see Matteo's text.

I've been asked to contact you about a job.

A job. That could mean anything from tailing someone's girlfriend to killing an errant informant. Coming to Hannaford Prep has been an attempt to close the door on my old life in Mounts Bay and to start a new, legitimate life. I had done things at Matteo's command that I wanted to leave firmly in the past. The trouble was Matteo had no intention of letting me go. I would always belong to him.

I'm not leaving Hannaford until summer break. The

food is free and good. Sorry.

I chew on my lip for a minute, and then I dig out my emergency bottle of whiskey while I wait for his reply. I'd smuggled it in on the first day but hadn't felt the need to drink it until now.

I owe a lot to Matteo. He's the reason I'm alive today. I could just have easily stayed with him in Mounts Bay and dropped out. He had encouraged me to, he wanted to bring me into his organization and have me run it with him. If I hadn't gotten the scholarship, I would have been inducted and become one of his pawns. I'm not a fool, I know he's the head of a gang. I know he sells drugs.

I know he kills people.

I try to think about those years in foster care as a story, something that happened to some other girl. It's easier to do now that I'm here in the sheltered halls of Hannaford. I have a real buzz going on before I finally take that trip down memory lane.

Once upon a time, a young girl finds herself orphaned and at a group house. Another kid takes her under his wing. He protects her and cares for her for an entire year. She is lost and hungry, but she thinks someday she will know what it means to be happy.

And then one day he tells her he's named her in the Game. She doesn't know what that means, but he tells her it's the only way she will ever be safe and free. So, she learns. She learns how to fight. She learns how to disappear. She learns how to make others disappear. And then she competes. She is broken beyond repair. She will never run again. She is covered in scars. She can't sleep at night, she can't bear the sound of her own voice, she sleeps with a knife, she startles at every sound, she's scared of what hides in the shadows, she can't breathe—

She wins.

She is crowned the Wolf.

She could become a leader. Have a gang of her own, make millions, live an untouchable life. She goes to school instead. Gets a scholarship. Disappears. Tries to forget all the things she did to get to where she is. She does forget, most of the time. She forgets until the Jackal calls her home.

It's the Boar. He'll pay cash or a favor. Whichever you prefer. The job is small enough. It can wait until summer break.

Despite what the spoiled kids here think, I don't actually need the money. The favor makes it tempting. I'm owed a lot of favors, and I like having them up my sleeve. I could have Joey taken out of my life as permanently as I wanted. It amuses me that Ash and Harley warn me about him.

If only they knew who I really was.

Ten

"Joey wants to see you in the chapel after the assembly," Harlow says to me with a smug look on her pretty face.

I'm sitting in the dining hall on the first day back after the break, lamenting all the noisy students after my week of peace. I also have a teensy bit of a hangover after finishing off the whiskey, and I'm not in the mood to deal with Joey's bullshit. I stare Harlow down until she finally gets the picture and stomps off. I cradle my piping hot, black coffee and try to absorb the superpowers of the caffeine. The school doesn't serve hot coffee, but I have a small stash in my room for emergencies.

Today is an emergency.

I'm having a moment when I hear Blaise's voice down the table from me. I'm proud to say I can now listen to it without wanting to die, but I still can't look him in the damn face. I glance over and see he's only a couple of seats away, surrounded by other students in our grade. I can't help but listen in.

"My parents are pissed at my scores. Father wants me to spend more time at home, and Mother is backing him up for once. I think she's still pissed I went on a tour to Europe without asking her first."

The group around him laughs, and I can hear the fake tones from where I sit. How awful it must be to have to entertain all these kids who are just trying to gain social status by sitting with you. I'd feel bad for him, but he's a rock god with millions in the bank and an established career. He doesn't need my sympathy.

"Father wants to get me on track to take over Kora from him. I have no interest in technology and manufacturing. I'm not going to pull my grades up just for his dreams," he continues. His eyes are guarded and sharp, and I can't look at them for longer than a second. Kora is his family's business. His dad became a billionaire in his twenties by manufacturing computer parts during the first big technology wave.

"At least you're doing better than me in math. Maybe you should study more and mess around on your guitar less."

A wounded look darts across Blaise's face, but he covers it with a smirk effortlessly and the girl who spoke doesn't seem to notice. The lyrics I've listened to and sung over the years that he wrote come to me all at once. Living a lie, wearing a mask, walking alone. None of these kids understand him. No one here really knows what it feels like to have melodies creep into your subconsciousness while you sleep and steal your soul. None of them have listened to the same words over, and over again, until they're burned into their being. None of them understand what it means to be Blaise fucking Morrison. If you had told me two years ago that I'd be listening to Blaise have this conversation at school one day, I wouldn't believe you.

"Never mind. Obviously, you'll do what your father wants."

Blaise gives the girl a look, and I realize I recognize her. She's the girl I saw in the woods that night with Harley. A blush begins to crawl along my cheeks as I think about the white streaks that painted her pretty face. She's stroking Blaise's bicep possessively. He doesn't pull away from her, even though he's obviously pissed. "Why would I give up my music, Annabelle? I'm already successful, I've made my own money independently. Why would I give that up for the stuffy, corporate life?"

Annabelle laughs again and the muscle in Blaise's jaw ticks, but he still doesn't move away. Is she his girlfriend? Is she cheating on him with one of his best friends? I can't imagine Harley doing that. Maybe I don't know him at all.

"Your parents are worth *billions*. You don't give up money like that for some singing and dancing."

I snort. I can't help myself; it just happens. Breakfast has wound down enough that Annabelle clearly hears it and looks over at me. I've never noticed her before, but she knows all about me. Everyone at the school knows about the Mounty trash amongst them.

"This is a private conversation. Inferior students aren't welcome." Her voice is sweet and her face a mask of placid joy. If I've learned nothing else about the human race, it is that the quiet ones are usually the worst. Best to nip this in the bud.

"Inferior? You've both just said you're flunking the lower math class, and you're not in any of the other top classes with me. Clearly *I'm* not the inferior student."

Annabelle doesn't flinch. She just flips her long, mousy brown hair over her shoulder and looks at me like I'm nothing. I consider slamming her pretty face into the table, but then I rein myself in. I don't need another rich kid hating on me. I need to learn to shut my mouth and keep my head down.

I need to stop feeling all these emotions for gorgeous rich boys.

Blaise is sitting there surrounded by people he's probably known his whole life, and yet none of them understand how badly he needs his music. None of them have looked past his handsome face and his bank balance to see the real guy underneath it all. I'm not stupid, I know he isn't just his musical talent, but I'm certain that I know more about him than this Annabelle girl does. She's vapid, shallow, and hungry for the immense wealth that being with Blaise would give her access to. "You could be the smartest girl on Earth, and you'll still never be someone worth our time." She laughs and looks around at the others they're sitting with to make sure they're laughing too.

I do not need the trouble opening my mouth will bring me. But I do it anyway. My temper is going to get me killed someday; Matteo says it to me all the time. I should really listen to him. He's killed people for dishing out less honesty than I am. "I'd rather be poor and smart than rich and brainless. You can't even tell how pissed off you've made Morrison."

I don't look away from my breakfast, but I can see her eyes narrow at me from the corner of my eye. Blaise doesn't say a word, and I wonder again if she's his girlfriend. She lets him go and turns on me, but I snort at her derisively and tuck back into my breakfast. "Well, that just shows you're a stalker and he should start sleeping with one eye open at night. I did hear you're obsessed with him. Don't you sleep in one of his band tees?"

I try not to blush, but I fail. Avery fucking Beaumont and that damned photo she took of me in my pajamas. Of course she's shared it around. I glue my eyes to Annabelle so my traitorous eyes can't flit over to Blaise. "Actually, it shows I like his music, and not his reputation or his face. But what am I saying? At this school, all the girls just like how much money a guy has."

She rolls her eyes at me, and I clench my fists at her. "Sure you don't. It doesn't matter anyway; he would never fuck trash. No guy with any self-respect at this school would."

I know I need to work on my poker face now that I'm not channeling the Wolf every day, but I manage to stare the little bitch down as I clear up my breakfast. I accidentally glance toward Blaise and see the look he's giving me, like I've just shocked the shit out of him. I pick up my tray and leave the dining hall without looking back. I tell myself I'm not going to hate Annabelle just because she's sleeping with two of the hottest guys in our grade, but I've never been good at lying to myself.

I'm still feeling hot and irritable with embarrassment when I take a seat at the assembly.

Blaise is sitting two rows in front of me, and Harley is with him. They're both laughing and nudging each other boisterously. The twins are nowhere in sight.

I look around to find Annabelle sitting among Avery's flunkies. She's gazing at the two boys with appreciative and possessive eyes. She could be sleeping with them both and hiding it. They could be sharing her. *I wish they'd share me,* I think, and then I shut that part of my brain down tight. I am Mounty trash to them. I need to get over my little crushes. They will never want someone like me, and the sooner I accept that, the better.

Mr. Trevelen stands on the small stage, and the chatter around me ceases. The twins still haven't appeared, and Harley looks around, concern clear on his face. Blaise joins in and he looks back at me. I feel a jolt of lightning in my blood as his eyes meet mine, and I look away quickly. I hate that I have somehow gained his attention, and I definitely shouldn't have come to his defense in the dining hall. He didn't need my help with anything but his studies. He certainly didn't thank me for interfering.

As the principal's speech starts and he drones on, I watch as Harley becomes more and more agitated. He's practically vibrating in his chair, his leg bouncing so hard I can feel it two rows back, and his hand keeps running through the hair at the back on his head until it's all mussed up. His concern worries me. I glance around and I see Joey isn't here either. Harlow and that idiot Devon are both present. I pick out all of Joey's cronies. Not a good sign. I have a sinking feeling that the violence Joey unleashes on his siblings is kept behind closed doors.

No wonder Harley and Blaise are antsy.

Harley makes as if to stand, and Blaise shoots out

an arm to keep him seated. I can't hear what they're whispering, but they're getting more and more heated. The other students around them are starting to take notice.

"Trouble in paradise?" Lauren murmurs. She's been getting braver about talking to me outside of our choir class. I give her a sidelong look and grin, and she wiggles her eyebrows in response. I don't question myself before I ask, "Hey, do you know anything about that Annabelle girl? The brunette over there?"

Lauren doesn't have to look to where I gesture.

"Yeah. Her family are old money, but not like Beaumont's. Her great-grandfather was loaded, something to do with oil, but then her grandfather made a lot of bad business moves. They nearly lost it all. Her father married her mom to pay back debts, and now they're stable enough. She struts around like she's royalty, when really her father is constantly skating on ice to keep them millionaires."

Huh. Calling me inferior when she's pretending her family isn't struggling? What an idiot. Especially if it's common knowledge. I guess that's what they call fake it 'til you make it.

"She's obsessed with Avery's boys. She drapes herself over them at every opportunity. Avery only allows it because she's discreet about whether she's actually banging them."

My eyebrows shoot up. "Them? As in…"

Lauren nods and eyes the back of Blaise's head with

pure lust. "She's totally doing them all. Her room is next to mine, and her roommate is constantly getting kicked out because one of them shows up."

Yep. I hate her. I think I might even hate her as much as I hate Joey. Damn my hormones. This must all show on my face, because Lauren grins at me again and nods, her own jealousy clear to see.

Mr. Trevelen starts handing out awards, and I try to focus again. I know I'm going to get one of the academic trophies, and I'm sure Harley will too. As students begin to take the stage and accept their framed accolades, I see Harley slip away. Blaise doesn't move, and when my name is finally called, I catch a glimpse of his face as I walk past.

He's livid.

His eyes are glowing green orbs and his jaw is clenched so tight, I'm worried his teeth will crack.

I take my award and stand on the stage to have my photo taken. Harley's name is called out, and when he doesn't come up, Mr. Trevelen grumbles into the microphone. I look down at Blaise again and I feel the dread start to take hold in my stomach.

I look around to see Harlow smirking at me. I'm not afraid of her summoning me to face Joey at all. I'm only really worried about what he's doing to the twins. I'm clearly crazy, because Avery is trying her best to get me out of the school and Ash insults me every opportunity he has.

Yet I'm still having trouble breathing.

When I arrived at the abandoned warehouse to complete the last round of the Game, I had been faced with the remaining members of the Twelve. There were only eleven men present, plus myself and the two other contenders for the spot. The Coyote and the Fox both looked at me like I was a raw piece of meat. It didn't rattle me; I'd spent weeks being put to the test, and I had gotten used to being the untried liability of the group. Only the Jackal looked at me like I was someone worth backing.

I wasn't afraid of Geordie. He was the bigger of the two other contenders, but he only really had his size to use to try and win. He wasn't bright, or cunning, he didn't know how to blend in, or take someone by surprise. He didn't have the skills required to seduce someone into taking a drink without sniffing it first, or to get out of handcuffs or an exemplary sailor's knot. He didn't know how to survive in the underground criminal world.

Xavier did. He only looked at me when he absolutely had to but when he did, I felt the piercing slice of his eyes on every inch of my soul. If I lost to him, he would take pleasure in what he did to me. Every cut his blade made would be savored, every ounce of blood would be intentional.

I know exactly what it means to look into the soul of a killer.

When I arrive at Hannaford Prep's chapel, the grin on Joey's face chills me to my core.

He's not pretending to be a decent person anymore. There's no fake civility. All I see is the evil that lives under his skin. An echo of Xavier rings out in my mind and the inventory of what it took to disable him. I can't believe I'd thought he looked like Ash and Avery. The differences in the siblings are so clear to me now that I struggle to see their similarities. I am no longer blinded by the good looks.

The girl I had put away to come to this school, the one that lived inside a box in my mind—her job wasn't quite done yet.

"Thank you for joining us, Mounty." His tone is conversational and jovial. I want to hit him so badly; I clench my fists to stop myself from lunging at him. "I thought we should all get to know you a little better. I took the liberty of looking into your records so we could get a better idea of who Eclipse Anderson *really* is."

My records, *fuck.* I manage to keep my breathing even. They can't know about Matteo or the Wolf. There's no written evidence of my position within the Club, or as one of the Twelve. I'd never been caught or implicated in any of my jobs. There's nothing he could have that would break me.

I wasn't wrong.

He doesn't break me.

But fuck it if I don't bend a little.

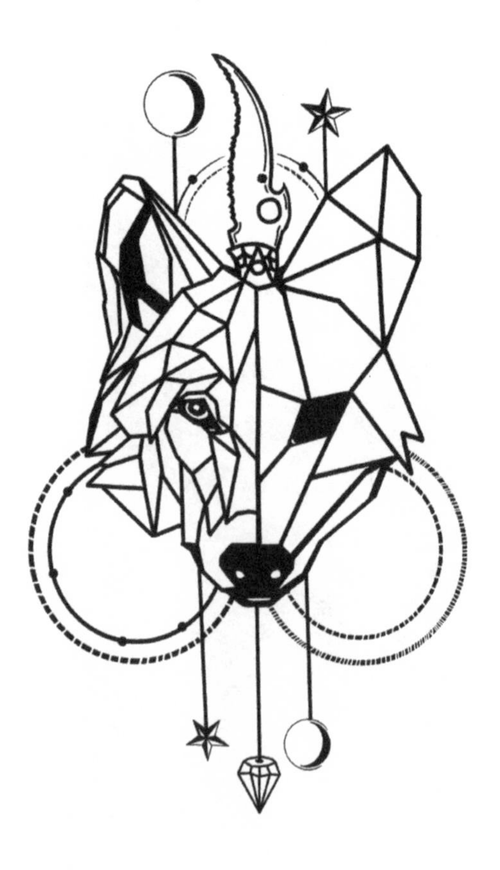

Eleven

I'm the only kid in my class who walks to and from school without a parent or older sibling. The area I live in isn't safe, not by a long shot, but my mom doesn't care if I make it home alive. She would probably rather I disappeared, so she didn't have to feed me.

The holes in my jeans aren't artfully placed or fashionable. The shirt I'm wearing has bloodstains from the last time my mom's boyfriend smacked me so hard my nose shattered. I still have the lump to remind me not to breathe too loudly around a guy so high on meth, he thinks his skin is crawling with insects and the walls are bleeding. My mom had told me it was my own fault as she threw a dirty rag at me to wipe up. I didn't have any respect for her left to lose.

My teacher had pulled me to the front of the class to sing happy birthday to me. I was embarrassed, and I didn't want to admit it was the first time I'd ever been sung to. What kid wants to admit their mom never remembers the day they were born? I only knew when my birthday was because of my enrollment at school and the teachers adding my name to the class birthday tree each year.

I hear sirens in the distance as I approach the front steps of our house. It's barely a step up from sleeping on the streets. It's ancient and decrepit and it belongs to my mom's dealer. He arrives twice a week to take his payment from her, and she makes me sit outside while she gives it to him. I can still hear them.

The door is locked, but I don't need a key. I jiggle the door handle until the lock springs free and the door opens. The room is dark as I enter, but that's nothing out of the ordinary. I kick my shoes off and sling my bag to the floor, wincing as I feel the straps pull. It's threadbare and ratty, like everything else I own. I've had to use duct tape to fill in a hole, and I know I'm a few short weeks away from having to find a replacement. I have no money and no way of making money. Well, there are ways I could make money, but the thought of getting down onto my knees in the bathroom of the gas station on the corner and doing… that stuff is inconceivable to me. I know girls my age who are doing it to eat at night. I'd rather starve.

I do starve.

I start toward the kitchen, and as soon as the door cracks open, the smell hits me. I gag and step back. It smells like vomit and shit and rotting meat. There had been a heatwave happening in Cali for weeks, and the temperature had gone over a hundred degrees every day that week. We didn't have air conditioning or even a fan. I'd learned to just sweat it out. It helped that I was skin and bone.

I know now that the heat had accelerated my mother's decomposition.

She had overdosed. Vomited and shat herself while she fitted on the dirty kitchen floor. I might have even been home that morning when it happened and not noticed. Her eyes are bloodshot and milky. Her hands are rigid and twisted like claws, and one of her fingernails is ripped out at the nail bed from where she clawed at the floor in her dying moments. Her hair is lank and matted. Her lips are blue and stretched over what is left of her rotting teeth. I can see the burn scars that cover her arms and belly, the gray hue of her skin distorting the look until I'm sure she's made of wax and this is all a nightmare.

It takes me a while to realize I'm screaming.

The smell has crawled up through my nose and down into my lungs and I think I'll never be able to get it out of my body again. I'm rooted to the ground. I can't move my arms or my legs, every fiber of my being has turned to stone. I just stand and stare and bear witness to the demise my mother had been crawling toward my entire life.

I'm only nine years old.

Eventually, long after the sun has set and the traffic has

picked up on the road out front, I shake myself out of the trance I'm in. I need help. I need to call someone to get her and take her away. I just want someone to take her away.

There's no landline. I don't have a cell phone, but my mom has one. I do a quick check of the house with shaking knees. There're only really three rooms to check, so I'm quick about it. Then I realize, with a stuttering heart that just won't pump the way it's supposed to, that I can see the outline of the cell in her pocket.

I have to touch her to get it out.

I sit and hug my knees. I let myself cry for the first time, but I hate the feel of the fat, hot tears sliding down my cheeks. I think the smell has dissipated, but really, I've just grown accustomed to it. My body has absorbed the unthinkable stench of death, and now I'm immune.

The feel of my mother's skin slipping from her bones as I wiggle the cell out of her pocket will stay with me forever. If I ever need to vomit on command, that is the memory I recall. I open the back door to vomit on the rickety wooden steps.

My hands shake as I dial 911.

I pause before I hit call. I'm a smart kid. I know what will happen if I call emergency services. There are girls in my class being abused by their foster dads. I could just run away. I could leave and let the neighbors call it in when the smell finally hits them. It's tempting, but then I think about the girls kneeling in the gas station restroom, and I finally hit the call button.

My voice shakes.

I am only nine years old.

As the recording of my 911 call plays over the PA system, I have two choices. I can give in to the chaos of my trauma, or I can retreat into the dark and survive. It's not really a choice. *I can never lose myself again.* I had climbed out of the pit of Mounts Bay tooth and nail. I would never be forced back into the desperate form I'd once been.

I let the calm wash over me instead.

I let everything drop away from me. Everything that is destroying the little scraps that remain of my soul slips away and, instead, I open the box in my mind, and I let my senses out to play. I'd honed these senses for two years under the watchful eye of the Jackal. I'd learned how to walk in and out of a building without a single eye touching me. I'd learned how to endure extreme, bone-shattering pain without screaming out. I'd learned how to kill a man. I'd left all this behind me when I'd arrived at Hannaford, but now I let it all out.

I'm surrounded. There are two exits, the door I just came through and one on the far side of the room. I see a familiar flash of blond hair, but I put that aside. I don't need to be distracted by gorgeous, intelligent, ruthless boys. There're wooden bench seats in neat rows, littered with students gaping at the scene playing out before them. Joey has chosen the spot with careful consideration to maximize the audience and my humiliation. I don't have any allies in this room, I don't have my knife, and there isn't much I can do to stop the recording. The damage is done.

Joey is smirking at me, and he's flanked by his usual group of guys. Every last one of them has approached me for sex, every single one has tried to win the bet. I look at each one of them long enough to commit their faces to my memory. I will never forget their willing participation in this. The girls who flock them are all laughing behind sly hands, fanned out. If they try to attack me, I know exactly what to do. I may not have my knife, but I don't truly need it. As long as my busted leg holds together, I know I have a chance of getting out of the room. I doubt the girls have ever raised a fist in their lives, and the guys… well, I doubt they've ever had to fight for their lives. I don't make the first move. I don't need to. One of Joey's flunkies grabs my arm, in an attempt to stop me from leaving.

Big mistake.

My body is in survival mode. Not private school, I'm-so-sad survival mode, but true life-or-death survival mode. The type of survival you need when your back is against the wall and a guy three times the size of you is coming at you for blood. The type you need to survive your leg being smashed to pieces and someone looming over you with a knife. The type of thing none of these rich kids could ever understand. My eyes lock with Harley. He's standing at the end of the chapel, and he's the only one not laughing. He's the only one who can read the cold, dead calm in my eyes. He doesn't call out to help the girl who's touched me. He just stands witness.

Good.

Let him watch.

I swing the textbook that's in my arms and listen to the satisfying crunch as Harlow Roqueford's nose breaks, shatters completely under the sheer force of my swing.

Her blood goes flying, I'm spattered in it, and the room explodes with her screams. She drops to her knees and cradles her face with both of her hands. I get a fist full of her hair, and her hands scramble at me pathetically. I tighten my grip until she squeals, and her hands drop to her side. Her eyes meet mine and they're wide, petrified. Devon lurches toward us, but he stops when I jerk her body closer to mine. The PA system is still playing the 911 call, it's on repeat, and I can hear the nine-year-old version of me screaming, but the fifteen-year-old me, standing here covered in blood with a fist full of some rich bitch's hair—she is hollow. She is carved out until there is nothing but cold, dead calm.

She is the Wolf.

"Let her go. You can't take us all." Devon tries to command, but his voice trembles. Pathetic. My eyes stay on Harley. He's watching me with such a grim satisfaction that I wonder what this group has been doing to him. I wonder what torture his cousin had been putting him through. I wonder what he did to the twins today. I answer Devon without bothering to glance at him.

"Are you sure?" My voice doesn't tremble. It does, however, push them all back. Everyone except Joey takes a step away from me. He holds his arms out and grins at me.

"Looks like you're out, Mounty. This school is a zero-tolerance establishment. The principal has no choice but to throw you out like the trash you are." His words should inspire some sort of dread in me, but nothing can penetrate my frozen walls. I pull Harlow up to stand by her auburn hair, and her whimpers fail to incite any sort of remorse on my part. She's crying. Fat tears are rolling down her face and mixing with the blood pouring from her nose. I think about pushing her, bending her and seeing how quickly she breaks. I doubt it would take much. Her eyes are pleading on mine. Truly pathetic. She would never survive the Jackal. She's a child playing at a game she has no real place in.

"Run," I whisper, and then I let go. Harlow flings herself

into Devon's arms and he pulls her out of the chapel. The other students' part, and some follow them out. I see that the crowd is dispersing, and then I hear why.

"Miss Anderson. My office. Now."

The principal has arrived.

Joey looks at me, and the sick pleasure I see in his eyes melts the ice I've encased myself in a little. He thinks he's untouchable. Maybe. Maybe he just hasn't found the right opponent yet.

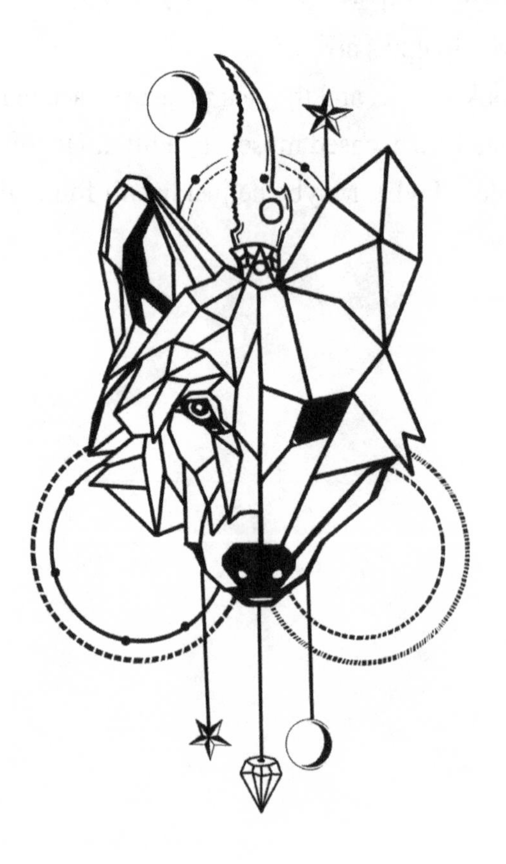

Twelve

Mr. Trevelen leaves me in his office to go and check on Harlow.

He's not happy with me, but he also hasn't expelled me yet. Joey didn't just play the recording in the chapel. I have to face the fact that the entire school has now heard the call. They all know about the worst thing that has happened to me.

Or so they think.

I wait for two whole minutes before I reach out and take the phone on Trevelen's desk. I punch in Matteo's number and I wait for him to answer. My eyes dance around and focus in on the watercolor painting of lilies over the bookshelf. It's pretty, but bland. There's no real passion in the strokes, just like every kid at this school. Pretty, vapid, empty, useless.

"How did you get access to the principal's landline?" he answers, and I wonder again if he has eyes in the school.

"They're going to expel me. I broke a girl's nose."

My voice is flat, emotionless. My eyes trace to the blood drying on my hands with detached interest.

Matteo chuckles, but he stops when I don't join him. I can hear the chatter in the background. He's at his house, I can tell by the sounds of the ocean and the low tones of the shitty jazz rap he listens to when he's plotting. I recognize all the voices as the henchmen he likes to surround himself with. A show of muscle to distract from the fact that Matteo is always the most dangerous man in the room. "What's happened, my Wolf?"

I'm not his. I will never be his. I will fight tooth and nail, with everything I have, to not be his girl. It doesn't matter, though. I can never tell him that; only bide my time until I can make an escape.

"I need your help. I'm willing to call in a favor."

I can hear him moving around and closing a door. His voice is gentle, soothing, but I'm not falling for his games anymore. I'm not the scared little girl on that 911 call anymore. I just need him to fix this for me, I need him to have my back again. "No favor necessary. Tell me what you need."

I twirl the phone's cord around my finger and stare at it with glassy eyes. I need to hold onto this calm apathy as long as I possibly can. "I cannot be expelled. I'm going to destroy the kid who is doing this to me."

"What is he doing? I can remove his piece from the

board, if you want me to." The calm offer to kill Joey for me is tempting. I'm definitely going to hell, because it takes me a full minute before I can reply.

"No. I'm going to destroy him at his own game. It's not satisfying if I can't do it myself."

"That's my girl. I'll fix it for you. No favor required, but I will ask that you make it to the Club meeting in the summer."

He's so intent on getting me to the meeting, so I take note, filing it away for inspection at a later date, when I can think clearly. I hear the principal coming back, so I agree and hang up. By the time I've straightened myself back into my chair, Mr. Trevelen strides back into his office. He sits down and begins to fidget with his shirt cuffs. He seems so nervous, and I feel bad for putting him in this situation. He believed in me enough to offer me the scholarship despite my emancipation. He'd had to fight with the school board for them to let me in. Now I'd just proved them all right. I'm just an angry girl from Mounts Bay who can't fit in with the polished, upper-society teenagers. I've failed him. *Don't lose it now,* I tell myself as I blink back the hot tears.

He finally clears his throat and opens his mouth. The phone rings. He frowns but holds up a finger to signal that I must wait. I nod, and he picks up the phone.

"Yvette, I'm sure I just asked you to hold calls."

He pauses, and then he turns ghostly pale.

"Put him through."

Sometimes I'm amazed at the reach Matteo has managed to achieve. I doubt he even knew Hannaford existed before I told him I was applying here. I also know the moment I got my scholarship; he would have started to reach out and find all the secrets he would need to use to manipulate these people. I wondered what Trevelen had done. I wonder what skeletons he was hiding that Matteo was threatening to shine a light on. From the look on his face, it wasn't good. He looked like he wanted to vomit up his breakfast all over his lovely oak desk.

After a terse 'of course,' Mr. Trevelen hangs up and then he looks at me like he's never seen me before. He looks at me like he's let a monster into his school.

He has.

"I'm going to let you off with a warning this time, Miss Anderson, in light of… new information. Harlow will also be receiving a warning for her prank on you. I will not be so lenient on you if you choose to retaliate." I stare him down. I'm sure he would turn a blind eye on anything I choose to do from here on out, now that he's been threatened by the Jackal. I nod obediently and stand.

"I'm going to go get cleaned up. I'll skip my next class, but I'll be in my Health Ed."

He nods and motions for me to leave as he drags a silk handkerchief over his sweaty forehead. I'm tempted to call

Matteo back and ask what his buttons were, but sometimes, ignorance is bliss. I'd rather not find out the depths of evil this man has stooped to.

Yvette stares at me as I walk out free and clear. Classes have resumed, so I don't see anyone all the way up to the girls' dorms. I head into the bathroom to shower and clean Harlow's blood off me. I take my bag into the stall with me, and I don't let it out of my sight as I wash down. The shaking starts when I dry off. It takes twice as long as it should to redress, thanks to the trembling. I will finish today with my head held high, and then tomorrow I will let myself crumble.

As I walk into the classroom, all the eyes in the room turn towards me.

No one expected me to last the day, and yet here I was, taking my seat in Health Ed and ignoring the lot of them. I would not cry. I wouldn't let them enjoy my tears. I'd survived my body being put through hell, but this sort of psychological torture grated against me. The Wolf has retreated, and I'm back to the little girl who cries and has crushes and wants to be liked. I kind of hate her. I can't wait to graduate and leave all this behind. So much for my new start.

I unpack my bag and set everything out onto my desk

in clear lines as the whispers get louder. I can't have any sort of control anywhere else but in my pencils right now, so I measure everything out with my fingertips. When that doesn't calm my racing heart, I start to count backwards from a hundred in French, my go-to for panic reduction. The over-complicated number system keeps enough of my brain occupied that I can usually fight back the panic.

As the bell begins to toll, Avery, Ash, Harley, and Blaise walk in and sit in their usual spot behind me. It's the only class we all share, and I'm pissed I have it today of all days. Thankfully, I don't have to sit next to Harley. I hear Avery snort out a laugh that doesn't suit her manicured appearance. She's the epitome of grace and beauty. When you think about the beauty that wealth can create, she's exactly what you would picture.

She murmurs, "Stupid Mountys," and then opens her books. She seems pissed about all of this, but I'm sure it's because she wanted to be the one to break me.

"Your brother really fucked up everyone's chances of winning the sweep." Harley isn't even trying to be discreet; I think he's enjoying my downfall more than anyone else. The guy who bore witness to the retribution I wrought isn't in this room at all, so I'm left with the pompous asshole instead. There's something in his eyes when he looks back at the sound of his voice, a recognition, that tells me he's still trying to figure me out. Well, good luck.

"She still looks at Blaise like she would enjoy a ride on his dick. Looks like the money is yours, man," Ash drawls, and I want to kick his perfect face in.

I turn to give him a scathing look, but they're all enjoying every second of this torture. Harley is looking at me the same way he was in the chapel. I try not to shiver at the intensity. Blaise looks over at me, and for the first time he actually *looks*. I squirm in my seat as his eyes trail over my scuffed shoes, nails chewed to the quick, and the mess of black ringlets that is my hair. I know I look nothing like any of the girls at Hannaford, and for the first time since I started here, I feel pissed off about it. I've never felt so out of place as in this school with all of these obscenely privileged kids.

"I don't fuck fans."

They all howl with laughter, and even Avery manages a smug look in my direction. I turn back to the front of the class and ignore the comments all around me as the other students snicker and join in. Only Lauren, who's still sitting as far away from me as she can to not be targeted by association, is silent.

I decide on the spot that I'm going to burn my Vanth Falling t-shirt and sleep in the nude from now on. I will never listen to his beautiful voice again. I'd rather die than admire this guy anymore.

After class, I go to the library and email in all my

classwork for the week, my obsessive need to be ahead working in my favor once again. I tell each of my teachers I'm feeling unwell and will not be able to go to any classes in the foreseeable future. Then I go to the dining hall and grab a box of protein bars.

I don't leave my room for a week.

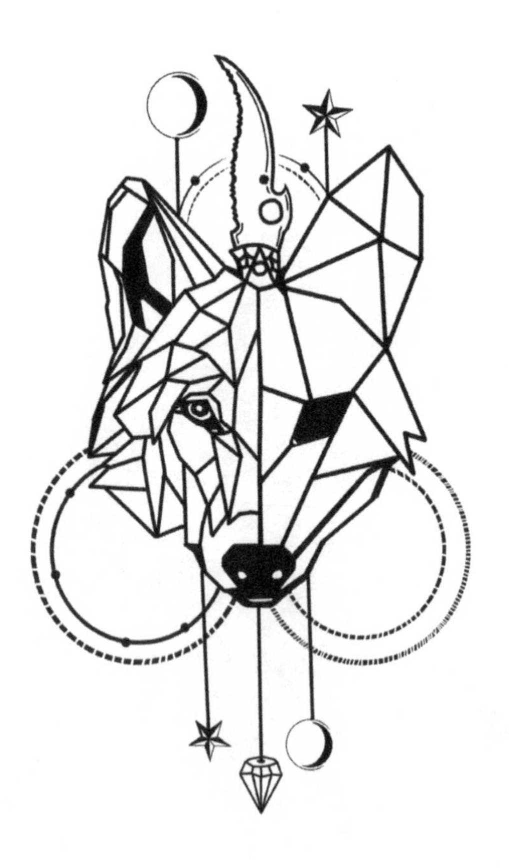

Thirteen

After my self-imposed sabbatical from my classes, I make an important decision: I'm going to unleash the Wolf on these wealthy assholes and show them some real-life consequences for their terrible behavior. Things the rest of us had to learn as children, things I had learnt the hardest way imaginable.

Sneaking around the dorms during classes is not the easiest thing to do. Technically, all the guys who live here should be in classes but there's the chance someone else is playing hooky or genuinely sick and hanging around. What I'm about to do cannot have any witnesses, so I'm extra cautious and I take my time.

The ballet flats I'm wearing are the softest soles I could find in shoes, and I've worn them enough to know exactly how to position my feet to go unnoticed. They are silent on the old oak floorboards. My black tights and tee are closely fitted and don't rustle either. There're surgical gloves on my hands from my first-aid kit, and my hair is swept under my biggest knit cap. I've become the living shadow I've had to be hundreds of times before.

I remember the path to Joey's room, and I slip through the unlocked door easily. This will teach him to lock the damn thing.

I wait until I'm sure he's not here, and then I begin the slow and careful process of checking for security cameras. There're no obvious lenses, but I'm sure he's more imaginative than that. The living areas and the bathroom are clear, but I find a small camera that faces the bed.

Typical. Fucking. Rapist.

Collecting trophies is the usual predator MO, but I'm still pissed to see it. Did he still have the footage of him trying to force himself on me? Was he planning on sharing around the video of the assault as proof he'd won the bet? He had told me that nudes were so common at this school that no one really cared about them, but what about sex tapes? Would the other students care about seeing a rape, or would someone be willing to report Joey? I already knew the answer to that.

I swipe it, tucking it into my bra. I'm sure I'll find something abhorrent on it that will come in handy later, but I'm here for one thing.

His stash.

I walk back to the front door and start a meticulous search for his drugs. He's certainly not shy about all of the contraband in his room. There's alcohol everywhere, whiskey and rum mostly, and there's even glasses half-full still in the sink, like he was interrupted before classes this morning. I wonder if he's ever truly sober. He must be a high-functioning addict to be getting away with it. Hiding the scent alone is tricky, and to sit tests while buzzed must be an experience. I've never smelled it on his breath, but there's ways around that.

The bathroom turns up dozens of bottles of prescription medications. I snap photos of all the labels in case there's anything of interest there. But still no drugs. They have to be here somewhere. I'm getting antsy and frustrated at how long it's taking to find something worth finding. I should have hours before Joey is due back, but he doesn't come across as someone who cares about the rules at Hannaford. I begin to pace the rooms as I think.

On my third trip around the living room, I finally hear it.

There's a loose floorboard in the sitting area in front of the luxurious leather couch. I drop down to my hands and knees to run my fingers along the edges of the wooden plank. The gap is razor-fine, just barely registering on my fingertips, but it's there. I have to use a knife from the kitchen to prize it open, but when it does, I could crow with happiness.

Inside a small recess there's a tiny box, no bigger than

the palm of my hand but a little longer. I open it carefully and find three bags of coke, a fake ID, and a stack of crisp hundred-dollar bills. I flick through the cash and make a quick estimate of ten grand. Pocket change to this guy, but enough to buy a lot of drugs for one person. I take a photo of the ID to check it later. I try not to touch the bags at all, but as I move the box, I hear the tinkling sort of rustle of something else sliding around. I use the flashlight on my phone to look for the culprit.

There's a small, heart-shaped locket. It's obviously pricey, I'd guess the stones on the front are real diamonds, but it's nothing special when you consider the Beaumonts are billionaires. My fingers catch on the raised edges of the back, and I flip it over. There's a delicate, tiny inscription on the back.

You before my blood,

My soul, my life,

My heart. Iris Arbour.

Arbour. Joey has taken this from Harley, probably earlier in the year when Avery was in damage control and Ash told her to let them fight it out. I stare at the words. They are lover's words, something private and sacred. I would guess that Iris was his mother. Had she died, and this was something he has left to remember her? Joey is the kind of heartless psychopath to enjoy taking something of that sort of value.

I slip the necklace around my neck. I don't have any pockets, and I'm afraid I won't feel it if it slips out of my bra. The metal feels cold against my skin.

I slip the box back into the gap and take photos of the placement. As I slip out of the room and head back to my room, the necklace swings against the hollow of my neck in an unfamiliar way. It feels like a win against Joey already.

When I arrive at the second-period class I share with Harley, he frowns at me as he moves his books from my desk. I know I'm radiating my smugness out for everyone to see. I'm using it as my armor for the day, so I don't feel any of the barbs being thrown at me. I've already had two teachers pull me aside and offer counseling because of the 911 call. The students are less kind about it. I've had to watch a couple of juniors do a dramatic reenactment in the dining hall over my early breakfast. They both looked at me, baiting me to hit them and risk another run-in with the principal, but the Wolf doesn't make rash decisions, and today I am the Wolf. I just watched them with a blank face and then gave them a slow, deeply ironic clap that echoed through the dining hall. Their bravado quickly dried up, and I got to watch them gulp and run away.

"Where were you this morning?" Harley says as he gives me a sidelong look. I watch him out of the corner of my eye, but I don't give him any extra attention. My mind is on bigger things today. "Are you still in a bloodthirsty rage, or have you mellowed enough to talk to me?"

"I have nothing to say to you or your little friends," I reply, and then I tune him out completely. He gives up trying pretty quickly.

The class drags, but only because I'm waiting for the big reveal I know is coming. When the bell finally goes, I shove everything into my bag as quickly as I can. Harley notices and does the same, his eyebrows drawn in tight as he stares at me.

"If you enjoy watching Joey get what he deserves, you should probably follow me," I murmur, just to get to see the look on his face. It doesn't disappoint.

"What did you—fuck it, lead the way, Mounty." He gestures with his arm, and I take the lead. He falls in step with me and he's got his phone out, texting with one hand. We get some looks as we walk together, the other students aware of the animosity between us.

"The twins might have a heart attack if they see this, so you might not want to tell them," I say as we approach the crowd that is slowly building in the front courtyard. Harley gives me this sort of dazed look, but he shakes his head and shoves his phone back in his pocket. I push through the crowd, and when I finally get to the front, I school my face into a blank look, so the shit-eating grin doesn't accidentally pop out.

Joseph Beaumont Jr. is in handcuffs.

The crowd is full of gasps and whispers already, and all the voices are laced with a reverent kind of fear. To see the self-appointed king of the school being subjected to something so pedestrian, so scandalous, as being put in handcuffs. There're three police officers, and while one holds Joey's wrists, another is talking to him quietly. The third one, a tall imposing man, is talking to the principal in a heated discussion. I'm sure this is a first for Hannaford.

"What. The. Fuck," I hear Blaise say behind me. I glance behind me and see he's standing with an arm slung casually over Ash's shoulder. They're both dressed for the gym, the track team if I remember correctly. Ash's face is ghostly white, and his eyes are haunted as he takes in the scene. Harley nudges me and leans in to whisper in my ear, his breath dancing over my throat.

"Please explain to me what the fuck you did?"

"Did you know he's an addict? Cocaine was found in his room this morning. It seems the police were called in without Trevelen's knowledge, what a shame Joey couldn't talk his way out of it before law enforcement arrived."

Harley swears under his breath and leans away from me quickly as Avery arrives, with Rory close behind her. Harley shoots him a dark look full of loathing, but he doesn't say anything, and Avery doesn't notice. She doesn't have the same haunted look Ash does. Instead, she stares at the police officers reading Joey his rights with calculating eyes. Joey doesn't struggle or make any sort of scene; he just nods along amicably. I suppose he knows his dad will bail him out the second his ass hits the bench at the station, so why bother putting up a fight? Avery looks over at me, and she really looks at me for the first time. She's trying to read me, get some insight on my involvement. I wonder how much Harley put in the text message to her.

"If this was your doing, you'd better hope he never finds out," she says, and I shrug. I know they're all looking at me again, but this time I feel powerful. I've made my own move on the board, and now I have to wait to see what Joey does next.

Mr. Trevelen finally notices the huge crowd and starts to order us all to disperse. Avery tugs Harley away. He's hesitant to go, like he'd rather watch Joey be dragged away until the image is burned into his corneas for life. My eyes trace the tattoo that curves along his jaw: *Honor before Blood.* The necklace is in my pocket. I think about giving it to him now, but there are too many people watching. It feels wrong to keep it.

I wait until the crowd has thinned right down and Joey looks over to catch my eye. He doesn't look upset or surprised, he tips his head at me and grins. It's his maniac grin, the one that lets me know he will never be a good or kind person. I tip my own head back just a little and let him see the challenge I'm setting him. Let him come for me.

By dinner, the entire school knows about Joey's arrest and subsequent suspension from Hannaford.

I fill my tray with all the meats and vegetables I can fit—I'm starving and a little worried about possible scurvy after my week of surviving on protein bars—and then I find a seat at the long table. No one spares me a second glance, which I'm smug about. I get to listen to the rumors already circulating about what Joey has done to land himself in handcuffs. My personal favorites were prostitution, money laundering from street fighting, and involvement in his family's business.

Avery and the guys are also at the table, and Harley is staring my way. He's not trying to be discreet, just openly glaring my way as he chews on his meal. Avery is chatting to Blaise and, though their tones are light, I can see the strain in her shoulders. Ash is scowling at his plate. No amount of cajoling by Avery will get him to talk. I'm busy observing them, so I miss Harlow arriving at the dining hall. She doesn't miss me.

"Move, idiot," she snaps at the guy sitting across from me. He startles and glances between us both. I get my first real look at the damage I'd done to her face as he scrambles up and away from us, leaving his tray behind. Both her eyes are black and swollen, her nose has been taped and braced, and her cheeks are mottled with bruises. None of her pretty features are visible anymore. She looks horrific, like she's been the victim of a violent crime, and the smile I give her is all teeth.

"Is there something you want, Roqueford? I'm busy." A hush falls over the dining hall. Even the teachers further down the table have stopped to watch our confrontation. I wonder if they've been warned off from me as well.

"You're dead. The minute Joey gets back, he's going to fucking kill you, Mounty scum." She spits at me, literally spits; I feel it land on my cheek. I fight the urge to wipe it away.

"Why would he bother with me? He's already extracted his revenge for me turning him down." I laugh at her, and she flinches back at the icy sound.

"He's not stupid. Obviously, it was you who snitched on him." Her knuckles are white as she grips the chair. I let my eyes roam over her face again with pride. I really do feel proud of what I did to her. There's only the strong and the weak in this world, and it didn't matter what Joey and his fucked-up flunkies did to me. I'd always be stronger than them.

"How about you prove it?" I whisper and smile at her again. She curses at me again and turns on her heel to storm out. The room seems to hold its breath for a second, and then the conversations resume, quietly at first and then with some gusto.

I enjoy my dinner and I don't waste another second thinking about Joey Beaumont.

He's out of my hair for a few weeks.

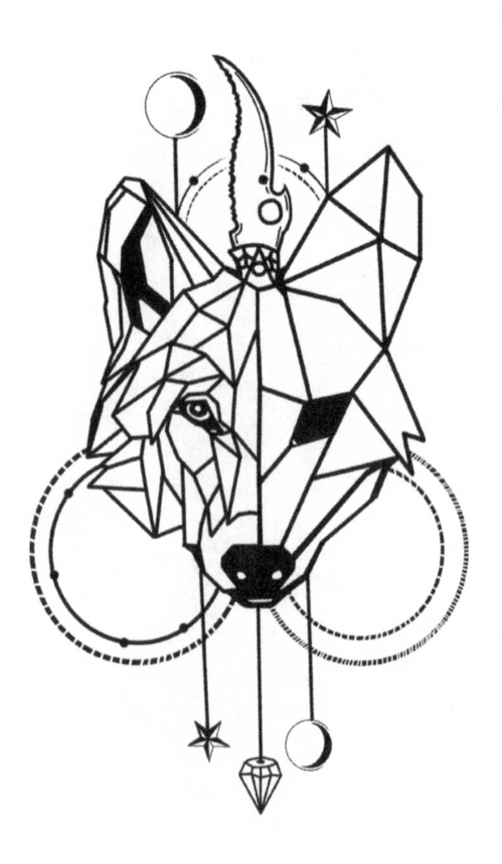

Fourteen

I get a week's reprieve from Avery and her minions. I don't know if I've rattled her, or if she's still recovering from whatever it was that happened between her and her siblings, but I enjoy the silence. I throw myself back into my studies and focus on my vocal work for choir. I have worked out that if I wear earplugs, I can go through the exercises Miss Umber has assigned us, but that means I have no idea how I sound. If the class didn't directly affect my overall grade, I wouldn't care whatsoever about it, but my scholarship required a near-perfect GPA to stay eligible. There was no way I was letting my PTSD lose my chances at a decent future.

During my training with the Jackal, I'd been subjected to torture. There was no other word for it, no pretty little name that changed what happened into a useful lesson. I'd been taught how to withstand extreme levels of pain without screaming. The side effect of that training was that now I couldn't hear my own voice, screaming or singing, without the bone-deep fear of the consequences the Jackal had set for me. I had the scars to show for the punishment I was dealt, and the thought of going through that again made my brain switch firmly into fight-or-flight mode.

It was one of many reasons I had run away from Mounts Bay, and why I could never love Matteo the way he loved me.

Sometimes, when I didn't keep myself busy or on high alert, those memories would creep into my mind unbidden and I'd find myself shaky and nervous, twitchy even.

I was in one of those moods when I sat in the library for my usual study session with Ash.

He'd blown off our other session for that week, so I had no real expectations for him showing up today. If anything, I hoped he wouldn't show up. I didn't want him questioning the tremor in my fingers as I answered the math equations in my workbook.

I get fifteen minutes of peace before Blaise arrives. He looks around the library as if he is looking for someone else to help him, and then sighs and sits down in the seat Ash usually uses. I don't look up or acknowledge him as he empties his bag and gets settled in his seat. Once he's set up, he clears his throat to get my attention. I look up and focus my eyes at the tip of his nose instead of staring into those gorgeous green eyes. He shifts in his seat, and I think about feeling sorry for him. Then I remember his cold words when he'd publicly humiliated me on the worst day of my time at Hannaford so far—*I don't fuck fans*—and I give him the tiniest glare instead. God, I am pathetic.

"I'm going to fail math if you can't perform a miracle on me."

I take the paper he slides across to me and see the mess he's made of his own workbook. It's bad. It's not completely hopeless, but he's definitely going to fail if he hands this in. I start to mark it and jot down observations in silence, trying to ignore the slight tremble of my fingers. I can help this arrogant, gorgeous, talented, swoon-worthy asshole without having to look or speak to him. I am just that good.

He squirms in his seat.

"Look, if you don't want to help me, then I can find someone else."

I snort at him derisively without stopping my methodical work. "Harley is on par with me in math. Why don't you ask him to help you? Then you wouldn't have to ever look at me. I could continue to stay as far away from you as possible, and you could forget I even go here."

He clears his throat again and looks around the room. His tie is off, and his shirt is unbuttoned enough that I can see his tattoos peeking out. I try my best not to think about them and finish marking the page, sliding it back across the table to him. When I pick up my own work again, he finally answers me.

"Harley is really impatient. He used to try and help me, but we would end up at each other's throats. He doesn't understand how I don't get it. It's all so easy to him that he's removed from the work the rest of us have to do to understand."

It's an honest statement. Something revealing and raw. I nod at him, and then I sigh, looking up to walk him through the work verbally until I'm sure he's got a decent understanding of the formulas. He's obviously smart, but it takes a few tries to find the right explanations to help him get a good grasp on the sums. It's pleasant, much nicer than the antagonistic banter with Ash, and I find myself enjoying him being there. We get the workbook in a solid A condition, and I even help him develop a great page of notes for the upcoming tests.

"So, how did you first hear Vanth?" he asks as I do a last read-through.

The question throws me, and I just barely manage to keep hold of my pen. I glance up to see his eyes fucking twinkling at me, and I choke on my tongue.

"I heard your early covers and I bought the albums." I don't mention what I had to do to get the money to buy them. I don't know how well he'd take me gambling with my body in the fighting scenes of Mounts Bay middle school.

He groans and rubs a hand over his face.

"How did you find the covers? They're terrible! You must be a very dedicated fan to go looking for them."

I know logically that he's joking around with me, but he hits a nerve. The same nerve he'd struck uttering those words to me in Health Ed. My face flames, and I slowly put my pen down with a glare at him. His face drops, the smile sliding right off his features.

"I didn't go looking for them. I'm not a fucking stalker. I meant that I heard them when you released them. I'd been listening to your shit from the beginning, and I followed your career from there to Vanth. But don't worry about going to school with a fan, I'm certainly not one now. I've fucking burned the shirt and deleted your shit from my phone. I have no interest in listening to music from a stuck-up, spoiled, rich brat. I'll listen to music from people who are real and write lyrics from the heart."

I've managed to strike a nerve with him too. I know all about his insecurities, how he didn't want to use his parents' money to prop up the band in their early years or use their connection to get a record deal. I know exactly what to say to piss him off, and that's what I've done.

He leveled me with a look so dark, my mind flashes to Ash sitting across from me. I take in every inch of his fire and give him back my own. I may never be able to speak to him again, but at least I've told him exactly what I think of him, exactly what his dismissal of me did to me.

Now Avery might actually kill me. But fuck him and fuck her.

Two things cross my mind when I get back to my room after dinner the next night: Avery Beaumont works fast; and where the hell could I get some locks that would keep the bitch out of my room?

I thought the urine was the worst thing they could throw around my room, and I guess it was a stinking biohazard. However, piss could be washed out. You could splash enough bleach around to disinfect and clean the damage done to the room.

You can't wash out pure, industrial-strength black paint.

When I open the door and switch on my light, the blackness eats it up so much, for a second I think the light has blown. There isn't a single inch of the room or contents that isn't now black. My clothes and shoes, my books, my fucking pillow. I take a step forward and I feel the tackiness of the floor. The paint isn't even dry yet. They must have barely finished before I got here. I can hear the tittering of their laughter, a sound that will probably haunt me for life once I've left this damned place behind, but I don't look back to see who it is. I know that no matter who held the tin and brushes, Avery is behind this. I'm grateful that I've made copies of all my classwork, so at least I don't lose that work, but I now have nothing. I'll have to spend some of my stash of funds to replace my uniforms and my clothing. I've lost every damn thing I own. Well, not everything. My safe hidden under the floorboards is fine.

I have no choice but to call the administration office and report the damage thanks to the black walls and floor.

While I wait for help to arrive, I pick through my destroyed belongings and start a mental list of what I'm going to have to replace, the bare minimum I'll need to survive. It's frustrating that Avery knows exactly where to hit to cause the most damage to my life. While Joey uses big, sweeping acts to attempt to break me, Avery knows the small pressure points that chip away at me. The bet and the guys chasing me for sex is annoying, but manageable. Even Joey trying to fuck me against my will was something I could deal with; a knife to the dick is pretty persuasive. The 911 call was closer to the mark, but he underestimated my mental walls.

The exhaustion of cleaning out my room constantly, of checking for cameras, of showering as quickly as I can, of replacing everything I own—that was all much more likely to get me to quit this school, and honestly, if my only other option wasn't returning to the Jackal, I might've walked away by now. But I know the second I go back to him; I will never get out. I'll be stuck as his second in command in his gang, and probably even his girlfriend. I'll be his to own and control. I can't ever belong to him again.

Avery's face is the perfect picture of innocence when Mr. Trevelen arrives. I don't have any evidence to say it was her, but there isn't a doubt in my mind that she's responsible. I'm escorted down to the sick bay in the nurse's office to sleep for the night, and Mr. Trevelen informs me I'll be reimbursed for the items lost. I don't kick up a fuss, there's no point, and when I lay my head down, I sleep like the dead.

When I wake up in the sick bay, I'm handed a day pass, a packed lunch, and ten crisp hundred-dollar bills. There's a small town, with the cutesy name of Haven, twenty minutes away from Hannaford, and I have a school car and personal driver waiting to escort me there to replace my destroyed belongings. Mr. Trevelen explains to me that my room will be cleaned and painted by the time I return in the afternoon and he's barely looking me in the eye. Whatever Matteo said to him is sticking.

During the drive, I tap out a quick text to Matteo and ask him for some recommendations on pick-proof locks. I'm willing to pay big bucks to keep the other girls out of my shit from here on out. His reply is immediate and coddling, but I take it. He'll send me what I need.

It's a Saturday, so the town is full of students. I've never seen the appeal in venturing outside the school. I don't want to spend money or run into one of Matteo's men out here, but the town is one of those cookie-cutter-perfect places with cafés and boutique stores, and I have to admit it's nice. There isn't a big box chain store in sight. Giant trees line the brick streets, and they're all decorated with hundreds of white, blinking fairy lights. It's magical looking, even for my jaded heart, and I let myself stare out the window at it all a little wistfully.

A thousand dollars isn't enough to replace what I need if I stick to these higher-end stores, I'd be lucky to find a single item of clothing for that price, so I ask the driver to drive around for a while until I spot what I'm looking for. Tucked away off the main street in a tiny alleyway, I find a thrift store. I ask the driver to wait, and he informs me with a curt smile that he's mine for the day and to take my time. Rich kid perks, I guess.

The store is teeming with designer labels I care nothing about, and I dig through the shoes until I hit a jackpot. A pair of cherry red Docs that hit me mid-calf. They're a touch too big, but with thick socks they're perfect, and my spirits are instantly lifted. I trawl through the jeans until I find three pairs that work for me, and then I look for some booty shorts.

An hour later, I leave the store with more bags than I've ever carried out of anywhere before, and the driver has to pop the trunk and help me pile my haul in. It's still early enough in the afternoon, so I decide to stop to get a coffee. I shouldn't be wasting money on something as frivolous as coffee, but I think of it as a reward for all my hard work and perfect marks at Hannaford so far.

I choose one of the smaller shops, because the bigger ones are overrun with Hannaford uniforms and I do not want to be accosted by one of the Beaumonts or their loyal followers. I order it to go, eager to get back to my room and get my life back in order. I chat to the barista, Emily, and I enjoy just being a teenager for a moment. She doesn't know anything about me except that I go to Hannaford, and the shock that I'm speaking to her at all is evident on her face. I find out the other students have a reputation in this town for being assholes. What a shock. When she hands me the coffee, I thank her warmly, and then slip back out to the alleyway.

I should have ignored the sounds coming from the tiny back parking lot.

I knew what I was hearing, I'd heard it a million times before, but curiosity killed the cat and it may someday kill me too. I move slowly and try to be silent, which is hard in the kitten heels I'm forced to wear as part of the Hannaford Prep uniform. As I round the corner, I get the disgusting view of Rory's bare ass as his hips swing. He's got Avery bent over his garishly orange Lamborghini Huracan. I can't see her face, only the skirt pushed up over her hips and twisted in Rory's fists as he pumps away at her. He's grunting and swearing under his breath, and I startle at the sharp crack of his palm hitting her ass.

Why would they be fucking out here instead of just doing it in the dorms? The zero-tolerance bullshit Trevelen spouts means nothing to any of these rich assholes, so why risk public sex? Maybe they're voyeurs and Rory needs the thrill to get his dick hard. I smother the snort I have at the thought. I'm tempted to take a photo and send it out, give her a taste of her own medicine, but I won't stoop to her level. Plus, the guys all told me it wasn't her and, while I don't believe them, I prefer to extract the right forms of punishment. Just as I turn to leave them to it, Rory grunts and pulls Avery up by her hair so roughly, I wince. It doesn't look sexy at all, more controlling and dominative in a shitty, misogynistic way. He turns them both so he can sit on the car and she can straddle him reverse cowgirl to finish the job. Her head is down, but I don't need to see the face to know that's not Avery riding his dick. The hair isn't the perfect black curls of the devil that's torturing me.

It's Harlow Roqueford.

She tips her head back, and I see her nose is still taped, but the bruises have all faded enough to be covered by makeup. She's moaning loudly, seemingly uncaring of being caught, and she's bouncing on him with gusto. I'm shocked enough to freeze for a second, gaping at the sight of them both, but after a heartbeat I get my wits about me. I get my phone out and snap a photo, not to share around, but if I decide to tell Avery, she won't believe me without some proof. I take a short video for good measure, and then I sneak back down the alleyway and out to the waiting car. I flick through the photos and smile as I sip my coffee and the driver pulls back onto the highway.

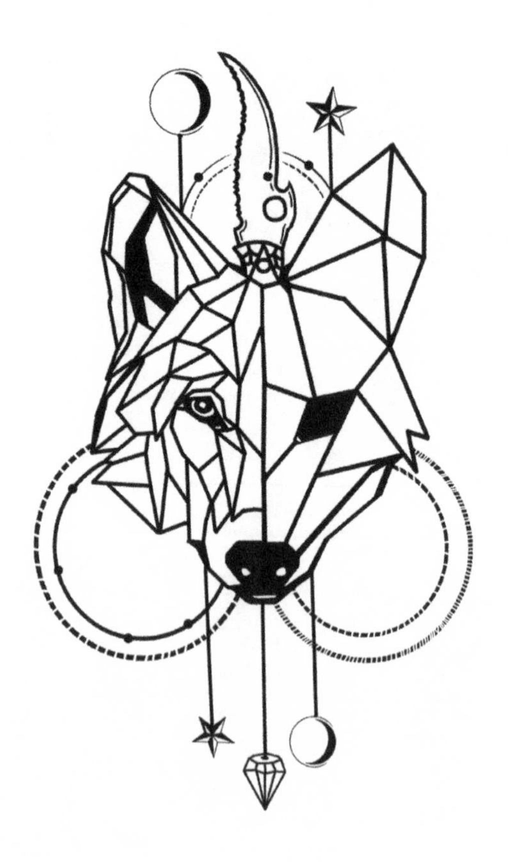

Fifteen

My room is now freshly painted, white and crisp, and the new bed I've been supplied is even more comfortable than the last one. The sheets and pillows are also brand new, and the thread count must be higher than my postcode. I feel like I should send Avery a thank-you note. I grin to myself at the mental image of her reading all about her little prank backfiring. I'm also in love with my new boots, and I spent hours trying them on with all my new clothes to see what I like best. Hannaford is quickly teaching me to take the good with the bad.

True to form, the lock Matteo had promised me was already installed by the time I arrived back at Hannaford, and the single key is on a chain around my neck. If anyone wants access to this room, they will have to pry it from my cold, dead body. I'm sure nothing would give Joey more pleasure.

My great mood lasts until choir, and then I'm overcome with nerves. I arrive early, having sprinted down the halls and shoving other students out of my way, so I can corner Miss Umber and persuade her to take pity on me. Our class assignment is to sing a solo in front of the class, and there is no way on this earth that I'll be able to do it. I've been practicing at every available opportunity and I've become decent at distracting myself, but the second my concentration wavers, I get the shakes and lose my stomach contents. If I perform in front of the class, Avery will not only have photos of my disgrace, she will also have a new weakness of mine to exploit. Now that I've managed to lock down any access to my room, I'm not looking at giving her a new avenue to explore.

Miss Umber looks right through me. There's this puzzled look on her face, like she's trying to place my face, and I grumble under my breath. Such is life when you share a class with the fabled lead singer and guitarist of Vanth Falling. I'm not sure she remembers any of my classmates, only the shining god that joins us each lesson. It doesn't matter to me if she doesn't remember me. All that matters is convincing her to let me have a private assessment. It's not an easy sell.

"Part of the mark is your ability to perform to a crowd. I alone am not a crowd, Miss…er-And-Anderson." I ignore the stumble over my name. I've already had to tell her what it is twice.

"I understand that, but I'm currently undertaking

extensive therapy to be able to do so, and my health care professionals aren't comfortable with me stepping out on stage to more than a few people." Lie-lie-lie, I don't care. I'll keep spewing out falsehoods until I get what I want, and if she asks for proof, I'll call in a favor. Fuck, I'll call in ten favors. Whatever it takes, I'm not getting on that stage.

"Oh. Yes, okay. That's a different case. We wouldn't want to upset your parents and have them in here, would we? You can come after the winter break, and I'll assess you privately. Now, take a seat and start your warm-ups! Mr. Morrison should be here soon, and then we can start."

I thank her and slump onto my usual chair, relief coursing through my veins. I'm still feeling prickly with irritation and relief when the rest of the students arrive. Avery has her hand tucked into Blaise's, and they're chatting happily with their adoring fans. I nod to Lauren when she joins me, but my mind is on Avery. What is the best way to get back at her for everything she's been doing to me without becoming a bully myself? If I get caught, I'll lose my scholarship, but it's more than that.

I've never done anything out of spite. I've hurt people, I've stolen, I've lied. I've beaten someone until the life left them. But never have I done anything with the intent of hurting someone purely to get back at them. I'd only ever acted in self-preservation or defense. That was the moral high ground I clung to, so I didn't lose my mind about all the wrong I'd done. What am I willing to do to Avery as revenge?

"Oh, Lord. You're staring at Avery again. Should I be worried? Is another Beaumont about to be taken out in handcuffs?" whispers Lauren, breaking my chain of thought. I give her a sidelong look, and she grins at me. I don't know how she guessed about my involvement in Joey's arrest. Maybe the whole school has already guessed.

"What do you think of our oh-so-benevolent overlord?" I reply. Lauren is nice enough. If she thinks Avery is the devil, then maybe I could be spiteful just this once. Lauren glances over to her, and we both watch as she plays around on her phone, not a care for the teacher and lesson going on around her at all.

"I think she's lonely. I think she comes from a fucked-up family and her brother is so scared of anything happening to her that she's now isolated. Did you hear that Rory and Blaise got into a fight over dinner last night? Rory came back from his football game and Blaise said, in front of the whole dining hall, that the pussy he could smell on him had better not be Avery's." Lauren giggles at the shocked look on my face. "I think he was just saying it to bait Rory into spilling about their sex life. Ash was there too, and everyone knows he'll murder Rory it he touches her."

"But why? If any of the rumors are true, they're all

fucking half the damn school between them. Pretty damn sexist to say she can't sleep around if she wants to." I did not want to think about any of the whispers I've heard. Or about Annabelle. Ugh, fuck Annabelle.

"I know. It's an old money thing. My parents would also have a lot to say if I started dating, and I'd murder my little sister if I found her hanging around someone like Rory." Lauren shrugs and settles back in her chair.

Ash Beaumont is lying to me.

I'm not stupid, and it's starting to be really obvious. He doesn't need my tutoring at all. I watch as he follows my explanations on his physics assignment, and he's not even listening to me. He knows every damn thing I'm saying to him.

Why the hell is he torturing me by being here, then? He's more distracted today than he usually is, so I test out my theory by purposefully explaining the theory wrong, and then I watch him answer the questions. He gets them all correct. What the hell is his problem?

"I told you during our first session that if you're not here to learn, then you shouldn't come," I say, my temper rising. It doesn't really matter if he's learning or not, I get the credits just for being here, but I feel duped. Like he's just here to push all my buttons, or to find ways for Avery to torture me.

"And I told you, if you want the credits, you'll sit and teach me." He doesn't look up from his work as he speaks, which is probably for the best. I'm seething even as I survey his stunning eyelashes. It's a crime that he has naturally sooty eyelashes that curl beautifully. I wonder how many girls have stared at them enviously before me. He looks like he's wearing eyeliner, a dark frame around the cerulean blue irises.

"If you're not actually learning anything, then we could just sit and study together in silence. I could get my work done, and you could… do whatever it is that you're here for, without me having to ramble on uselessly."

He glances up and catches me ogling him. I refuse to blush; I tell myself I'm staring because I'm pissed. He gives me a slow smirk and leans back in his chair, cocky as he crosses his arms over his chest. I forget sometimes that he's built. The uniform hides the physique of the male students far better than the legs and curves of the females. Sexist bullshit. If the guys get to see whether, or not I've shaved my legs this week, I think I should be able to see who bench presses my bodyweight on the regular.

"Enjoying the eye fuck?" he drawls. Oh, no. That self-flagellating tone will just not do. I need to take him down a notch.

"I'm assessing your weak spots, so I'm confident in

my aim when I have to take you out." He doesn't back down. If anything, my words egg him on. His smirk turns into an entirely too-confident flirty grin. I haven't been this close to swooning since Blaise's appearance at the school. This guy is devil spawn.

"Sure, you are, Mounty. And will you be aiming for my eyes, then?"

I nod and attempt a glare. "Blinding you gives me a much better chance at survival. You're twice the size of me, so unless you're well trained at fighting in the dark, that should even the playing field nicely."

He chuckles and lets his eyes roam over my chest and down my legs. I hate people looking at my legs. The scars may have faded to white but they're still plain to see. I can't wait until I'm a junior and I can wear thigh-high socks. Cute, and a satisfactory cover up. His gaze is heated, I think he's flirting with me, but with no prior experience I don't want to jump to conclusions. I might be mistaking things because of how badly I want Ash. He's such an asshole but, fuck, I'm attracted to him.

"Don't sleep with any of the boys." I look up to see Ash looking at me with such intensity, my knees think about shaking.

"What the fuck?!" I splutter out, more at my reaction than his words.

"I know it probably goes against your Mounty nature,

but you'll just dig a bigger hole for yourself if you fuck any of them." How do I find him so attractive when he's such a dick to me?

"My Mounty nature? I'm not some sexual fucking deviant! Why is every boy in this damn school so far up their own asses?"

He smirks at me and shrugs. I don't know what to do with him or how to reply, so I drop my eyes back to the assignment in front of me and get back to marking it. It's all correct, because of course it is, he's fucking with me by being here.

"Joey has decided he's going to fuck you. That's why he started the bet in the first place. He likes to prove how powerful he is. Every year he picks some big, elaborate goal, and then we all get to sit back and watch while he crushes, breaks, and mutilates everyone around him to achieve it. This year it's you." I think I've stopped breathing. This should be over. He can't possibly be saying I'm still going to be a target for Joey to *rape.* "If you fuck any other guy, Joey will probably kill you both."

It's become so commonplace to use the word 'kill' flippantly. They'd kill for those shoes, they'd kill you if you tell on them, they'd love nothing more than to kill that person. Ash isn't saying the word kill like that. He's saying it like he's seen his brother choke the life out of another human being. I give him a curt nod. It's not like I had any plans to date at this place. I'd always planned on waiting until college to lose my cherry, so what difference did it make if Joey had a say in it too?

A fucking big difference.

Now I wanted to fuck half the school just to spite him. Well, not really. I wanted him to think I had, because I didn't want my celibacy to look like I was bowing to him and his whims.

"What do your parents think of Joey and his actions?"

It's the wrong thing to say. I watch as Ash's face sets and a thunderous look rolls in. I shouldn't have asked. The gossip mill here at Hannaford is active enough that I could have just asked around instead. I was bolstered by his kindness in warning me, and I forgot myself. I forgot for a second that, to this man, I will always be trash.

"How about I'll answer that when you answer something for me. Did it hurt? When you found your mom, did it cripple you, even though you always knew it was going to end that way?"

My chest collapses in on itself like a vice is squeezing the life out of me. I should know by now that Ash always goes for the low blow in a fight. It did cripple me, but I'm not that girl anymore. I think about my life as the me before, the one who had to fight for food but had a mom, and there's the me now. I don't have to fight for food anymore, and I have a safe place to sleep every night.

I'm at the best school in the country. I already have the attention of several of the top colleges in the state, and I have plans to start reaching out to others further away from home. I did a lot of bad things to get to where I am today, my hands are filthy with it. I don't feel any better now than I did before.

I am truly alone.

"One of these days, I am going to show this school what it takes to survive at Mounts Bay High and foster care." My voice shakes, and he smirks at me.

"I'll take that as a yes."

He turns his attention back to his homework, and I grit my teeth. Why, oh why, did I have to do this for extra credits? I finish my page of sums in seconds, my affinity with numbers making this all child's play, and then I crack open the required reading for my literature class while I wait for him to catch up.

"Hey, man! Just in time, as per usual," Ash calls out, and I cringe. I know what that sarcastic tone of voice means. My other student has arrived.

Blaise looks like he would rather be anywhere but here. I've lost the fire within me that had enabled me to speak to him callously, so I stare at his ear lobe again and wait for him to sit down.

"I need help with my Lit assignment, and no one else has been able to help me like you did with the math shit.

Can you please help me?" he grinds out from between his clenched teeth, like the words are hurting him. Ash watches us both with raised eyebrows and a half smile.

"Sure. Sit down and show me what you need." The cool tone replaces the snarky one I was using, and he gets even more curious.

"What the fuck went down with you two?"

Blaise ignores him, slumping in his chair, and I consider doing the same. Ash throws a pen at me, and I sigh. "I informed Blaise that I burned my Vanth shirt because I don't listen to music written and performed by assholes, and he ran off to tattle to the spawn-of-Satan you shared a womb with, and she destroyed my room to avenge his hurt feelings."

"I didn't fucking tattle! She asked me why I was pissy, and I answered," Blaise hisses back at me. Ash's mouth drops open as he watches us.

I snort. "So, you're put out that I don't fucking worship you like you think you deserve, and in return I lose every single thing I own at the hands of Avery's minions? Fair trade. Fair fucking trade."

Ash leans back in his chair, the glee at our spat rising in him quickly. "Everything you own is here at Hannaford?"

"I'm emancipated. Of course it is. No, was. I have nothing now, until the summer break when I can go back to Mounts Bay. Happy now, Morrison? Got your revenge?

Great. Show me your assignment and let me fix it so you can tell your billionaire daddy how fucking great you're doing at this hellhole."

Blaise is gaping at me like I've just kicked him in the balls and asked for his gratitude for doing so. I raise my eyebrows at him until he hands over the assignment, and I start in on it.

The evidence of Rory's unfaithful ways is burning a hole in my consciousness. I want to get the shit off my phone and out of my mind as quickly as possible. Plus, I caught Avery making out with him on the couch in the girls' dorms again. If he's cheating on her, if they're not in some weird polygamist relationship like the guys are, then I hate the idea of him getting away with it.

I can't email her the video. There're too many risks of the school administration finding out about it. I know for a fact that all our study and interactions online are monitored. Texting it to her is another option. The only way I can get Avery's phone number is by either breaking into the administration office or asking around for it. Neither are good options.

I end up in the library printing off copies of the photos. I feel gross even looking at them, and I'm twitchy about being caught. I did not want to explain all of this to Matteo if Mr. Trevelen catches wind of this. He'd probably insist on using the photos as blackmail against Rory and Harlow, and while I did enjoy the thought of them sweating it out at the hands of the Jackal, it would complicate my life.

I don't want to think about Matteo anymore. I'm so confused about him. His gentle tones on the phone when I called him for help made my chest ache. I used to love him. Back when I first went into foster care, he was the cool kid. Someone in my corner who loved me back. I truly thought he loved me too. Now I know that he sees me as a valuable pawn on the chess board. Nothing more. But I still feel guilty for having certain feelings about Ash. And Blaise and, fuck, Harley. I can't forget the feelings I have for Harley.

I get back to my room and deliberate over my note to Avery. Fuck, I should be so happy to be able to crush her with this, but it feels so underhanded. I don't want to break her with a guy. I want to outsmart her. Outplay her. I want to survive everything she throws at me, and then dish it back twice as bad.

I'm not Joey. I don't enjoy cutting people where it stings the most. I'm not cruel. I'm no angel, but every rotten thing I've done has been to survive. Someday I'll be able to shed all of this and just be kind.

I slip the photos and the note under Avery's door before I head down for dinner. All the other students will be leaving for winter break in the morning, and I need her to know before she goes.

Taken three days ago. Dump him.

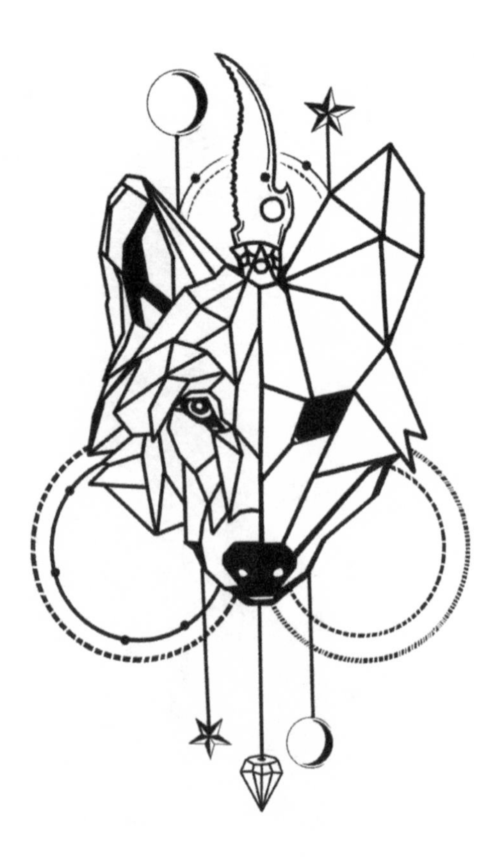

Sixteen

The entire school is empty for winter break.

At least that's what I think, until day three when I spot Harley sitting in the dining hall eating a massive pile of eggs by himself. He freezes when he hears the door, and then glares over at me. I pile my own plate full of pancakes, fruit, syrup, and ice cream, and then sit as far away from him as possible.

I wasn't expecting to see anyone, so I'm wearing tiny shorts, an old, torn shirt, and thigh-high socks. I'd been sliding my way around the school and squealing like a toddler all morning. There was only a skeleton staff still at the school, so I hadn't felt any shame in doing it. I now cringe at the thought of Harley catching me.

It was uncomfortable eating in silence, knowing he was at the other end of the table. A few times I thought I could feel his eyes on me, but when I glanced up, he was scrolling through his phone. He was probably texting the others about how ridiculous I look. I sigh into my fruit and prepare for how much shit I'll get from Avery when the break is over.

I'm contemplating my future doom when Harley gets up and leaves the hall. As he walks past my chair, I meet his eyes and keep my face blank. He sneers down at me, and I roll my eyes.

Stupid rich kids.

When I'm finished, I head back to my room and start the colossal pile of homework I have. It's not the fun winter break I think the rest of Hannaford students are having. I think back to when my mom was still alive and it was Christmas time, but we never actually did anything. Too broke for presents, too sad for a tree or good food. My only really good memories from then were watching the Christmas specials on TV by myself while my mum got high and walked the streets. Fuck, if that's where my brain was going, I was going to have a miserable break.

I have a scholarship to keep and not much else to do, so homework it is.

The most pressing is to do my vocal work.

I can't practice in my room when the other girls are here. I'm too nervous that they can hear me and even with my headphones on, the anxiety triggers my PTSD. I've picked my song, having ditched the Vanth Falling song for good now that I've met Blaise, and I just need to practice it enough that I can zone completely out while I perform.

I will never admit this to another living soul, but I pick Pompeii by Bastille because of Blaise's cover of it. It sucks that so much of my own musical story is intertwined with his because of my past obsession with him, but I need something I've sung a thousand times before to get through the assignment. No one will ever have to know it's all because of him.

I'd rather die.

I decide to skip lunch to keep practicing, and then finally my stomach drags me to the dining hall for dinner. The menu is very festive, and it takes me a second to realize it's Christmas Eve. I feel bad for the kitchen staff who have to be there to feed me, a scholarship student, and then I remember Harley and the giant mountain of money his family would have paid to send him here, and I feel a bit better.

I fill my plate with such a feast I feel bad for the kids back home, and then I sit and tuck in.

Harley is in his usual seat, so I situate myself at the other end of the table again. Not long after I sit down, I hear him get up, and to my utter shock he sits down across from me. His plate is only half-empty, and he gets back to eating as soon as he's sat down.

"Rumor has it you're emancipated," he says without looking up at me, so I have to do more than nod. My voice is barely more than a croak.

"Yeah."

"How the fuck did you manage that?"

I can't figure out his angle. Is he fishing for information to use against me, or is he just curious, bored, feeling the Christmas spirit?

"I was already in foster care and I proved I could provide for myself, so it was one less kid the state had to take care of. Took me a year, but I just kept trying."

He grunts and leans back in his chair to study my face. I try desperately not to flush scarlet under his gorgeous stare.

"How the fuck can a Mounty provide for herself? You have a sugar daddy or some shit?" He doesn't speak like the other rich kids. It jars me, because he may look like the most heavenly being I've ever seen but he speaks like a roughneck kid from the streets. He sounds like me. It's comforting, even while he's all smirks and asshole nature.

"I'm not selling myself to anything except my scholarship."

He scoffs. "That's vague."

"Why do you want to know? Mommy and Daddy pissing you off? Why aren't you home celebrating the holidays with them?"

His eyes narrow to a glare, and he clenches his teeth. I could apologize or change the subject, but he started it. He looks away from me and I can see his brain at work.

I give him a minute of silence before I prod him again. "I answered you honestly. Is there no honor among rich kids?"

He gives me a dark look, and I tuck back into my dinner while I wait.

"My dad's dead. My mom is locked up. I'm thinking about applying for emancipation too. My caseworker won't say a word to me about it, she just tells me it's not for me. So, I'm offering you a meal of peace for the information. I know you're smart, you wouldn't be here if you weren't, so I'll take you at your word."

Huh. He was an orphan like me. So why does he treat me so badly? And why does Avery protect him so fiercely?

"Are you on a scholarship too?"

"Fuck no." Like it's something to be ashamed of, like I didn't spend half my life working to be here instead of paying my way in. I give him my own dark look, which he promptly ignores.

"Then you must have the means to provide for yourself. It should be an easy process for you."

He stabs around at his plate violently. I almost feel sorry for the beans.

"I don't have access to any of the money my dad left for me. Or… well, any of the money that's rightfully mine. So, no, it won't be."

I shrug at him. "If you have an estate that pays for you,

then that will count too."

"Don't have one of those either," he grumbles.

I set my fork down and fold my arms over my chest. He watches me, and then mirrors my movement. Is he fucking with me? "Who pays for your school tuition, then?"

"Avery."

Holy fuck. "Is she in love with you? I see her tongue down that dickhead Rory's neck all the time, so I wouldn't have guessed it."

He snorts and looks at me incredulously. When I stare at him blankly, he shakes his head. "We're cousins. Our moms were sisters. Avery takes that shit very seriously, so I'm here with her and Ash because she couldn't bear the thought of me going to a public school back home."

Cousins! They look nothing alike. Harley is a golden god, and Ash is like a dark prince, with all that dark hair and brooding. I look at him closer and think maybe around the nose there's a hint of similarity, but nothing obvious.

"Well, fuck. I don't know how to advise you with only half your story. So, either tell me it all, or go spend weeks researching it online like I had to."

He looks at me again, and then sighs, rubbing his hands over his face like he wanted to scrub years off it. His biceps flex invitingly with the action and I resist the urge to reach out and squeeze them. "Fuck it. I have a large inheritance from my parents, but to get it, I'd have to fulfill certain…

obligations that I refuse to do. I won't lose my soul for the money. My mom has nothing. Avery pays for all my shit. How do I get emancipated?"

I push my tray away, the meat now cold and unappealing. Every time I'm interrupted by one of these guys, I end up missing out on good food. The kitchen staff had put out an amazing spread for only two students, and now I'm not even going to finish my plate. So damn wasteful.

"You would have to have enough money to cover all of your expenses for the next four years in a bank account, and a plan on how you would use them. Detailed, like an itemized list, down to how much soap you use in a year. Can Avery give you that?"

He doesn't answer, he just grits his teeth again and picks up his tray. I huff out a breath, feeling dismissed, and then he calls out to me as he leaves, "Thanks, Mounty."

I grab my own tray and head back up to bed.

I don't get out until Christmas Day is over.

Boxing Day is not a good day for me.

I decide to go down and eat breakfast, and Harley pours me a cup of juice as he passes by my chair. I stupidly think it's a nice gesture after how much information I gave him at our last meeting. I should know better by now.

He'd put laxatives in it.

I could not leave the girls' dorms for the rest of the day.

I am so angry about the juice that I throw caution so far into the wind, it ends up in fucking Kansas.

I know Harley is on the swim team because it's the only class we don't share, and I've heard Blaise and Avery talking about it in our choir and voice development classes. I also know that being as unbelievably gorgeous as he is, he must be very attached to his looks and, especially, his immaculately coiffed silvery-blond hair. You can't be *that* hot without also being vain.

I have no access to any beauty stores, but I'm an inventive sort of girl. The kitchen staff are very happy to help me out with my science project and armed with two bottles of food-grade dye, I find his shampoo and conditioner and pour an entire bottle in each. I'm not sure Harley is the type to pull off the Smurf look, but *good god* am I ready to find out.

Being the only two students in the school gives me an extra dose of bravery, like I'm untouchable over the holidays, when really I know that Harley will tell his friends, and then I'll have to face whatever it is they decide to retaliate with. Avery had already proven herself to be an unconscionable bully, and that was without me ever fighting back. It was a sobering thought of what she would do once she finds out. But for now, I'm going to enjoy the sport of beating this gorgeous guy at his own game. It's nice to be able to mess with him in such a low-level way.

I get to dinner early and sit at the far end of the table in the exact chair that he usually sits. I enjoy ten minutes of silence and steak before showtime. When the door at the far end of the dining hall swings open, I don't look up, and it's a struggle not to smirk. I can hear him filling his plate and then the sound of him walking toward me. I roll my eyes that he would insist on sitting at his chair even in an empty hall, and I prepare to stare him down but then he pulls out the chair across from me and sits. I glance up and snort.

Between the bright blue tones and the tattoo, he looks like he belongs in an eighties punk band. The shocking part is that his eyes are twinkling with laughter rather than the malice I expected.

"Good shower?" I prod at him.

"Great. Just what I needed. How's your bowels?"

"Lovely and cleared, thanks for asking."

He snorts with laughter and digs into his plate. It's weird to sit with him, but I can't move away without seeming weak or bitchy. Plus, he's just as alluring as the first time I saw him, so hot it hurts to look right at him.

"Which dictator did you pick for history? I'm going to wipe the floor with you." His eyes are still twinkling, and it makes me feel lightheaded. Is he flirting? He can't be. I clear my throat.

"Avery Beaumont, but Ms. Aurelia said I can't choose someone still in power, so I went with Mao Zedong. Who did you pick?"

He smirks and shows off his perfect teeth.

"Like I'd tell you." He gives his juice a sniff before shrugging and drinking from it. I regret not messing with it. He sees me watching him and says, "I'm sure you've thought of something worse, but if you have spiked it, I needed some fiber anyway."

I smile and hope that not knowing drives him a little crazy.

"I bet you've picked Hitler like every other student ever. Predictable. Boring," I taunt him, but he just smiles. Even his smile is deadly. I can feel it slicing into my soul.

"Have you finished yet? Is it printed out and ready to be handed in?" His voice is soft and sweet, and fuck if it doesn't make me nervous. And a little turned on, but mostly nervous.

"My breakfast, my assignment, or fucking with you?"

He leans back in his chair and crosses his arms.

"I don't expect you to ever stop fucking with me. You came to this school swinging, like we wouldn't swing back. I meant your assignment."

My eyes narrow. This is a trap. He is far too smug right now.

"It's a shame about the computers," he says innocently.

"Sounds like they'll be out for the whole week."

Fucking *bastard.*

"Seriously? That's all you've got?" I say with confidence that I'm not feeling, and I stand up with my tray. I walk out of the hall to the sound of his raucous laughter.

It takes two seconds in the library to discover that he has in fact messed with all the IT systems in the school. My completed assignment is stuck on the little USB stick I'd been forced to buy. There's a chance the computers will be fixed before classes resume, but I'm not really one for taking chances. It's such a rich kid thing to assume that he's won because I can't access the computers, and yet the school has a bigger and better stocked library than my home town does, so I pull a dozen books and spend the day rewriting my assignment before he decides to burn the library down instead.

After six hours of intensive work, Harley shows up with a smug look that only falters on his face for a second when he spots me in my fortress of books. I give him my own smug look and finish off my attempts at perfect penmanship, though I can never completely disguise my scratchings successfully.

"I didn't expect to see you here. I thought you were

so out of touch from the library that you wouldn't know where to find it."

He grins wolfishly at me, and my breath catches. Goddamn it, why is he so hot!

"I know the library well." He pulls a chair out across from me and straddles it. "I've fucked quite a few girls in the stacks."

A shiver runs up my spine. I should feel disgusted, like I had at every other boy who's said that kind of thing to me, but all I can think is how much I want him to take me into the stacks. How sick is that?

Maybe foster care messed me up more than I thought.

A slow grin spread across his face.

"Don't worry, Mounty, I don't want to fuck you. There's at least three guys in this school who don't want you."

Himself, Ash and Blaise. My stomach drops, and I want to scream at myself. Why the hell do I want them so much, when they are the ones torturing me? Some secret part of my brain whispers to me that the last few days hadn't felt like torture. They've been the most fun I'd had since I'd come to this pretentious school.

"What a relief. I suppose none of you need the money."

His eyes tighten like he's taken a hit. I open my mouth to ask him why, but he cuts me off.

"Not enough to fuck trash, no."

I would have given anything to be able to stop myself from blushing, but I couldn't. I tell myself it's a flush of anger, but its shame burning in my gut.

"You might want to bury your nerves a bit deeper, Mounty. Putting them on display like that just gives us all a target."

He winks at me, *fucking winks*, and then leaves me.

I tell myself I'm not gutted.

But I am.

The students all arrive back Sunday night.

By Monday morning, Harley's head is shaved, and he looks at me like I'm nothing again.

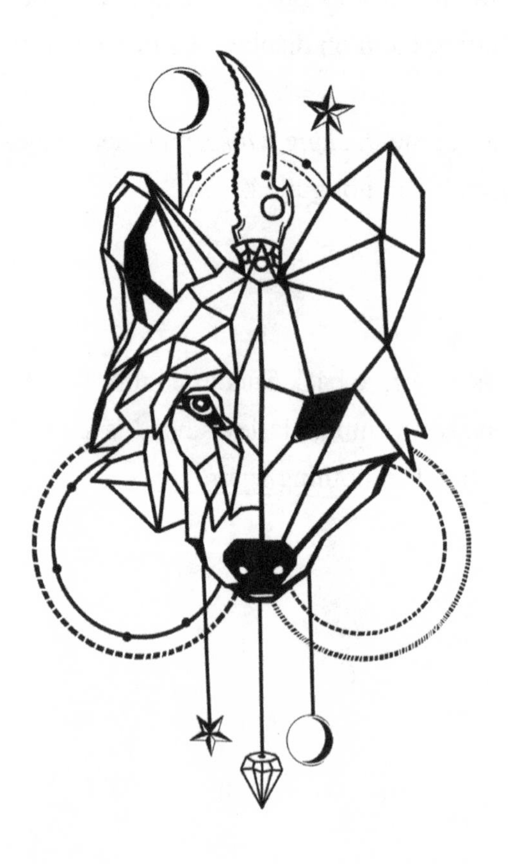

Seventeen

Miss Umber is late to my choir assessment by twenty minutes, which is coincidentally just long enough for me to start sweating bullets at the thought of singing for her. The choir room looks so much bigger without the other students milling about. I'm glad she agreed to do it here, and not at the chapel. Standing on the stage there, where I'd heard my 911 call, I would've lost my mind. And my lunch.

"Right. You. Yes, of course. Which song did you pick?" Miss Umber sounds flustered as she drops her bag onto the tiny desk. She's far too old to be a Miss, she should have at least switched out to be a Ms. by now. Her startlingly white hair is chopped off into a severe-looking bob with bangs, and her glasses are too large for her face. On a teeny runway model, it would have looked fashionable, but on the aging teacher it looks unflattering. I'd much rather sit here and pick apart her appearance than start my assessment. When Miss Umber turns to give me a look, I snap to it.

"Pompeii. By Bastille," I croak. Not a good sign of my vocal abilities for the day.

"Good choice! Do you need music, or are you going to play an instrument?"

I hold up my phone to show her the instrumental song I have prepared. I had learned a handful of songs on guitar, this one included, but I didn't want to tempt fate by putting too much pressure on myself. I run through the warm-ups under her watchful eye, and I realize this is the most amount of attention she's ever given me. This is definitely the first time she's ever heard my voice, because I always hide among the other students in class.

Once I have the phone set up and the music starts, I slip my noise-cancelling headphones in, and then I sing.

My eyes slip shut and I forget Miss Umber is even in the room. For the first time I can focus on the feeling of singing, the rush of my body working hard at something that isn't entirely physical, and I lose myself in it. I sway and swing my arms for emphasis, the way I've watched Blaise do a thousand times before. I can hear myself, but the headphones tone it down just enough that I can immerse myself fully into the act of singing rather than the sound.

It's incredible.

I feel like a piece of me that I lost years ago has come back. It's healing to think that the damage done to me at the hands of the Jackal and the Game could be healed. I can someday be a whole person again. I can feel the tears prickling at the back of my eyes, and I know the second I open them, they will fall. If I can stay at this school and survive everything being torn down around me, I can pull myself up and out of the world I was born into. I can make something of myself through sheer will and perseverance alone.

When the last word slips out from my lips, my chest is heaving and my heart pounds wildly in my chest. I give myself a second before I open my eyes, just a moment to collect myself so I don't fall to my knees and sob like a child. When I pull the earbuds out, I hear clapping and I grin at Miss Umber. She's looking at me the exact same way she looks at Blaise when he sings, like I've exceeded all her expectations and dreams as a teacher.

"Miss Anderson! I've never—you are a rare talent!" She grips my hand tightly in hers and tugs me into a hug. I try not to freeze or flail awkwardly, but I'm not hugged often enough to be comfortable. I can't actually remember the last time I was hugged. As she lets me go, I turn and see Avery standing in the doorway, her jaw damn near hitting the ground.

She's heard me sing.

I feel exposed. Worse than even my 911 call, I feel like she can see inside me. I'd given up singing so long ago that not even Matteo has heard me. Only my dead mum, and she took the memories of my singing to the grave with her.

I break away from her slack-jawed stare and turn back to our teacher, a flush staining my cheeks. I don't know what to do with myself, and I nod along dumbly as Miss Umber gushes to me.

"I can't believe I've missed your voice so far this year! Your range rivals Mr. Morrison's. Has he heard you sing?"

Oh, god. There is no way I want him to ever hear me.

"I don't think so. It's not… I'm not interested in performing. I'd rather stick to the group sessions."

Once she's finished marking my rubric, I take the page and flee the room.

Avery hasn't moved from the doorway, and I have to brush past her to leave. She doesn't move to let me pass, and when I look down at her fist, I see the pages I'd slipped under her door crumpled in her hands.

Hannaford prides itself on 'encouraging' its students to excel by posting all grades publicly. It's never bothered me because I've always had top spot, or occasionally second spot if Harley beats me. I would feel bad for the other students here who land closer to the bottom if I didn't already know they were going to be millionaires the moment they turn eighteen and get their trust funds.

The first time I decide I hate this system is when the

choir marks are posted. That's when I learn Blaise has never come second in that class in his life.

I've beaten him by a teeny-tiny margin.

I take my usual seat with Lauren, Jessie, and Dahlia, and I try to ignore the eyes that are on me. Lauren leans toward me and then stops dead as Avery and Blaise walk in. I had expected Avery to have told Blaise about my singing, but one look at him tells me she didn't.

"What. The. Fuck."

He whips around to look at me, and I glue my eyes to Miss Umber so I can keep blanking him. The students around us start to murmur and gasp, but I don't let my gaze waver. Miss Umber claims first place in my list of favorite teachers by starting the lesson before Blaise can confront me.

"Mr. Morrison, Miss Beaumont, if you could both take your seats so we can begin! Please start our usual warm-ups, and then we can start discussing what each student can be working on to improve before our next assignments."

There is no way I want to discuss my singing with the whole class, but short of faking an illness, there is nothing I can do to get out of it. And then Miss Umber tumbles back down to the bottom of the list by ruining my life.

"Miss Anderson, can you please swap groups? I'd like you and Mr. Morrison together, where I can monitor your progress accordingly."

Every eye in the room is on me.

I flush scarlet and pray that a stroke takes me out. There is no justice in the world, because my heart continues to beat, and I'm forced to collect my bag and move across the room. Miss Umber holds out a seat for me, and then I'm sitting right next to the devil herself. Blaise is still trying to catch my eye, but I will not play his game.

Once the warm-ups are finished, my hands are trembling, and my stomach is a roiling pit. I can't half-ass it now. I'm stuck under Miss Umber's eye and Avery is watching my every move. I sit on my hands so she can't see how badly I'm shaking. The moment Miss Umber starts to write out notes during her explanation of the correct breathing methods we should be using, depending on application, Blaise leans over Avery so far, he's practically in her lap.

"Since when can you fucking sing?"

I take out my notebook and ignore him. I never take notes in choir, but it's a good excuse to ignore him. He's not an easy guy to get away from. "Mounty, how did you get a higher mark than me? Are you fucking the teacher?"

I snort and keep writing. I don't spare him a glance as I reply. "If anyone is fucking Miss Umber, it's you. Why would I take choir if I can't sing? I told you I liked Vanth for your voice. Did you not think I was telling the truth? It was one singer admiring the talent of another, that's it.

Get over it."

Avery pushes Blaise back into his own seat and off her lap. I'm a little wary that she seems to be helping me, but I know there'll be an ulterior motive. Blaise is mumbling under his breath and Avery slips her hand into his, and that's when I know I'm in trouble. That I'm about to be tormented by them again. Avery Beaumont is always the calm before the storm. While her brother and his friends get angry and loud about it, Avery is silent as she efficiently makes her moves to destroy me.

I shake my head at her and go back to my notes.

When the class finishes, I leave without looking at Blaise again. Classes are done for the day, and when I round the corner to walk back into the main building, I hear the footsteps right behind me.

They're both following me.

It's taco night and I've had to miss the last two taco nights because of Beaumont bullshit, so I head straight to the dining hall for an early dinner. I give them both a warning look when they sit across from me at the long table. Neither of them have bothered to grab anything to eat, so we sit in silence as I start to eat my tacos. They're good, but I can't enjoy them with my hostile audience watching my every move.

I break the silence.

"What are you planning on doing to me just because I

got a better mark than your little friend?"

Blaise's eyes narrow at me, and then he hesitantly glances at Avery. She's staring at me, down her nose like Ash does, and it sends my blood boiling. I've grown accustomed to being the poor little foster kid. Even at Mounts Bay I had people looking down at me for my drug addict mom, but no one makes me feel more shit about it than the Beaumonts do.

"Did you take the photos of Rory and Harlow together?" she says, completely monotone, like she's not discussing her cheating boyfriend.

I nod and drink my juice. I'm distracted enough by the conversation that I don't think twice about it. Blaise is staring at her, his eyes slits of rage, and his cheeks have deep red patches. I've assumed this far that they're all so close they don't keep secrets, but now I see I was wrong. He runs a hand over the back of his neck and blows out a frustrated breath. I wonder how long it will take before Ash is publicly beating the life out of Rory. Or will it be Harley this time?

"Why didn't you send them out to everyone? You're convinced I sent out your nudes. Wouldn't that be the best revenge for you?"

It's a trap, but I know no matter what, she'll hate me. Why not tell the truth? "I believed Ash when he said you didn't have anything to do with that. It doesn't matter, though. Even if you did, I wouldn't have sent them out. I don't do that shit. If I want revenge, I go straight to the source and do it properly, I'm not good at this social hierarchy stuff. I'm at this school to make a better life for myself. Whatever you guys do to me, it's nothing compared to what's waiting for me at Mounts Bay."

"That doesn't answer my question."

I blow out an exasperated breath. Why does this girl rile me up so badly? I'm giving her answers, and she still wants more. I should tell her to go fuck herself. I should tell her to choke, to jump off a cliff, to go and hide among the beautiful boys she hangs around and leave me the hell alone. I don't.

"Rory is a fucking scumbag. I'm not one of these brainwashed bimbos who thinks it's funny when other girls are treated like shit by guys. I think he's a dick, and I think you deserve to know *where* he's sticking his dick. Plus, I didn't see a condom in use so, you know. He's probably caught something truly heinous from that bitch, and you should get tested to make sure he hasn't passed it on to you."

As I lift my juice to my lips, I see a flash of regret pass over her face. I've never seen that sort of human emotion out of her before, and it makes me feel another pang of sympathy for her. We were both born into cages. Mine was poverty, drugs, the threat of gangs and violence. Her's is a gilded cage, but the bars work just the same. She's trapped by her blood and her name. I wonder, not for the first time, what her parents are like. Are they as beautiful as their children? Are they loyal and caring like the twins, or did Joey come by his cruelty honestly? I should really take a closer look into them, maybe get Matteo to dig around for me.

"For the record, none of this is because of what you did to Harley. It's not an eye for an eye anymore. If you stay here, Joey will kill you. He likes to break things. You're not shattering the way he likes; you're proving to be too strong. He doesn't let strong things survive." She's warning me. What has she put in place, what will I have to survive this time? I swallow.

"It's okay. I'll survive it. Whatever it is you've done, and then I'll survive your brother too. I have no choice but to survive."

She nods sharply and bumps Blaise to get him moving. He's not happy. He's watched our entire exchange with that frown on his face, and I do something entirely out of left field.

I smile at him.

Just a tiny, sad lifting of the corners of my lips, but he stares at me with heartbreak in those stunning green eyes of his.

He's in on whatever she's done, and he's torn about it.

He had probably convinced himself to help because I was a stalker fan in their eyes, and then I'd gotten that higher mark.

The last thing I remember thinking is that he wears heartbreak so fucking well.

And then my mind knows nothing.

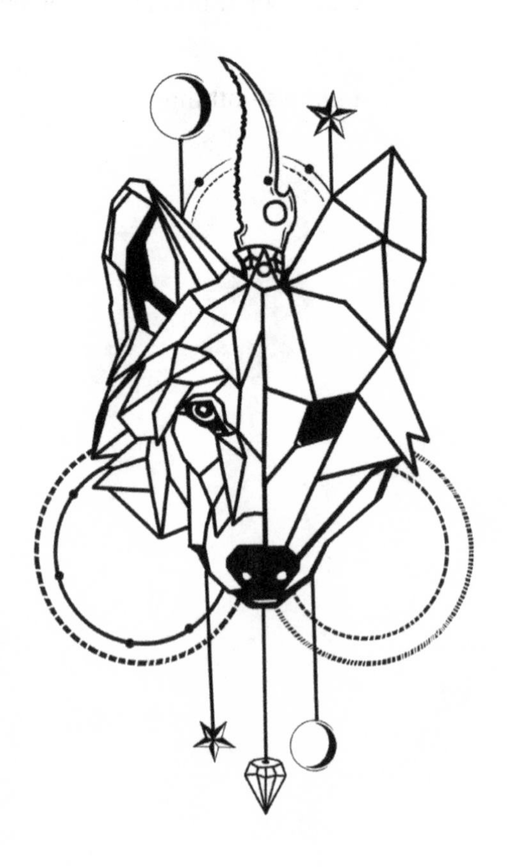

Eighteen

The blackout is so overwhelming that I have no memory of what happened that night.

I ate dinner with Avery and Blaise, and then I'm waking up in one of the seniors' bathrooms. I only know that for sure because I'd accidentally used it on my first day and had been bitched out by one of Joey's flunkies. The large, ornate mirrors are a dead giveaway. The door is locked from the inside, so I know I've done that myself, and I'm freezing. My whole body is shivering uncontrollably. It may be the temperature, or it could be the aftereffects of whatever it is Avery drugged me with.

I swear under my breath at my own idiocy. It must have been slipped in the juice. I'd forgotten the number-one rule of being around these assholes: never accept a drink from them.

I push myself up to stand on my shaking legs and look in the large mirror. I still have all my clothes on, which is a relief, but there's vomit all down my shirt and splattered on my legs. My hair is a mess and there are deep, black circles under my eyes. I can't see any new bruises or scratches, and I hope that Avery's moral code includes making sure I wasn't assaulted while I was out of it. I look as though I've been out drinking all night, and I'm sure that's the end game here. Underage drinking by paying students is frowned upon and will result in a warning, but I'm held to a different standard here at Hannaford. I'll lose my scholarship if I'm caught and breathalyzed.

I pull my phone out of my bag and thank whatever guiding hand led me to this bathroom while I was out of it. I take a deep breath before hitting call. I know Matteo has the resources to help me. How else had he gotten me out of breaking Harlow's nose? He answers right away, and I don't even bother with pleasantries, I just dive right into an explanation of what has happened. He listens intently.

"It's bad, Matteo. I'm going to get kicked out if you can't help me."

"Maybe you should come home, kid." His cool tones do nothing to soothe my nerves.

"Fuck that. I'm not going to get run out of this place by spoiled rich kids. Please, just… help me."

He sighs at me, like I'm being unreasonable. I know he's getting pissed at me for not just leveling the damn building and being done with it, but if I have to, I can start calling in favors.

"Give me ten minutes."

I hang up and slump down on the wall again. The vomit on my shirt is still wet, it's cold, and the smell is truly horrendous. I can't wait for a hot shower and my bed. Fuck these rich dicks. I wipe down my shirt and my legs as best I can to clear away the vomit. Tacos have now been ruined for me forever. Thanks, Avery. I stare at the wall and I must zone out, because when my phone pings again, it makes me jump.

All sorted. Just walk back to your room. Call me if you need anything else. M.

I exhale and open the door. There are students standing around in the hall, and I can see Avery's little flunkies with their phones out. I step into the hall and I can hear them whispering and giggling among themselves. I keep my head high as I start to head back to the dorms. I get as far as the main staircase before I'm faced with Avery, Ash, and Blaise. Avery looks victorious, but the boys both look a little sick at the sight of me. Clearly, they're not fans of girls covered in vomit, which is mildly reassuring. There's a teacher I don't recognize standing with them, wearing gym clothes.

"Mr. Embley? I found Miss Anderson. She's a little worse for wear, and I think I can smell alcohol." Avery's voice is saccharine, and I could vomit again at the sound of it. Mr. Embley steps out from his office, and I try not to cringe. Did Matteo know I'd be facing this teacher? How did he think I'd be getting out of this? Fuck, I'm doomed. Before I can spiral any further into a panic, Mr. Embley ushers me forward.

"Miss Beaumont, please let Miss Anderson pass. She doesn't look well."

I sigh in relief. I shouldn't ever doubt Matteo. His reach is unparalleled, and he makes Avery look like the child she is. He may be infinitely more dangerous, but at least he's the devil I know. I start back up the stairs as the whispers get louder and more insistent.

"Mr. Embley, aren't you going to breath test her? I saw her drinking last night." Avery's voice changed back to the sharp edge she always reserved for people she thought were lesser than her. It was the first time I'd heard her use it on a teacher.

I level her with a look as I go to pass her. I feel like we've come to some sort of an agreement where she'll dish out punishments, and I'll take them just the same. Ash steps in front of me so I'm forced to stop. I think about stepping into him and getting my vomit on him but stop myself. He's looking at me, at my face and the bruises under my eyes. For a second it looks like he's checking to make sure I'm okay. He seems uneasy about what his sister has done to me.

"Let her pass. She needs some rest. Do you need the

nurse, Miss Anderson? No? Then head straight to your room, please. The Jackal sends his regards."

Ash's eyes widen slightly, like he's never heard anyone disobey his sister before, and Blaise crosses his arms. I smirk at them both. The moment would feel a lot more victorious if I wasn't cold and disgusting.

"Looks like you're not the only one with connections, Floss," I whisper so only they can hear me.

Ash finally moves, and I walk back to my room, slowly and with my head held high. As I round the corner to the girls' dorm I see Lauren and Jessie studying in the sitting area. They look up and see me, their jaws drop. Lauren scrambles to get up, but then she glances around the room to check and see who else is watching. I clench my jaw and give her a quick shake of my head. I'm frustrated at how afraid she is, how easily she bows down to the whims of the more popular students.

I make it to my room, and I grab my shower bag. I make it four steps away from my door when Harley steps out of one of the other girls' rooms and directly in my path. Annabelle steps out after him. I had no idea she lived two doors down from me, that the guys had been fucking her two doors down from me, and as irrational as it may seem, it pisses me off to know how close I am to that.

If looks could kill, Annabelle would be buried by now.

Harley glances at me, and then levels her with a glare

so dark I'd be worried if I were in her shoes. She ignores him completely. The smirk she gives me only lasts as long as it takes me to flip her the bird as I shove past them both and into the bathroom to shower.

I remember to take everything into the shower stall with me this time.

"Out."

Harley's voice bounces off the bathroom tiles. I've stripped out of my dirty uniform, and I've barely got the shower running. I think for a second he's talking to me, and then I hear the other girls leave and the door to the communal shower close and lock.

"I'd rather not be locked in here with you," I say, my voice still raw as I wrap a towel around my naked body. I don't know if I think he'll burst in here with me or what, but it feels too intimate to be naked with only the stall door between us.

"Just have your shower. We'll talk once you're clean."

I wait a minute, and when he doesn't go on, I drop the towel and get under the spray. The heat from the water pierces my skin and soaks straight through my bones until I'm left tingling. I just stand there and try and get warm for a moment before I start scrubbing my skin to wash away the vomit and grime. The smell at first is vile, but after my second pass over the washcloth, I'm able to just enjoy the shower. Once I'm happy with the state of my body, I brush my teeth, and then again for good measure.

My mind keeps skipping back over to Harley being in here with me. He can't see me, at least I hope he can't, but there's something intimate about me washing myself with him in the room. I begrudgingly admit to myself that I like the feeling. He's probably hating every second of standing here and waiting for me, but my mind is still too foggy. I really couldn't give a damn about what he's thinking.

When I shut off the water and wrap myself back up in the towel, I wait for the steam to dissipate enough to start dressing. It's a Saturday, so there's no classes for me to get to, only extracurriculars, and I'm not going down to the dining hall after last night. I may never eat down there again.

Once I've pulled my pajamas on, I look down at myself and see the bruises that have formed over my arms. There're two perfect hand prints, one on each arm, like I've been grabbed roughly. I place one of my own hands over the prints, and it fits near perfectly. A girl has put them on me. No guy at this school has hands as small as mine. It was probably Avery. She would have grabbed me and shoved me into the bathroom so I was safe enough until I came to and she could get me expelled for drinking. That girl is an evil psycho, but I grin at the thought. Maybe it was stupid of me, but I've started admiring her work. She has a good understanding of the school rules, and she's working hard to exploit them and get me out of here.

I open the stall door and step out into the bathroom with my bag slung over my shoulder. Harley is propped up on the sinks, and he's glaring at his phone. He glances up at me and shoves the phone into his back pocket like it's offended him. His eyes roam over me, like Ash's had down at the staircase, like he's looking for injuries, and it makes me fucking livid.

"Is there something specific you need, because *I* really need a nap," I croak out, my throat still sore. I need water and something to eat. I need ten hours of sleep.

"What happened to you? What the fuck did Joey do this time?"

I laugh at him. Was he the only one who wasn't in on it? Why had Avery left him out? "I'm fine. I'm still standing. Go back to Annabelle and enjoy your weekend."

I make to move around him, and Harley's hands shoot out to grab me. They land right on the bruises, and I grunt at the sharp sting of pain. His eyes widen and he loosens his grip on me as he pulls me into his chest. It's not a hug, not even close, but now I'm pressed up against him and I can feel every inch of his rock-hard torso pressing against me until I want to melt into him. Danger, Will Robinson. Big fucking danger.

"Fuck Annabelle, she's in on this. Did Avery do it?" His eyes dance around my face, and I think he's judging how willing I am to kiss him. A shot of fear shoots through my blood. I can't kiss him. For one, I have no idea how to even kiss someone. My experience so far is just the forced kiss from Joey, and I mostly just laid there for that. For another, if he kisses me now and then leaves this room and goes back to hating me, I will break. I want him too much. So instead of facing my fears head-on, I focus on the tattoo on his jaw like a coward. It's moving as he clenches his jaw, and I think of the little heart pendant I have back in my room that belongs to him.

You before my blood. If I tell him what Avery had done, would he put me before his blood? Did I want him to? Now that I had started to question Avery's motives, I wasn't sure I wanted to drive a wedge between them.

The longer I stay silent, the more agitated Harley becomes, until his chest is heaving, and his hands begin to shake where he holds me.

"Fuck, can you just stay alive? Can you just leave and keep breathing? Is that too much to ask?" he ground out.

"Afraid your cousin is going to get life for my murder? I'm sure he can buy his way out of it. I'd rather risk death than leave here. Do you hear me? I'd rather die here than go back to Mounts Bay and become what's waiting for me there."

He stares down at me, his eyes burning into my skull, and then he shoves me away from his body with a vicious curse under his breath. When he rubs the back of his head, he glances over at me with a calculating look. I don't like it; I don't like feeling that he's assessing me and found me wanting.

"Don't worry about today. I'll live to die another day, and it won't be at your cousins' hand. Go back to your friends."

He doesn't fight me as I swing the door open. We find Annabelle waiting on the other side, close, like she's been eavesdropping on us both. I ignore her, walking straight out and toward my room as she begins to yell at Harley. I intend to ignore their lovers' spat altogether, but then I hear the slap of her palm across his cheek and I glance over my shoulder at them both. She's crying, and he's looking at her with a bored expression that doesn't gel with the tightness in his shoulders. She takes another swing at him, and he catches her wrist.

"It's pretty fucking simple. I don't take orders from my cousins. You've just proved that you do, so you can kiss my ass goodbye."

He drops her wrist and turns to leave. Annabelle grabs his arm and screams at him again.

"Over the fucking Mounty? Maybe Ash is right, maybe you are soft over her."

Harley whips around and, using his chest alone, he backs her up against the wall so quickly that the other girls watching scatter. Again, no one steps up to help her. No one cares if he does turn out to be violent. My eyes collide with his for a second before he leans down to her. I think he's going to kiss her, and if he does, I'm going to vomit all over again.

"If you think I'm the soft one, then you're dumber than I thought."

And then he leaves her. Annabelle is panting, tears are streaming down her face, and the crowd is lapping up her humiliation. She's always enjoyed the attention she's had for being shared by them, but I don't think she'll enjoy being dumped so publicly by him.

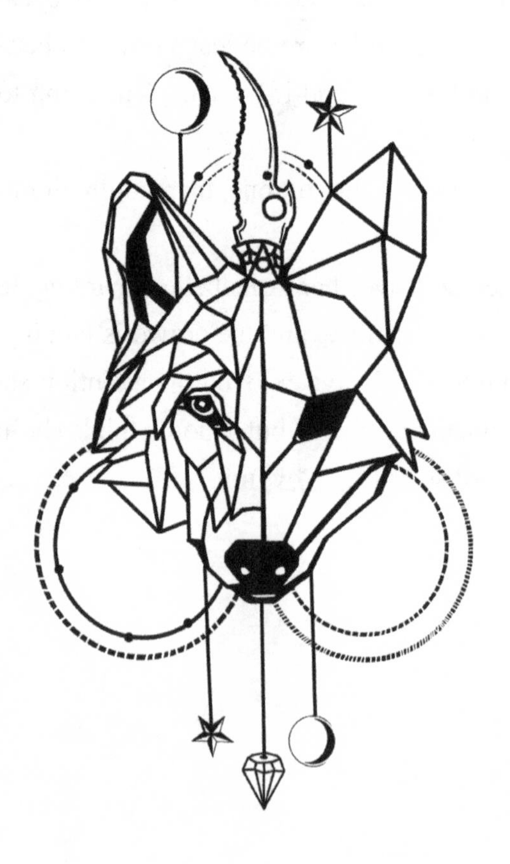

Nineteen

I wake on Monday to the news that Avery has dumped Rory.

There isn't a single freshman that will look at or speak to him, or Harlow for that matter. Neither seems to care all that much, but Rory is now walking the halls of Hannaford like he's got a target on his back. By the looks he's getting from Ash and Harley, it's obvious they're the ones that have put it there.

I watch the entire spectacle of Rory trying to find a seat at lunch with a grin on my face. I must look like a lunatic, but there's something incredibly satisfying about seeing his football team turn their backs on him. After a cold glare over at Avery, he ends up sitting with Harlow and Joey's flunkies. Ash glances over and sees my glee, and we share a moment. He knows I gave Avery the photos and, angry at Rory as he is, he's fucking ecstatic about the way this is all panning out. *Join the club, Beaumont*. It feels weird to be on the same side for once.

My joy quickly evaporates when the dining hall doors open and Joey walks through, his suspension finally lifted.

He's looking much healthier than the last time I saw him. There's meat on his bones, and the dark circles that were ever-present have faded. I wonder if he's been in rehab. He's been gone long enough to have finished a twelve-step process, but I snort at the very thought of him sitting around a facility and making nice with people there. Still, it would explain his appearance. Maybe the suspension was really the school covering for him at his parents' request. I'm sure Mr. Trevelen is on their payroll; he's certainly on Avery's.

He doesn't bother to grab a tray. After giving his siblings a sarcastic little wave, he joins his flunkies and gives Rory a once-over.

"Weren't you fucking my sister? Have you lot let a spy into my house?" His arrogant tone cuts through the rest of the chatter at the table.

"He got caught sticking his dick in someone else's hole, so now he's sitting with us. You always said anyone who fucks with the twins is welcome here," is Harlow's dripping reply. She doesn't mention that she was the hole. She's still open for Joey's business, first and foremost.

Joey tips his head back and laughs too loud for the echoes in the room. Ash gets up to leave, and he tugs Avery along beside him. He's practically vibrating with rage but, aside from her ashen face, Avery looks unaffected by their behavior. Blaise leans back in his chair and stares Joey down. I wonder whether new money would win over the old if those two had it out.

I'd bet on Blaise in the physical fight any day of the week. His shoulders were easily broader and more defined than Joey, and I knew from concert photos he was ripped. I'd also heard the rumors of the fights he'd won here over the years. The boys' dorm was basically a fight club half the time, fighting over girls and money. None of those three ever lost.

The problem was the old adage that the Jackal had told me over and over again: new money can't become old money without getting dirty first. Amongst the Twelve, it was crucial to our domination and survival. If you can find a family close to turning and get in with them, become indispensable, then you can amass power as quickly as money. Matteo had done it dozens of times, and now he was the most powerful man in the state.

The Beaumonts were old and dirty. The Morrisons were unparalleled in their wealth, but squeaky clean. If Blaise took on Joey for what he's doing to his friends, then his hands wouldn't stay clean for long.

From the look on his face, I'd guess he didn't want them to.

"And how fares my little Mounty love?" Joey calls out

to me, breaking my train of thought. I've been staring at Blaise for too long. Instead of being embarrassed about it, I just flip Joey the bird.

Gasps ring out around me. People begin to get up and move out of the way, desperate not to be noticed by Joey. I take a bite out of my apple and chew slowly, sending a glare down the table at the teachers hearing all of this and ignoring it completely. What a bunch of pussies.

When the bell tolls its warning, I get up and walk out of the dining hall calmly. As I push out of the dining hall, I feel the heat of Joey's gaze on my back, so I turn to look at him.

The little smile on his face is manic, feral, and edged with insanity.

He's not sober.

The time away has given him the chance to get a grip on himself and hide the addiction better, but the dancing flames in his eyes tell me all I need to know about what's running through his veins right now. He winks at me, and I let the door swing shut behind me.

Joey's return to Hannaford means I have trouble sleeping again.

It doesn't matter that I have the best lock system money can buy now, thanks to Matteo. Every time I shut my eyes, I see that raging psycho's face as he pinned me to his bed, and that fucking wink in the dining hall. I've slipped my knife into the pocket in the hoodie I'm wearing like a safety blanket but sleep still evades me.

Usually I fight my insomnia by throwing myself headfirst into my studies, but I've just about finished all my assignments for the entire school year. I could go over my notes for my upcoming tests and the end-of-year exams, but I know that I already know everything, that I've already crammed it all into my head and it's stuck. I could also start on the reading required for next year, but nothing is holding my interest at the moment.

I feel restless. Like my skin is crawling and my mind is climbing the walls of my skull and trying to get out. I can't stop moving or jiggling my legs. My mind is currently torturing me with images of Matteo doing to me what Joey tried to do. I know someday his patience will wear thin, and he'll want to take what he thinks he's owed. It's why I have to do well here at Hannaford, so that someday I can disappear somewhere even the Jackal cannot reach.

I'm thinking the Caribbean.

I have no idea what job I'll do there but fuck it if I'm not resourceful. Everywhere needs doctors, so my original career path works. I'll just have to figure out how to go to med school there. I can figure this out if I put my mind to it.

I'm two hours into a deep internet research spiral when I hear a door slam.

I glance over and see it's three a.m., so not the usual time for loud noises in the girls' dorm. It's possible someone has gotten up to pee or is even sneaking a guy into their room, but my mind is currently a vortex of spiraling anxiety and what-ifs. I carefully roll out of bed; thankful the creaking mattress has been replaced and I can be silent as I sneak my door open.

My stomach bottoms out.

Joey is sitting against Avery's door, his phone in his hand and his face lit up in the dark as he texts someone. He's wearing dark slacks and a polo shirt, loafers on his feet, like he's just left some elitist gentleman's club. He doesn't notice me watching him, and I think about calling the student helpline to report him being up here to get him out. My hand reaches into my pocket, and I grip my knife. If he spots me and rushes toward me, I'll only need one good swing to take him out. I will use his momentum as he rushes to let the knife sink deep into his throat. It's a smaller target than his belly, but more effective at getting him taken out fast. I'd seen guys stabbed in the gut go on to run through the streets for hours during the Game. It was a good lesson on picking out the weakest spot and aiming true.

I don't know how long I sit there and watch him. My ass

goes numb and my fingers ache from where I'm gripping the knife handle so tight. I can't look away from him, even for a second; my eyes refuse to blink. I jump when the door opens, and Joey pushes himself off the ground to face Avery.

I've never seen the two of them interact. It's weird to think we've been at the same school for months, eating meals together and passing each other in the halls, and yet I've never seen them so much as look at each other.

"Dad's not happy you called the cops on me, Floss," he says in a sing-song voice. Avery's eyes are cool, even as her shoulders tremble.

"Don't call me that. Is that all you have to say? Because we both know it wasn't me that called them."

The clock was ticking. Joey was going to make his next move on me soon. "Nevertheless. Just telling you what dear old Dad thinks. He asked me to pass this on to you."

Joey's hand cracks across her cheek so hard, she bounces back against her door. Her head makes a sickening thud, and I open my door up wide, the light from my room cutting through the darkness. Joey doesn't look up at me, but Avery's eyes grow wide.

"Goodnight," he says in that same tone, and he walks off.

I take a step toward Avery, and she pegs me with a look of such loathing I stop dead in my tracks. She tucks back into her room and shuts her door quietly, and I'm left with my own thoughts again.

My head is pounding with an intense headache from lack of sleep the next day. Aside from preparing myself for Joey's next tantrum at me, I've put his little visit with Avery out of my head completely. She didn't want my help when it happened right there in front of me, so I assumed she still wanted me to stay the fuck away from her—so it was a surprise to arrive at history and find her leaning against my desk.

Harley has a habit of getting to all his classes mere seconds before they begin, so he wasn't the reason for her visit. I give her a cool look as I take my seat and gather my supplies.

"Something has been bothering me, Mounty, and I want some answers. I own the teachers at this school. I have since middle school, so how is it a lowly little scholarship student could override my instructions, hm? I've had a chat with Mr. Embley, and he nearly went into heart failure at my questions. It seems you're now scarier than I am."

She's deflecting. She's running interference so I don't question her on her brother or her fucked-up family dynamics. I play along with her little game in the hopes that she'll leave me alone so I can focus on Joey instead.

"Did you know that money isn't the only thing that can influence people? Some people have other buttons, and all you need to know is where they are."

She smiles slowly at me and Harley walks into the classroom. He frowns when he sees Avery speaking to me and hurries over to us both. "I'm well acquainted with manipulation. What I'm asking is how you did it."

I drop my gaze down to the assignment I'm due to hand in today and I give it a once-over, even though I know it's perfect. Harley drops his bag onto the floor at my feet and stands over me with his hands on his hips, frowning. I look up and find Avery still staring at me with an expectant look fixed on her features.

"That is absolutely none of your business, but a word of warning: you should think twice about who you target at this school."

Avery glances between Harley and me, and then smirks and takes her own seat. The teacher arrives and starts calling for quiet, and Harley drops down into his chair.

"The fuck was that about?" he whispers at me, leaning in so I'm drowning in his delicious smell. Would it kill the guy to be average for once and not smell like living ambrosia? Ugh.

"Just discussing tactics, nothing to worry yourself with. Your cousin is fine," I whisper back as I breathe him in. I hope it's not too obvious that I'm turning to putty over him again.

He shakes his head at me and goes back to his work, a small frown creasing his brow.

He doesn't ask me again.

I think that will be the end of the confrontation with Avery, but once again, I've underestimated her. It's another hard lesson to learn.

I walk into the sitting room in the girls' dorms after dinner and stop dead when I see Avery holding my bag. Gritting my teeth, I curse under my breath at her. I should have known this was coming. I had seen too much and gotten too close to the Beaumont family once again. No good deed at this school goes unpunished.

She holds the lighter up, and I cringe.

It's replaceable. I did the sums once, I can do them again, but they're due tomorrow and I'd slaved away at the workbook for weeks. It's the culmination of months of learning, and it's worth seventy percent of my overall class mark. I'll have to pull an all-nighter to have a chance of getting them done in time.

"I'm quickly learning that personal humiliation isn't the way to get you out of here. I'm tempted to look into what happened to you at your Mounty school to make you so resilient, but who has the time for that, hm? You need a 3.75 GPA or higher to stay here, right? How low do you think flunking math will drop it?"

I shut my eyes and take a deep breath. When I open them again, she can see the resolution I've come to.

"Burn it, then."

The flames eat the paper ravenously. Avery drops in into the bin, and soon the whole thing is engulfed in flames. The smile she gives me as she walks away is infuriating, but I give her my best serene face in return. There are things I know better than most about myself and the ways of the world. A night of no sleep won't kill me. A week without food won't kill me. Finding my mother's dead body rotting on my kitchen floor won't kill me. A bullet to the shoulder won't kill me. The bullying at Hannaford Prep *won't kill me.*

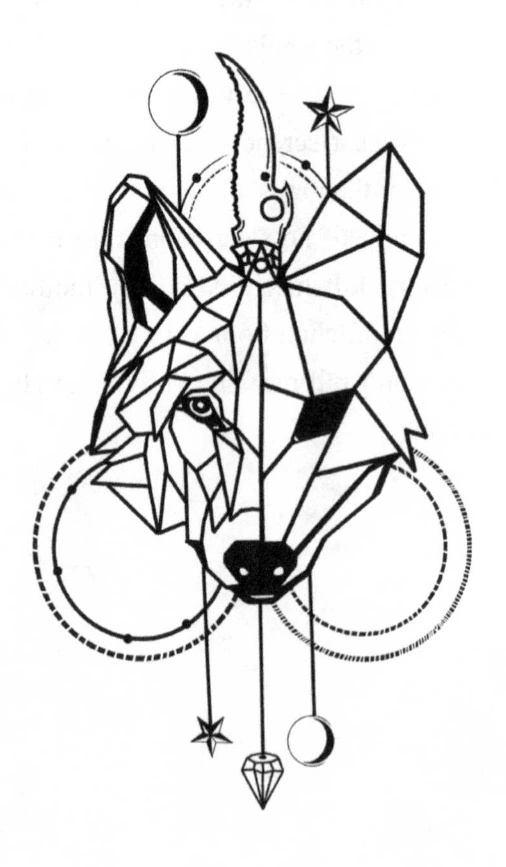

Twenty

Lunch is the only meal of the day that is at a set time for me. Since my drugging episode, I had started skipping breakfast and eating dinner at 10 p.m., right before the dining hall closes, and I am usually only ever joined by teachers. Still a risk, as I know Avery has most of the school staff under her impressive thumb, but there were only so many protein bars I could eat and meals I could skip. The small amount of weight I had put on is quickly disappearing off my body, and I miss my boobs already. I also miss the French toast with syrup and strawberries that are only served at breakfast. Ugh.

For lunch each day I select a sealed drink, either an iced coffee or a bottle of water, and a couple of apples and bananas. It's barely enough to stop the intense hunger pangs in my empty stomach, and I still have to listen to the rumbling for most of the afternoon. To every other student, it looks like I've gone on a strict diet, which is common among the girls here. I know for a fact there are at least five girls I share the bathroom with that are vomiting after their meals in an effort to be supermodel thin. One of them even confronted me and asked my secret to being so small. When I answered poverty with a blank face, she snarled at me like a rabid dog. Calorie deprivation can turn even the nicest girls into bitches.

My phone pings as I sit, and I'm careful to keep my eyes on my food while I fish around in my bag to grab it and see what Matteo needs from me.

You never call to chat anymore.

I stare at the screen for a second while the other students around me eat and talk and laugh like normal teenagers. What I wouldn't give to be one of them. To be worried about what my parents think about my grades, or what I'm going to wear to the next party I attend. Instead, here I am trying to decipher obscure text messages from gangster kingpins while planning my next move against billionaire sociopaths.

I need to catch a break.

I wonder what it is about me that appeals to these types of guys. Matteo had hand-picked me out of hundreds of foster kids at age nine to train to someday become the Wolf. Joey had taken one look at me when I arrived at Hannaford and decided I would make a good game. If I knew what it was that appealed to them, I could try and snuff it out, or at least conceal it. Instead, I'm stuck dealing with the ramifications of their desires.

I shove my tray aside and tap out a reply. I can use this opening if I'm smart about it; I want to try and clear my summer break from any Club business. I need some downtime.

I'm fielding a lot at the moment. I'm making some good connections. A lot of future leaders in my classes.

I pick up an apple. I like the wholeness of it. I can see if anyone has tampered with it, so now I'm surviving on fruit. Lauren sits down across from me and gives me a little half-smile. I return it with a sigh.

I've heard some disturbing things about you, Starbright.

Ugh, I hate it when he calls me that. I'm sure he is one of the last people on this Earth that knows my middle name. He enjoys teasing me with it. Nothing makes my blood boil quicker than hearing the name my doped-up mother assigned me. Eclipse Starbright Anderson. The second I turn eighteen, I'm changing my name to Claire, or Kylie, or fucking Frances. Anything normal, anything that people just write down without making a smart-ass comment about.

I'm acing my classes and I'm finally looking like a girl instead of a skinned rat. What's so disturbing about that?

Avery and the guys walk in and line up for food. Harley is back to laughing and joking with them all, my drugged night of vomit clearly forgotten. Avery looks dimmed from her usual smiling overlord shine. I watch them all out of the corner of my eye, and I don't miss the looks Ash sends me. Curious.

Why does Joey Beaumont want you dead?

My stomach drops. So Joey is running his mouth about me so much that now even Matteo has heard it all the way back at Mounts Bay? Rationally I know the Jackal has eyes here as well, and any of them could have passed the information on, but it still makes a shiver run up my spine. I know how badly Matteo wants to own me, mind and body, so this at least I can work to my favor.

He wants to fuck me. He's made a game out of it. I have no intention of fucking any guy here, and when I expressed that to him, he tried to rape me. He was unsuccessful and doesn't take kindly to the word no.

I think Matteo gets a kick out of the idea of me being untouched. I think he fantasizes about being the one and only person to be inside me someday. I know this is the best card to play. Maybe I am learning how to play the political game.

I will pay little Joey a visit. Do not argue with me on this.

I glance over to watch Joey as he presses over his group of flunkies like he's their king, and smile. Occasionally, it's a good thing to keep Matteo's dreams about me alive.

I wouldn't dream of arguing with you, Jackal.

As I grab my tray to head back out of the dining hall, I see Joey frowning down at his phone, and it feels like a victory to me.

"You should talk Avery into taking some self-defense lessons."

Ash stares over the library table at me like I've lost my goddamn mind. Maybe I have, but I've also lost the ability to give a fuck at this place anymore. I decide its sleep deprivation. I only got twenty minutes of sleep after finishing the re-do on my math workbook, but I'm confident I'll get at least an A-minus on it, so it was worth it.

"And why do you think I should do that?" He speaks slowly, dragging out the words like I'm very simple.

"Maybe next time your sociopath brother takes a swing at her, she can plant him on his ass like he deserves."

His eyebrows show the exact toll my words have taken on him. He's fucking devastated, and my heart drops to see it. I guess she didn't tell him about Joey's homecoming. I feel weirdly guilty, like somehow, it's my fault his twin was hurt.

"When did you see that?" His voice is as raw as his face. I look down at the page in front of him, and I realize he's shaking. Fucking Joey, he ruins everything he touches.

Even his siblings have been broken by him.

"Last week. I tried to speak to her about it and she freaked. She should at least learn enough to make him think twice about touching her."

Ash groans and scrubs a hand over his face, all long tan fingers I try not to stare at. It's jarring to see real emotions on his face this close. He's usually so reserved, so cut off, that I never see his face without a sneer in my direction. It's oddly comforting.

"I've tried. She said if she fights back, it'll only make him more violent toward her. We always make sure she has one of us with her." He groans again and cradles his head in his hands.

There're so many questions I want to ask him, but I don't want to break the spell that has him opening up to me. Does his father hit them both, or was Joey lying? What does their mother think about this? How much time are they forced to spend with Joey outside the school year? How does Avery have access to enough money to pay Harley's tuition, which I know for a fact is over eighty thousand dollars a year?

Why does Ash lie about needing help with his classwork?

I'm still deciding if I'm brave enough to try and ask him any of these questions when Blaise arrives. We've been studying for twenty minutes already, so I give him a look. He's still doing his best to not look at me at all, so he doesn't see it. My temper flares.

"How kind of you to grace us with your presence." Sarcasm drips from my words. Blaise ignores me, but Ash chuckles from where his head is still pressed into his palms.

"He does what he can for his people."

"Yes, yes, you're both so fucking amusing. I had to re-sit a test for history, because apparently Mr. Smithton gets hard over ruining my life. He called my dad, so now I'm truly fucked. Why can't I just drop out and make music and fuck groupies and get fucking blind drunk every night? Why do I have to learn inane bullshit about dead people? Why?"

"Ah, good. The dramatics have started, Mounty, settle in. We're going to be here for hours while he gets this out of his system."

Blaise slumps into his chair theatrically, and I scoff at him. He looks like a poor little rock star, forced to be a scholar. He groans and tugs at his hair roughly, so it stands up everywhere. He has sex hair at the best of times, but now it's bordering on obscene. I can't tear my eyes away from it no matter how hard I try.

"I hate this place and I hate my dad's business and I hate the expectations he has for me."

Ash drops his hands and looks over at his friend with

fake sympathy, nodding at him.

"Yes, so unfair to be the sole heir to a billion-dollar empire that your father sold his soul to be able to create. So sad. Do you want a drink, Mounty? May as well drown this tirade out while we have the chance."

Ash starts snapping his fingers, like a bartender is going to appear out of nowhere. I smoother a laugh in my blazer sleeve. My chest aches at being so close to their friendship and playful banter, my favorite blend of sarcasm and fondness. The world is a cruel place to put this so close to me, but so wildly out of my reach.

"You know what, fuck capitalism. If we could be happy with what we have instead of constantly striving to be at the top, I wouldn't be in this mess. Let's be fucking hippies instead. Let's make music and throw away all of our worldly possessions and ask the moon what it thinks about our problems."

That strikes a familiar chord in my chest. My mom used to get high and talk like that all the time. It's how I got my name, for god's sake.

"No, no, I won't be growing a beard and smoking joints out of a van like a fucking pedophile. Get it all out, though. Bottling it up will only make it worse."

I tune out their banter, as amusing as it is, to look over Blaise's classwork. He's started bringing in bigger and bigger piles, and it's clear to me just how far behind he really is. How he managed to convince his parents and the faculty that he could afford to miss the first few weeks of the year is beyond me. I'm good, but I'm not sure even I can work this miracle, given how little time we actually interact.

I'm about to interrupt the pity party to suggest we start in on the mountain of work when I feel someone walk up behind me. I tense, expecting it to be Joey, and a dark, hidden part of my mind expects him to have a knife. Ash and Blaise fall silent as the chair next to mine pulls back and a student I don't recognize sits down. He's blond and broad, but with none of the grace or stunning features that Harley has.

"Can I help you?" I say, aiming for a light tone.

"Sure you can. I wanted to discuss the sweep Joey started."

For fuck's sake. I cut him an icy glare, but he just smiles in return. His teeth are too straight, a fake white row that makes him look like an android. Everything about him makes my teeth clench so hard my jaw aches.

"Look, it's admirable that you're taking a stand and refusing to fuck anyone for the sake of the money. It shows you have more integrity than the average Mounty. At some point, someone is going to fuck you and get the money. Why not give Joey a taste of his own medicine and let me fuck you for it? I'll even give you a percentage of the sweep for your troubles."

A percentage. For my troubles. I silently weigh up my options. There're three librarians, and two are within eyesight of our table. If I slam his face into the desk and break his pompous nose, there'll be too many witnesses. If I ignore him, he might go away, or maybe he'll start stalking me instead. I could call the Jackal and have him murdered in his sleep.

The guy, who still hasn't even told me his name, slings an arm over my shoulders and his hand ends up hovering over my chest. I have what can only be described as a full rage blackout.

One minute he's laughing and touching me, and the next he's howling and clutching his now-broken hand to his chest like it's a baby bird. I'm much faster than he is, and while he's flailing, I slap a hand over his mouth, so the librarians don't assume he's being murdered and come over here to stop me. He could push me off, but he's too busy losing his shit over his mangled hand.

"What's your name, asshole?" I whisper. He's swearing and sweating too much to answer, so Blaise surprises me by doing it for him.

"Mounty, this is Samuel Hanson. He's a sophomore and he's at risk of being kicked out by his parents because he's been caught gambling away his trust fund. Is that why you need the money, Sammy-boy? Run out of funds to feed your addiction?"

Samuel manages to stop screaming, so I let my hand drop away from his face. He's panting and his eyes keep rolling back into his head. It's pathetic.

"Your pain tolerance is worse than a child's," I hiss at him, and Ash snickers, but I don't spare him a glance. I need to make a point with this guy. It's been too long since I hurt someone for propositioning me, and they've forgotten what I can do.

"I won't fuck you. I won't fuck anyone at this school, not for a hundred grand."

"The pot is sitting around the seven hundred grand mark now, Mounty," Ash drawls. I don't let the shock show on my face. These fucking wealthy bastards.

"Well, I won't fuck you for that either, even if my *percentage* was a hundred percent. If you so much as look in my direction again, I will *bury* you. Do those rumors make their way up here about us Mountys too? About how easily I can and will kill you for insulting me?"

He's managed to pull himself together enough to kick back into obnoxious rich-kid mode. "I will report you, and you'll be out for this, you little cunt."

I. Hate. That. Word.

My mom's boyfriends all used to call her that, or me, or they'd tell me all about my mom's gaping cunt. I was six the first time I realized what they were talking about. It still sends me to a crazy place in my head to hear it uttered.

"No, you'll walk your ass out of here, and you'll do exactly what she said," Blaise says, and I've never heard him so angry. "See, you're encroaching on my study time, and she's the best tutor I've ever had, so if I have to beat you senseless myself to keep her here and teaching me, then I will, Hanson. Are you ready to bleed by me again?" Blaise cracks his knuckles to drive home the point, and Samuel stands. The chair falls as he lurches out of the room and out of my life.

"Is your crisis over now? Can we get started on the important stuff?" I say as I shake out my hand. The force required to break bones is less substantial when you know exactly where to strike, but that didn't mean I wasn't paying for it.

Blaise finally glances at me and nods like he didn't just defend me.

None of us talk about how exactly it is that I know how to break someone's hand using only two fingers.

Twenty One

Hannaford is a writhing snake pit of gossips.

I didn't even make it to my room after my tutoring session with Ash and Blaise without being asked about Samuel. It was late by the time we finished up, and I'd been forced to skip dinner.

My stomach wakes me at 5 a.m. and I know for certain I can't skip breakfast. Harley will be pissed if he has to listen to the grumbling of my stomach all through our classes. The dining hall opens at 5:30 a.m. and I reason with myself that I'll be safe to eat at that time. What other students would be willing to eat that early?

I'm pissed to find that there are a heap of students waiting at the door for the dining hall to open. It turns out the swim team, track, and the row team all meet at 6 a.m. to torture themselves. It's all elbows and swearing to get to the front of the line, so I hang back and survey the crowd. Harley is on the swim team but he's not here. The room he shares with Ash and Blaise probably has a fully stocked kitchen and a personal chef, for all I know. Yes, I'll admit I'm hungry and bitter. I need to come up with a better system to keep me from turning into a hangry bitch.

My mouth waters when I see the French toast, and I decide to risk a second roofie episode. I pile on the cream and strawberries, drizzle so much syrup it drips everywhere, and I'm a sticky mess.

I'm a happy, sticky mess.

When I've literally licked my plate clean, I dump my tray onto the pile by the door and start back toward the girls' dorm for a quick shower before classes. My belly is full, and I even catch myself humming cheerfully under my breath. The perfect morning.

Rough hands grab me and pull me into an empty classroom.

I shove at them, but I have a six-foot guy on each side of me, neither of whom I have spoken to before. They're upperclassmen for sure. I grunt and pull at their arms, only to have their hands tighten around my biceps. Avery isn't the only person who is swift in their retribution. I'm sure this is Samuel's doing. I'm convincing myself to stay still and meek when a third student steps into the classroom.

Spencer Hillsong.

He's the guy who approached me after the naked photos of me were sent out. I'd forgotten he even exists, but he hasn't forgotten me.

Now that I know how much money is on the line for having sex with me, I'm sure that's what he's here for. Even rich kids must be tempted by seven hundred thousand, especially those who don't have unlimited access to their parents' wallets.

"My sweet mother would be so disappointed," he says as he steps toward me. He's smiling cruelly, but he's got nothing on Joey or Matteo. Still, he could rape me for the cash all the same.

"That you'd forced yourself on a girl? I should hope so."

He laughs right in my face. I swear to myself that I'll start carrying my knife with me from now on. It was stupid of me to believe I wasn't in danger of this now that I'd dealt with Joey. I'd only really dealt with him, not all of his blind followers.

"I would never put my dick in trash. Lord knows what commoner diseases you have. No, I'm going to show you what happens to girls who don't do what they're told."

The crack of his hand across my face leaves me dazed. He's certainly not holding back on account of my gender. I weigh up my options while he looks at me with glee. I could attempt to fight them off. Three to one, not great odds but doable. They're big guys, I can feel the muscular frames on the two holding me, so my chances of success aren't great. I tug my arms a little to gauge the reaction and their grips tighten. So they're both committed to playing their part, neither of them seeming to care about me suggesting they were here to sexually assault me.

Spencer seems to be the only one interested in actually hitting me. When he punches me in the stomach, I feel the guy on my left flinch even as my breakfast roils in my belly. So, if I stand there and take the beating, I'll only be hit by one guy. If I pretended to be more hurt than I actually am, I might be able to minimize the damage.

I moan when he punches me again. It feels strange after having spent so much time learning how to stay silent, but I lay it on thick. When he lands another blow to my head, this time behind my ear, where my hair will cover the bruise because he's a sneaky fuck, I see stars and swear roughly. I could vomit, and I swear under my breath at the thought of wasting that beautiful, fluffy toast.

"You should think twice about messing with Joey. He owns this school. If he says jump, then the whole damn building moves."

How utterly pathetic. Spencer is just openly admitting he's Joey bitch. And for what? Doesn't he realize Joey doesn't have the capacity to make friends? There's no loyalty in him at all. Spencer is just another child playing a man's game.

I don't have to fake the grunt that's pushed out of me as I feel my ribs snap. It hurts like a bitch, and I'm forced to pant instead of taking deep breaths.

"Fuck, c'mon, Spence. The bitch is done. If you keep going, we'll get caught for sure."

Spencer is panting and sweating from using my body as a punching bag. I don't know how many hits I've taken, only that I've got a concussion and several broken ribs.

"Don't be a pussy, Kyle, she can take a bit more. I'm sure she's been slapped around before and fucking loves it."

He pulls his arm back for one last hit, but the guy on my left drops me. I lurch to the ground, and the guy on my right gives up on holding me too. I manage to put my arms out to catch myself, but the intense roaring pain has them collapse, and I face plant onto the carpet.

Every breath feels like I'm drawing glass into my chest cavity and inviting it to shred my lungs to nothing. I think I have at least two broken ribs, and I have to remember to baby them a bit, so I don't puncture a damn lung. I know the score, I've done this all before, but I dream about the day that I never have to worry about being beaten again.

It takes everything in me to get dressed for the day and then make it back down the stairs to start the school day. When I arrive at my history class, Harley is already present, and he watches me ease myself into my chair with knowing eyes. The rest of the class filters in behind me, and the teacher shuts the door firmly as she starts the class. I grunt as I lean down to empty my bag, but he doesn't offer me any help. Only after I've completely set myself up does he speak to me.

"Who did that to you?" His voice is so soft, I know Avery hasn't heard him. Whether he's afraid to attract her attention or he thinks the answer is she's responsible, I can't even begin to guess.

"A junior. Joey's getting desperate," I murmur back. I don't want his help, but I can't afford to have him say anything to Avery and get me in the shit with her again. I physically could not fight her off right now.

"Which junior?" He's still whispering, but the words are distorted, like he's barely squeezing them out. I swivel in my chair to look at him, though it pains me. He's not looking at me, he's taking notes in his beautiful, even handwriting, and no one would guess that he was taking any notice of me. I shake my head at him and try to ignore the pain and focus on the teacher's words.

The teacher announces a pop quiz in our next lesson, and the class erupts with groans and whining from the other students. Harley uses the distraction to lean in to me, to whisper into my ear. My body is still firmly in defensive mode, so I startle, grunting at the white-hot pain that threatens to take my vision, sucking air into my ravaged lungs too quickly. As I cough and hack into my palm, I can taste the coppery tang on my tongue, and I know the wet spot on my palm is blood. Harley's hand wraps around my wrist carefully but firmly, like he knows I'll try and pull away from his touch. Even with my whole body lit up with intense pain, my skin tingles underneath his touch as he looks down at the evidence of my internal bleeding.

"Tell me who the fuck did that to you, or I'll tell the teacher you're spreading Mounty diseases by leaking blood everywhere."

Typical Harley. He can't even be sympathetic about my beating without acting like an ass. I tilt my head back to meet his eyes. I don't know what to do with what I see on his face.

He's staring at me how he looks at Avery, like I'm something precious, and my mind scrambles to figure out why. I gape at him and try to find my voice.

"Why would you care who did this to me?" I croak.

His eyes quickly shutter and his jaw twitches. From the corner of my eye, I see Avery turn to stare at us both. Great. Now I'm going to be attacked on my way to the toilet at midnight and I'll probably rack up some medical bills I can't afford to sort out.

"Spencer Hillsong. He had a couple of friends, but I didn't recognize them."

Harley gives me a curt nod, and then I nearly fall off my damn chair as he stoops down to pick up my bag for me and starts to pack away my books. Avery is still watching us, and while she's not outright glaring, I wouldn't call it a friendly sort of stare.

"Harley, you shouldn't—"

He cuts her off with a sharp tone. "Shut it, Floss. Messing with her shit is one thing, beating her bloody is fucking disgusting. I'll *end* that dickhead."

I snort at him and take my now-full bag, slinging it gingerly over the shoulder that isn't bruised. He gives me another look and then gently takes my elbow to steer me out of the class. I'm shocked enough to let him, and I can feel eyes following us both down the hall. Avery falls into step with him, but she doesn't glance my way again.

We round the corner to get to our shared chemistry lab when we run right into Ash and Blaise. I cringe and try to pull away from Harley, but his grip only tightens. Blaise looks shocked to see me, but when he recovers, he is back to refusing to look at me. It's like yesterday didn't happen at all. That works for me. I'm doing my best to forget he exists. Ash is more curious about my appearance; his eyes take me in, inch by painstaking inch. It was possibly the worst time to start coughing up blood again. It becomes clear to me that if Harley wasn't holding me up, I would collapse from the pain radiating around my chest, and my vision blurs threateningly again. Why did I even try to make it through today? I'm losing my edge at this school. At Mounts Bay, I always knew my limits. I need to regroup before it gets me killed.

"I told you to stay away from Joey. All of this is his doing. Honestly, you have no one but yourself to blame for this," says Ash as he grabs my other arm. I grit my teeth, but I'm not sure if it's because of his words or if I'm trying to take control of my body once again. The edges of my vision start to black out, and I can't even choke out a retort.

"It wasn't Joey, it was Hillsong, and he's a fucking dead man walking," snaps Harley.

I shut my eyes as we walk. There's no point in fighting them, I barely have the energy to stay conscious. My mind is hazy. Not a great sign; I'm going to end up in the nurse's office.

"Do you really think he's acting without Joey's influence? Ash is right, she should have stayed away from him," says Avery. She doesn't sound happy at all.

It takes me a minute for my mind to catch up with our movements and to realize we're still walking. Our lab is only a few yards away, so it makes no sense. Panic claws up my spine, and I jerk my arms to try and get free. *They're dragging me somewhere secluded to finish the job, Harley hates me, there's no way he would care about some junior beating me!* I plant my feet and try to stop them from moving forward, but Harley and Ash are too strong for me.

"Calm the fuck down, Mounty. We're going to take you back to your room so you can die somewhere more comfortable than the lab," says Ash, and I can hear the laughter in his voice.

"Don't be a dick, Ash. She's probably suspicious we're helping her. Twice in a week, I'd be suspicious too," says Blaise, and I jerk my head around to see that he's trailing behind us. He still won't meet my eyes.

"Why are we helping her, again?" drawls Avery, not even bothering to look up from her phone. Her arm is linked with Ash's, and he's directing her as much as he's helping me.

We arrive at my room, and it takes me three attempts to fumble the key out from around my neck and into the door. When I pause, Ash finally drops my arm and lets Avery tug him away from me. She's probably scared he's developing a soft spot for me, but I could set her straight about that. There's no way the guy who snarls at me over the table in the library would ever feel anything but contempt for me. I have to admit, this rescue is pretty confusing for me. I'm struggling with my own feelings for all three of the guys, and their kind and gentle touches are just making this all the more difficult for me. It is not normal for a girl to be crushing on three guys this hard at the same damn time. I don't want one of them, I want all three, even after everything they've done to me. I need to clear my head. I need some space, and I need it now.

Harley won't move. I attempt a pointed look at him, but he just raises his eyebrows at me in return. When it's clear neither of us are willing to back down, Blaise groans at us both and then pushes between us to grab the key and open the door. When his arm brushes mine, I flinch away from him so hard I hit the doorframe and grunt in pain. My body is going to pay dearly for that move.

"Why the fuck does she flinch like that when you touch her?" Harley snaps, and Blaise backs up quickly like his ass is on fire. I shuffle into the room and drop my bag on the floor.

"How the fuck should I know? I've never touched her!"

I flinch again. I know that if I ever do touch him, and if he touched me back, I'd be ruined for life. It doesn't matter how angry I am at him, how badly he's humiliated me, how much he loathes me. He could destroy me, and I would ask for more. I turn and grab the door, mostly to keep myself upright. I'm so pathetic. Thank god the Jackal can't see me right now.

"I don't want him running off to your little shared fuck and telling her I'm stalking him or acting inappropriately.

The last thing I need is that bitch starting a vendetta on me. I'd say thanks for the help up here, but I'm sure you'll find a way to make me pay for it later."

I enjoy the twin looks of shock on their faces as I slam the door on them both.

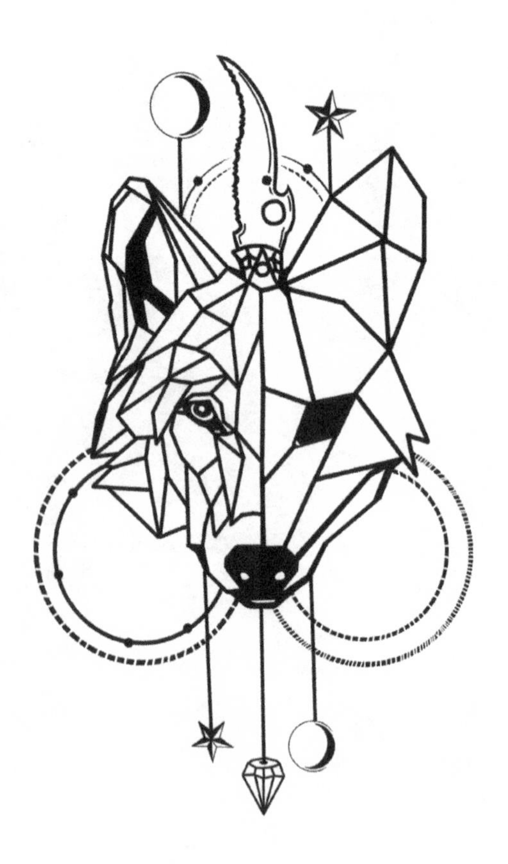

Twenty Two

It takes two days to be able to go back to class.

I still can't breathe without being able to feel exactly which ribs are broken, but my concussion has eased. For those two days, I can't sit up for longer than ten minutes without a migraine splitting open my skull and rummaging around in my brain matter. I'm once again saved by the fact that I'm so far ahead in all my classes.

When I take my seat in math class and I see that I got a solid A for my workbook re-do, I'm so relieved I could slump in my chair. I remember at the last second that the action would hurt me dearly, and I smile instead. It feels strange on my face. I've only winced and grimaced for days.

Only Harley beat me, a defeat I'll take gracefully thanks to him carrying me back to my room. He's smug about it, and I keep my mouth shut about Avery's little pyromaniac episode. Another boon I'm granting. I'm practically a saint.

At the end of our class, he waits for me to pack up. Avery doesn't share our math class, so I don't have to worry about the repercussions of Harley speaking to me. I look at him curiously, and when he gives me a slow smile, I fight the blush that's creeping up my neck.

"Let's take a walk, Mounty," he says with a voice full of honey, rich and thick.

We walk in silence as I let him lead me through the school. I forget sometimes how big this place is when I'm sprinting from class to class. I get jostled a few times by passing students, and I push out my elbow to try and force them around me instead. Being so damn short is a pain in the ass sometimes.

"Kyle and Nicky have both been expelled."

Harley doesn't look down at me as he says this. They must be the guys that held me while Spencer whaled on me. The pace he has set is brutal on my ribs, and I'm panting so hard to keep up with his ridiculously long legs. His sculpted, swimmer's legs. *Dammit, stop thinking about his legs!*

"What did you get them for?" I ask. I'm not sure if he'll give me a straight answer or not. I certainly didn't give him one when I'd led him out to watch Joey get arrested. Harley grins savagely.

"Kyle got done for doping. He was on the track team, and there are students on the fast-track to the Olympics.

They don't take kindly to their teammates taking banned supplements. Nicky… well, little Nicky Bianchi has some strange sexual adventures, and he likes to take pictures of himself doing what it is he does. Half of the classrooms in the school are closed for cleaning today."

I wrinkle my nose. Guys are disgusting. If I've touched that guy's DNA matter just because he's a fucking deviant, I'll be pissed.

"So what do you have planned for Hillsong, then? What skeletons hide in his closet?"

If anything, the grin on Harley's face gets even more savage. He looks imposing, vicious in the best possible way. The kind of darkness my heart reaches out for because it recognizes it. I swear to god my panties damn near disintegrate at the look of him right now.

"No explosion for Spencer. I told you, I'm going to end him."

A shiver takes over me. This could get out of hand fast, but that only makes it more exciting. "Give me details. I need to know what I'm signing up for."

I'm running through lists in my head, equations and formulas on how I can help. Minimize the witnesses, something to transport the body, clean-up crew so no evidence is left behind, a deep grave somewhere remote and unrelated to either of us. It's a lot to figure out on the fly but fuck it. I'm all in. I didn't become the Wolf because

I'm afraid of getting my hands dirty.

"I'm going to beat him bloody until he needs a tube to breathe. Anything less and he's getting away too lightly. It'll be hard, but I'll stop myself from taking him out. I'm not sure you'll be able to keep your scholarship if you're aiding and abetting a murderer."

"The Beaumonts want me out anyway, what a way to go," I mutter. Harley either ignores me or he doesn't hear me as he steps into the rose-colored light streaming down in the chapel. A senior who is even bigger than Harley shuts the door behind us and slides the bolt into place. My hand slips into my pocket and grips my knife. I feel the urge to put my back against the wall. After everything that's happened to me in this room, I guess it's to be expected.

Spencer Hillsong is already there, bare-chested, frowning over at us both.

"Why the fuck did you bring the Mounty? You know the rules. No girls."

The rules. Harley has challenged him to one of their little fight club matches. Spencer has no clue what he's in for. My heart surges in my chest as I watch them both circle each other.

"Fuck the rules and fuck you, Hillsong. You've already shown everyone what a coward you really are. You need your friends to hold a girl down while you hit her. That's fucking pathetic."

Spencer scans the crowd, but he doesn't find what he's looking for. I'd bet it was Joey. He's hoping the puppet master would leap to his rescue. What a dumb ass. Joey only saves himself.

Harley shrugs out of his blazer, and for a single heart-stopping second, I think he's going to take his shirt off too. Disappointment burns me when he rolls up his sleeves instead. Shouldn't he be worried about getting blood on his crisp white shirt? God, I'm such a pervert.

Harley glances down at me and gestures to one of the pews, right at the front where I'll get the perfect view of what's about to go down. When I'm comfortable, he dumps his bag next to me and then surveys the room. There're about fifteen guys all standing around, and the air is thick with their eager bloodlust. None of them spare me a glance as they watch Harley with greedy eyes.

"Anyone touches her or asks her for sex from here on out will get the same as Hillsong. You can film it and spread it around, for all I fucking care, but that's how it's going to be. We clear?"

There're nods, grunting, and a few phones make an appearance. Spencer laughs and puts his hands on his hips like he's preening under Harley's judgment. It's gross.

"And what about your cousin? Joey is the whole reason this started, are you going to beat him up? I'm not afraid of you, Arbour. You think getting a face tat makes you so fucking tough? You're just a pussy with a deadbeat dad and a fucked-up mom who's riding on your cousins' coattails."

Harley leans down to drop his blazer on his bag and I see the flames burning in his eyes. Spencer is a dead man.

"I can organize a cleanup crew if you want to kill him," I whisper, a smile playing at the corners of my mouth. Harley smirks at me and straightens.

"We can talk about how you have access to one of those later, Mounty."

He turns and steps into the proverbial ring.

I don't know who calls the ambulance, but I do enjoy watching them wheel Spencer Hillsong away. Harley grabs his shit and leaves the chapel without looking at me, so I guess his charitable mood has up and left him. His hands are a mess and there's blood all over him. Any teacher who comes across him would have to be on Avery's books to not call the cops. It's a good thing they all are.

I manage to convince the kitchen staff I'm an overworked, flailing mess, and they scrape together a tub of roast pork and sides smothered in gravy for me to take to my room to eat. I don't know why I didn't think of trying it before, and I'm thrilled when I sit on my bed and dig in. I mess around on my phone and try to tell myself I'm googling Vanth Falling news to keep tabs on my bully, and because I'm bored.

I didn't burn the shirt.

I did stuff it in the bottom of my bag to try and forget about it, but old habits, and devotion die hard, so I'm back to wearing it, and a tiny pair of sparkly booty shorts, when there's a knock at my door.

I panic.

It's embarrassing as fuck to think about any girl in this place seeing me wearing it after my tantrum at Blaise over it, so I scramble to find something else to throw on over it quickly.

"Mounty, for fuck's sake, I can hear you rummaging around in there. Open the door."

It's Harley. Oh *god*, I cannot open this door wearing the shirt. I will lose any credibility I've managed to gain with Blaise if he tells him. "I'm- ah- naked. Give me a second."

I find one of the new sweaters I bought from the thrift store in Haven—it's clearly a man's sweater, and it's three times the size of me—and I throw it over my head.

When I'm sure he won't be able to see the Vanth shirt, I throw open the door to his deep frown. His eyes trail down my body, and when they reach my bare legs, he starts to look around my room, his scowl deepening.

"Can I help you?" I say, breathless. He curses at me under his breath and pushes past me into my room. Rude.

“Please come in,” I say sweetly and shut the door behind him before I can think better of it. He may still have it out for me academically, but I’m not afraid of being around him. I snort at myself. I’ve just watched him pummel another student to the point the kid had to be intubated before he was scraped off the chapel floor by the EMT’s, and yet, that had proved to me that I had nothing to be afraid of. Funny old world.

“Is there a guy in here?” he says as he peers into my closet. My jaw drops.

“What—why would there be a guy in here?”

“You said you were naked. It’s five o clock, you haven’t just showered, and you’re wearing someone else’s clothes. Who did you let win the bet?” He’s damn near hissing at me. I look down at myself, sigh, and then rub at my face.

“I lied. I wasn’t naked, I’m wearing a shirt and shorts under this. I just—it doesn’t matter. This is my sweater. I’m not a wannabe model like the other girls here, and I like being comfortable. No guy. Not interested in seeing any guys here at Hannaford naked, thanks.”

Blatant lie. I’d be interested in him. Or either of his friends, really. I try not to think about the time I saw him come all over Annabelle’s face in the woods, but then it’s all I’m thinking of and my face heats up. Harley squints at me like he’s trying to decide if I’m lying. I roll my eyes at him.

"This place is a literal closet. Check under my bed and see for yourself that there's no one here." He actually bends down and does check. My blood heats, and not with desire. "What exactly gives you the right to police who I fuck, anyway?"

He smirks at me and shows me his knuckles. They're a mess; he hasn't cleaned them at all. From the look of him he's just thrown different clothes on, no shower. I should feel grossed out by that, but I lick my lips at the thought of the sweat that's still on him. He still smells fantastic—totally unfair, because I know for a fact that I smell putrid after that much exercise. I duck under my bed, pull out my first-aid kit, and grab out some antiseptic wipes. He drops onto my bed like he owns the place, and I start to clean up his wounds.

"I've just cleared your social calendar for you, I wouldn't want that to be for nothing."

I chuckle as I carefully wipe away the blood that's already dried, and he doesn't flinch. His knuckles are covered in raised white scars, crisscrossing and gouging into his skin. It looks more extreme than what a prep school fight club would warrant. I make yet another mental note to look into him and his past. He clears his throat to get my attention.

"So, which clean-up crew would you have called? Manning's?"

I snort. "Only if I wanted to be blackmailed with it later. Amateurs call Manning."

He smiles at me, a real one, and I have to focus to breathe. He's magnificent this close. I survive sitting next to him all day in our classes by not looking at him, but now I let myself just take him in. I tape some gauze over the parts of his hands that are still bleeding, and he lets me, watching me as much as I'm watching him.

"So, who then? Who would a Mounty call to get rid of a body?"

I can't really answer him. It would give too much away. I'd call the Jackal or the Bear. I wouldn't have to pay them a cent for their services, either. I'd call in a favor or make a deal with them on the spot, and then my problems would just vanish.

"That should hold if you don't shower until tomorrow. Or just get one of your friends to do it again for you. I'm assuming you have a kit of your own?"

He nods and watches me pack everything away. I feel his eyes on my legs as I bend to shove the kit back under my bed, but when I stand and face him, he's got his phone out. When he lifts it to his ear, I frown down at him.

"Nothing is wrong, Floss. Can't I call you to be social?"

I cross my arms and take a step away from him. I guess this is where I pay for making him bleed for me. Nothing ever comes for free, not here at Hannaford and certainly not back home.

"Okay, you're right I do need something. I need you to leave Lips alone. Stop trying to get her kicked out… No, I'm not joking… I'm not telling you to be her friend, I'm saying stop fucking with her on my behalf. I'm over it. I'm done…I don't like her, I owe her, and I hate owing people shit. Just drop it… if Joey wants her dead and she's too stubborn to leave to save her skin, then that's not our problem. You don't owe him a cleanup, Aves."

My stomach hollows out as I listen to him negotiate a ceasefire with Avery for me. He said he owes me; what did I do for him? I think back, but I can't remember anything I've done. Well, the necklace, but I haven't even told him I have it yet. I wince guiltily.

He hangs up and meets my eyes again. I wait for him to explain, to get up and leave, to tell me what I now owe him for this. I wait for him to tell me it's all a joke and I'm still trash to him. I guess he did tell Avery he doesn't like me, but he's not acting like that. When he just stares at me, nervousness bubbles up until I speak, just to break the intensity of his gaze.

"Why do you owe me? I don't remember helping you."

He grumbles and stands up. He looks almost bashful; it's charming as fuck.

"Joey set his eyes on you because of me. He heard me raging at Avery about you, and it caught his interest.

Whatever, you should leave Hannaford. You're stupid if you think you can take on Joey and survive."

I scoff at him. "Of course you do. What could a poor Mounty do against a billionaire sociopath?"

He shrugs at me and flexes his fingers. I can't stop thinking about the damn necklace, until finally I sigh and walk over to where I've dropped my bag. I've been carrying it around for weeks, trying to pluck up the courage to give it back to him.

"Don't ask me how I got this, and please don't start shit with me over it, just take it and forget this ever happened," I ramble. He quirks an eyebrow at me, but he reaches for me. I drop the little gold chain into his outstretched hand, and he freezes. The look on his face breaks my heart. He's so reverent, so gentle as he cradles the little heart pendant in his big, bandaged palm. When he looks up at me, his eyes are red-rimmed and glassy. I feel like scum for carrying it around for so long.

"I'm sorry I didn't give it to you sooner. I don't even have a reason, I just didn't. Like I said, please just forget I ever had it."

"Lips, this is… I've been trying to get this back for *years*."

I blink away tears of my own as I turn away from him. I wish so much that we had met under different circumstances and we could be friends. The fierce, protective nature of him draws me in like nothing else. I want him, but I want to be in his circle more.

I hear him moving behind me, but I don't want to look back at him. I should have slipped the necklace into his bag while he wasn't looking or given it to Ash to pass along instead. I feel the heat of his body press up along my back as his scent envelopes me. I freeze, and my heart stutters in my chest. It takes me a second to realize he's not attacking me, he's not trying to hurt me or get some sort of revenge, he's just close to me. I clear my throat like I'm going to speak, but I don't know what I would say to him. He's everything I wish I had, and it pains me to have him this close and to know it's only going to last for a second.

He leans down and brushes his lips to my cheek softly. My eyes fall shut, and I struggle to stop myself from leaning back into his warmth.

"Thank you," he whispers into my ear, and then he disappears, closing my door quietly behind him and taking his heat and delicious smell with him.

I feel gutted.

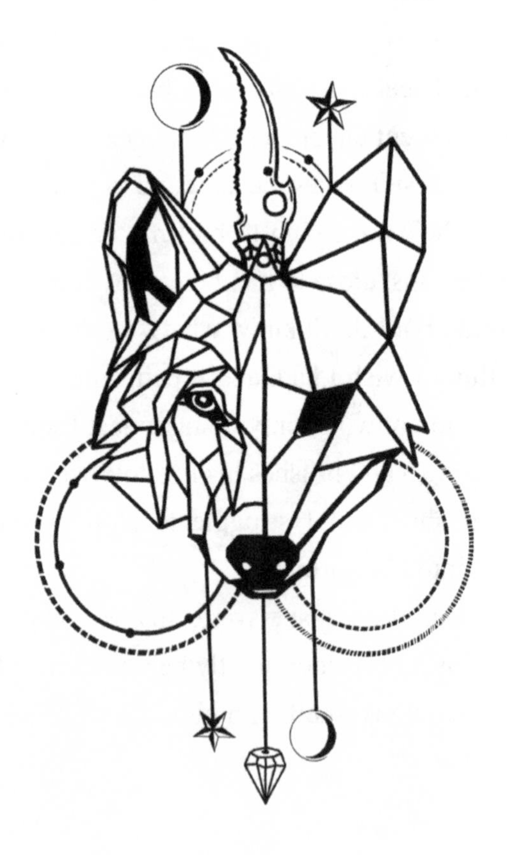

Twenty Three

My whole world has shifted on its axis a little after Harley's visit to my room.

I don't see him for the entire spring break, even though I eat every meal in the dining hall. I barely sleep, because I'm too busy freaking out about how much I actually like him. Like, not just wanting to ogle him or even consider making out with him, but to actually keep him. It's disturbing. I hate crushes so much, because they really do *crush* you.

When class goes back after the break, I make the perilous decision to trust him at his word, and I go down to the dining hall for breakfast. The lure of the incredible French toast is strong enough to let me test him out. I notice the difference the second I leave the safety of my room.

There's no whispering.

I've grown so accustomed to the constant gossiping that happened around me, because of me, that it's jarring to have the other students ignore me.

Avery Beaumont really is an evil dictator.

The dining hall is teeming with students, and I have to use my elbows as weapons to get a seat. I ignore the looks from the girls around me at the size of my plate—six pieces of French toast, thank you very much—and dig in like it's my last meal on death row. I'm starting my third slice when Blaise sits down across from me and actually looks at me. In the face. I wipe my chin in case there's syrup or cream splattered all over me, and I swallow roughly, trying not to lose what I've just eaten.

"Did you know that for the first time in my academic career here at Hannaford, I am sitting on a solid C in math? My dad called me yesterday and offered to buy me the Ferrari of my dreams if I get a B by the end of the year."

It takes me two tries to speak to him. It's far easier to speak when he's not grinning at me and being charming. "So you want my help to get the Ferrari?"

He smirks and makes a slashing motion with his hand. "Fuck the Ferrari. I can buy my own if I want one. I negotiated with him, and if I get a B-plus he's going to let me take three weeks away during the summer holidays to record my next album. I need a B-plus, Mounty. My career and my very soul need to get away from all of my parents' bullshit."

I nod sagely and sip at my drink, feigning a nonchalance, I definitely don't feel. He looks at me expectantly, and when I don't fall over myself to offer my services to him, he sighs.

"What's it going to cost me to get you to help me?"

A favor, Matteo's voice says in my mind. What would I even ask of him, though? I put down my cutlery and push my plate away, giving my food a mournful look. I can never eat around these guys, and the look on Blaise's face has butterflies dive-bombing deep in my gut.

"No cost. You need to ask for extra credit though; you don't have enough time left to bring your grade up without it. You'll need to come to every study session, on time, for the rest of the year, and you'll have to ask Ash very nicely if he can stop pretending he needs my help so I can focus on helping you."

"Done." Blaise grins at me and starts eating his breakfast. I don't know what to do with myself. I'm debating if I should get up and leave when Harley steps into the dining hall with Avery's arm tucked firmly into his. He sees us immediately and he frowns, his eyes darting between us both. I give him what I hope is a reassuring smile, but it only makes his frown deepen. Avery rolls her eyes, grabs a tray, and shoves it into his chest. I watch, curiously, as he fills it up for them both. I've never seen him dote on her like this. Usually Ash is the one who carries her things, but he's nowhere to be seen.

They walk past us, and Avery only pauses long enough

to kiss Blaise's cheek and murmur a *good morning* to him as she passes. She doesn't bother to look my way. Once Harley has Avery all set up and their food is portioned out, he stalks back over to us. Avery glares and shakes her head at him as he sidles up beside me.

As I glance up, the light from the chandeliers catches on the necklace around his neck, and I swallow. I don't know why I'm shocked that he's wearing it. If it means so much to him that he'd gotten choked up, then it makes sense he would want to keep it close. I can't pull my eyes away from it until he speaks and breaks the spell.

"What are you two doing eating breakfast together? People will talk."

Blaise leans back in his chair and looks every inch the rock star he is. He usually hides it well, like he puts away '*Blaise Morrison: Lead Vocalist for Vanth Falling*' when he arrives in the gates of Hannaford and becomes the spoiled rich kid everyone expects him to be. I've only ever seen the brash musician when he's around his friends. I get the feeling that this is the mask he wears to survive, that he protects himself and his music from this place, the way Avery protects those she loves.

"The Mounty has just offered to be my own personal tutor for the rest of the year. We're going to be practically inseparable; doesn't that sound fun?"

My cheeks flush, and I give him a look. A *don't-fuck-*

with-me-after-I've-agreed-to-help-you look. The cocky grin I get in return is something poets could write sonnets about. It's stunning and terrible and hot and heartbreaking.

"I could've helped you. Why didn't you ask?" Harley grumbles. I look up at him, and he looks away from me quickly, like he didn't want me to catch him staring. He is the most confusing guy I've ever met.

"No, you really can't. What's the problem, man? Avery's lifted the speaking ban. Any other reason I should be staying away from the Mounty?" His voice is too smug, and the smirk he levels at Harley makes my heart stutter. It's almost as if…they can't be fighting over me. They both have made their feelings toward me perfectly clear this year. Harley shrugs coolly—aiming, I think, to look unaffected—but I can see his fists clenching. He puts his elbows on the chair next to me and leans forward like he's going to whisper at Blaise. He's loud enough that the students around him here every. Goddamn. Word.

"Just thought you'd be more afraid of spending that much time alone with your stalker."

The blood drains from my head until I'm left feeling dizzy. There it is. There's the reason I shouldn't ever speak to Blaise without classwork in front of us. The sounds of sniggering and laughter start up around us from the students shamelessly eavesdropping. I stand up abruptly and grab my bag. Harley chuckles under his breath at me, but I refuse to look at him. He was right all those months ago. I need to bury my nerves better when it comes to him and Blaise. And Ash. *Goddammit.*

"Just get the extra credit work. I'll help you during the tutoring sessions, but don't talk to me otherwise."

I stomp out of the dining hall to the sound of Harley's roaring laughter and Blaise swearing up a storm at him.

I decided to arrive at our study group late.

Well, I actually decide to skip the tutoring sessions altogether, but then I think about my college submissions and I cave. I don't want to have to face Blaise again so soon. His opinion of me shouldn't matter. I'm the Wolf, for fuck's sake, but I feel hot shame wash over me whenever I think about him. He really does think I'm a sad little groupie. Not an awesome, sexy groupie. I've met girls like that before, I've been to gigs and seen girls that are so powerful with how they hold themselves up and live their truths.

My truth is I'm an inexperienced, blushing idiot with responsibilities no student at Hannaford would ever understand.

I wish I hadn't stayed quite so far away from guys back at Mounts Bay. Not that I wish I'd had sex with anyone, but if I'd dated guys or, fuck, kissed anyone before coming here, maybe I wouldn't be so awkward about this. Maybe Joey's little sweep wouldn't have been such a big deal. I can't think of a single girl in my last school who wouldn't jump at the chance to fuck a Hannaford guy, and maybe even get some cash for her troubles.

Ash and Blaise are already at our table when I get to the library. There's no laughing or joking going on this time, and Ash is taking stacks of paper from Blaise and flicking through them. My eyes narrow. It's all just more evidence that he's been lying about needing my help.

Blaise looks up at me with stark relief, and I take the chair next to him without a word, unpacking the bare essentials from my bag. "Thank god, Mounty, I thought—"

"I'd rather not have this conversation. Give me everything you have from the math class, and I'll work out a plan of attack." I hold out my hand and focus my eyes on a speck of dust on the tabletop.

Ash raises an eyebrow and hands me the stack. Blaise is twitching in his chair, but neither of them try and make conversation. We sit in total silence until I've flicked through everything he's given me. I glance up to see they're having a conversation entirely with their eyebrows. I'm oddly impressed.

"Here. Do this page so I can see where you're up to." I slide the page across to Blaise, and he murmurs a quiet, *sure* under his breath. I start to write out notes for him to study at night and to use during tests. I have to focus to keep my scrawling handwriting neat enough to be read by mere mortals.

Not that I think Blaise is mortal.

Or mere.

He gets straight to work. He's quiet, subdued from his usual flirty manner, and I give myself a second to breathe. It's hard to do, because I can feel Ash's calculating eyes on me. I wonder how much Blaise told him while they were waiting for me to show. I've always arrived at the sessions at least ten minutes early, so I would think Ash would have made a smart comment about my tardiness.

Ash begins to tap his pen in his hand as he says, "You should have asked Blaise to pay you for your tutoring. *He's* a millionaire and, someday, he's going to be the sole recipient of a billion-dollar empire. You're an orphan, Mounty, who has lost everything. There's only a few weeks left of the school year. Charge him, say, a grand a week. That's literally *nothing* to us."

I pause long enough to glare at him, but he just waves me off. "I'm not being an arrogant asshole, I'm just stating facts. Avery dropped more cash on hair products this week than what I'm suggesting he pay you. It's a business transaction. A legitimate one. You can replace all of your shit, and Blaise can stop moping around like a kicked fucking puppy because you're being nice to him for no reason."

Ash grunts as Blaise's foot connects with his shin. I think about it for about three seconds. I could increase my bank balance by thousands of dollars for doing something I've already committed to. I'm not going to lie, it's tempting. Then I think of something better. This is my moment to prove a point.

I set my pen down and fold my hands together, letting my face drop into a serene mask before I speak. "You're going to be a man of business someday, Beaumont, and I'm here to help Blaise out with numbers. So, let's look at some *real world* facts." Ash tilts his head at me and motions me on. "I have a full ride scholarship that covers food, shelter, and clothing for thirty-six weeks of my year, which leaves me with sixteen weeks to have to financially provide for myself. I have a hundred grand in the bank. At my current rate of spending, by the time I graduate Hannaford and move on to college, I'll still have more than seventy grand in the bank. I will get a scholarship for college, full ride just like this one because we all know I'm that good, so that money is going to keep sitting in the bank. When I start out in the career of my choice, I'm going to hit the ground running."

I pause. Ash is staring at me, rubbing his chin absently, and so I continue. "I know that to you that amount of money may sound pathetic, but to me, and to most people, I'm set.

Major, catastrophic disasters would have to happen for me to have to touch the money I've got. So, I don't. Want. Your. Fucking. Money."

I pick up my pen, expecting the conversation to be over. Blaise certainly thinks it is. He's frowning down at the numbers like he's waiting for them to give up all their secrets. Ash snatches the pen out of my hand.

"Inheritance?" he says.

I shake my head.

"Gambling? Are you a secret poker savant?"

"Nope."

"Shame. I could have used the pointers." Ash lets out a little gasp and leans in. His torso is long enough that he easily covers the distance between us. "Did you steal it, Mounty?"

I smirk and lean in to him. Once my chest is pressed against the table and my lips brush his earlobe, I whisper, "I earned it from a dead man."

I lean back and see that he's staring down the front of my blouse, where the small amount of cleavage I have is pushing up lusciously.

"Why, Mounty, I didn't think you were the type," he drawls, and I don't know if he means my chest or my money-making methods. There's this little grin on his face that makes me want to scream. I think he enjoys the push-pull banter we slide into the moment we're near each other.

I have no idea how to flirt, but I think this might be it.

I open my mouth, unsure of what I'd even reply, when we hear a scream.

I jerk around in my seat to look toward the sound at the back of the stacks. Students start moving en masse, but the librarians are nowhere to be seen.

"Avery?" says Blaise urgently, and Ash replies, "Harley took her down to her ballet class."

There's another shriek and I'm up and out of my chair, pushing past students to find the source. I have a sinking feeling as I make it through the crowd, Ash and Blaise pushing through behind me, and I stop dead.

Joey is standing over another student.

A dead student.

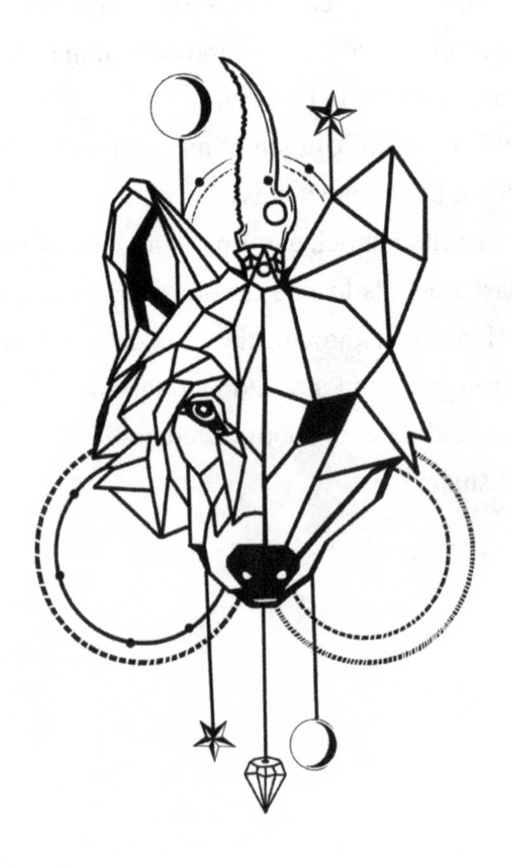

Twenty Four

Joey's chest is heaving.

There's a sheen of sweat on his forehead and his eyes are glassy, bouncing around the room like he can't focus on anything. I spare him a second before I grab Ash's arm and haul him over to the dead student. Joey begins to laugh. It's an awful sound, too loud and hyper, and tears stream down his face as he clutches at his chest.

I've learned a lot of important, life-saving shit while in Mounts Bay, but I don't know if there's a damn thing I can do for this guy. He's a freshman—I recognize him from my social studies class—with mousy brown hair and a dimpled chin that makes him look younger.

"Call 911, Ash," I say firmly. Ash startles away from me. He's watching Joey's every move like he's waiting for him to strike again, but he fumbles his phone out of his pocket and makes the call. Only seconds have passed since we got to the kid, but I know exactly how critical time is. I check his airways, clear, then his breathing…nothing. His throat is already looking mottled.

Joey has strangled him.

Ash starts talking down the line to the operator, and I start CPR. I'm focused entirely on the kid, counting compressions and singing the stupid song in my head to keep time. When I stop to do the breaths, Ash switches his phone onto speaker and takes over the compressions.

"Like this?" he asks, and I start to sing *Staying Alive* by the Bee Gees softly, just loud enough for him to catch the rhythm. I hear a scuffle behind us, but I ignore it. No, I trust Blaise to keep Ash and I safe while we try and help the kid.

No other students step forward to help.

I lose any respect for them, any shred that I had, because only a monster would step away from this without helping out.

He's just a fucking kid.

The 911 operator tells us the ambulance is at the gates, and I bark at the crowd to send someone down to lead them up. The scuffle gets louder, swearing and spitting and wood snapping, and then a palm touches my shoulder blade. I flinch and look up to see the EMTs have arrived. I slide away from the kid and Ash stops the compressions. As his hands leave his chest, I hear a wet, sucking, gurgling noise, and then a moan.

He's alive.

I scramble away and Ash catches me by the elbow, lifting me off the ground. I can't take my eyes off the EMTs while they load him up and start working on him.

"What's his name?" I say, and Ash pants back, "Matthew. Matthew Steiner."

When they're wheeling him away, I finally look over to where Joey was standing. Blaise and Harley have him pinned to the ground, but just barely. Blaise is bleeding profusely from a deep gouge in his forehead. Avery is standing over them, scanning the crowd with a keen eye. She's making her assessment, planning out the damage control required to minimize her brother's attempt at murder. I see red—seething, maniacal, bleeding red—and I step forward only to be stopped by the vise grip of Ash's hand around my wrist. He doesn't look down at me, but he gives it a little squeeze.

A warning.

"Anyone get it on tape?" Avery even sounds like her usual icy self.

Two girls step forward and hand over their phones. Avery taps away at them, her phone pings, and then she hands them back. I watch the crowd. I want to memorize the faces, so I know who the truly weak and apathetic students are. As easy as breathing, I start to notice the behaviors. There are three students, all guys, who are digging their phones deeper in their pockets subconsciously, like they're trying to push them out of Avery's reach.

I do not trust Avery.

But Ash just stepped up to the plate. He's earned my respect where a whole group of kids just failed. I now have some level of trust in him.

"There's others who have the footage." Ash looks down at me, and then when I point them out, he starts calling names, sharp and authoritative. The guys lurch forward at his command. Avery arches an eyebrow at them while they fumble over themselves to make excuses. Avery takes a copy of their footage and wipes the phones.

There're other ways to do it. Software and coding that can be done to hack into the phones and get whatever you need out of them. I might suggest it to Ash later, an extra sweep to make sure this stays buried.

I still don't know *why* we are burying it.

"Go, Mounty. You don't need your name attached to this." Ash lets my wrist go reluctantly and gives me a gentle push toward the door. It occurs to me that there are still no teachers or librarians here, and that Avery and Harley made it, but no adults have yet. If I hadn't rushed forward, that kid could have died. I mean, he might still die or have a brain injury, but at least we gave him a chance.

I glance back at Joey one last time before I leave. He's stopped thrashing about, but he's hissing at Harley instead. He's not looking at his face, his eyes are lower, his neck—

The necklace.

He's spotted the necklace I stole from his room the day I called the cops and had him arrested. I turn and walk away, shoving past the crowd, not giving a damn who I hurt with my bony elbows. I only stop at the table long enough to grab my bag and throw my supplies back in it.

I get to the far side of the school, where the staircases to the girls' dorms are, before I see Mr. Trevelen and the librarians rush past. Too little and far too late, thanks to the interference Avery ran.

I lock my door, check it's secure, and then collapse back onto my bed.

So I now have two lists I'm compiling.

One is an ongoing list of everything the Beaumonts can get away with, which now includes murder.

And the second is a to-do list.

I'm going to need to call in a favor.

"A phone call, Starbright? Is the school burning down? Have you castrated a young, enamored boy? Are you finally coming home?" Matteo's voice settles into my skin like a throbbing wound. I feel like I need to scrub my skin the second I get off the phone, regardless of the fact that I only just showered. The banter didn't feel fun anymore; it hasn't felt fun in a long time. Now all I can hear is the possession in his dulcet tones. He's speaking to someone he thinks he owns.

I won't ever let him own me.

"I need to call in a favor," I say sweetly. It sounds fake because it is. I'm not sweet.

I'm fucking tired.

"Tch, kid, this is getting out of hand. You know, you wouldn't have to keep running to me for help if you did some recruiting of your own. There are dozens of suitable candidates, all clamoring to sign up under the infamous Wolf. I could move some of my crew around for you. As a member of the Twelve, you have to have people behind you. This is why you need to come to some meetings."

I roll my eyes. He wants to give me some people to start a gang with. His people, so he can always have loyal eyes on my back. In his mind, it'll make it easier for when he claims me and have the two gangs amalgamate to become one super criminal organization.

It's much easier to lie to him on the phone. "I've been giving it some thought, and I've got a few leads. I'm looking for very specific skill sets, and if I'm going to do this, I'm doing it right. I gave you my word I'd be at the next meeting over the summer, didn't I? Is my word not good enough anymore?" I finish with a teasing tone. Some might even call it flirty, but I just call it a necessity.

I hear him cover the mouthpiece and bark out orders.

If you're with the Jackal, you're always at war or starting a new one. When I was just a kid and Matteo had first taken notice of me at the group home, he'd told me he looked up to Alexander the Great. All he wanted to do was build an empire. He enjoys the thrill of the chase, the outsmarting, and the kill.

I think I caught his interest because I was strong.

I think I've kept it because I won't give in.

"We can talk about your leads at the meeting. I'm interested to know who you have your eye on." The censure in his voice is clear to me. Great, something else I need to think about and plan for. "Let's get back on topic, I have someone waiting for me. Someone…went on an unsanctioned holiday and needs to be reminded of their duties. What do you need?"

He has a defector in his office, tied to a chair, listening in on our every word. They can listen because they will be dead by morning. I have seen Matteo work so many times, I don't even need to shut my eyes to see it. I know which knife he will reach for first, I know where he keeps his blowtorch, I know which hand he will wipe clean first.

"Joey Beaumont is deteriorating quickly. I need all the information you can give me about him, his family, their businesses, and their history. I need to know how I can safely neutralize him, because I'm going to have too. Soon."

I hear the knife at Matteo's waist slip out of its sheath. I do not want to have to try and sleep after listening to the defector scream. *Hurry up, asshole.*

"I'll send Diarmuid up with a copy of my files. He'll be happy to come visit; he has a nephew who goes to school with you."

My eyebrows shoot up.

Dairmuid O'Cronin was the son of an old Irish mobster. Forty years ago, the O'Cronin family had held a large territory. They'd exclusively run the docks and controlled the importation of drugs and weapons into Cali. Then the institution of the Twelve started and the family had lost members, lost loyalties, lost three-quarters of their territory, and rumor had it the patriarch of the family, Liam O'Cronin, had started to lose a grip on reality. Dairmuid had defected and became a gun for hire ten years ago. He is an unparalleled assassin, a terrifying driver, and he has a shitty attitude. I like him. The Jackal is one of the very few who can afford his price, so I have spent some time with him over the years.

"Who is his nephew? I can't imagine an Irish mobster going to Hannaford."

I hear the swing of Matteo's knife in the air and his grunt as he impales the poor idiot's leg. He doesn't scream, he just lets out a grunt of his own. *Buddy, you want to scream. If you don't, he'll only get more creative.*

"Kid goes by his mom's name. Arbour. Blond and blue-eyed like her, too. Apparently, he looks fuck-all like the O'Cronins."

My heart stops.

Harley.

Harley is the mobster's son.

'Honor before Blood'

Holy.

Fucking.

Shit.

"Diarmuid will pop in and see him, and then drop off the file. Does that work for you, Starbright?" I hear fabric ripping, grunts of pain, and Matteo's labored breathing. I hope to god he's just carving the guy up and not…doing anything worse. I don't want to think about it.

"Yeah, thanks. You'll only owe me two favors now."

Matteo agrees, which comes as a little bit of a shock. He'd been so adamant that he was just being nice and doing things for me this year that I thought I'd have to fight him. "I'll send you the diamond back with Diarmuid, if you trust him with that."

Oh, did I mention I have millions of dollars' worth of cut diamonds, all of the favors I'm owed, hidden in the safe under my floorboards?

Yeah.

My life is too complicated.

I sit in my doorway, pretend to read a book and eat a protein bar for an hour. I've changed into my old man's sweater, a pair of shorts, and thigh-high socks. I like to cover the scars on my leg, and it's already too warm for pants. I'm getting impatient waiting for Avery to appear. Every minute that goes by is a minute closer to Harley being ambushed by his uncle, and it's all my fault. Not that I can tell him it's my fault. I can't tell him I'm getting information on the Beaumonts without starting another war. My stomach turns. I have to tell them something.

When Avery finally arrives and breaks my spiraling thoughts, she's being escorted back to her room by Ash. It's a pain in the ass, because I was hoping it was still Harley's turn to babysit her. Now I'd have to actually come up with some excuse for them to get Harley up here.

"Too poor for a chair, Mounty?" drawls Ash, Avery's ballet bag slung over his shoulder. I've told him about my stash, so I know he's baiting me. It's the next step in our push-pull game.

"I was waiting for you guys to get back." I haul myself up off the floor and prop my hands on my hips.

Avery doesn't acknowledge me; she just grabs her bag and saunters into her room. Ash smirks at me, but I can see something has changed in his eyes. There's a soft edge in them that wasn't there before. It's like every one of our interactions so far has chipped away a little at him, and he's opening up. I shiver and rub my arms uselessly. I'm not cold. Someone should tell my pebbled nipples that fact too.

"I can't give you any answers, Mounty. But I can say thanks for helping out and shutting up about it." He leans back into the door frame, and my eyes run down the long line of his legs. Focus, Lips, fuck.

"Look, it's not about Joey. I need to speak to Harley urgently. Can you text him to come here? Or meet me somewhere else on campus?"

A frown appears on his brow, and he straightens. Whatever expression I have on my face is concerning him. He slides his hand into his pocket, but then Avery pokes her head out of the door again.

"Stay the fuck away from my cousin." It's the first time I've ever heard her swear. Cousin. I forgot about that; the Beaumonts have a mobster for a cousin. This is a fucking mess. I'm in too deep and I need to get out.

Deep breath.

There's no way out. Only through it.

I dart across the hallway and grab Avery's arm. She freezes and so does Ash, the tense lines of him pressed against my chest where he's trapped between us. I make sure my grip is gentle, so she can't screech at me and he can't attack me over touching his beloved sister. I don't need to be rough, though; I have their attention.

"Does the name Dairmuid O'Cronin mean anything to you?" I whisper, and then I watch as they both turn to stone. "He's on his way here to speak to his dear nephew."

Ash breaks first, cursing long and hard under his breath in creative and colorful ways. I nod curtly and let Avery go.

"Fucking call him. Now."

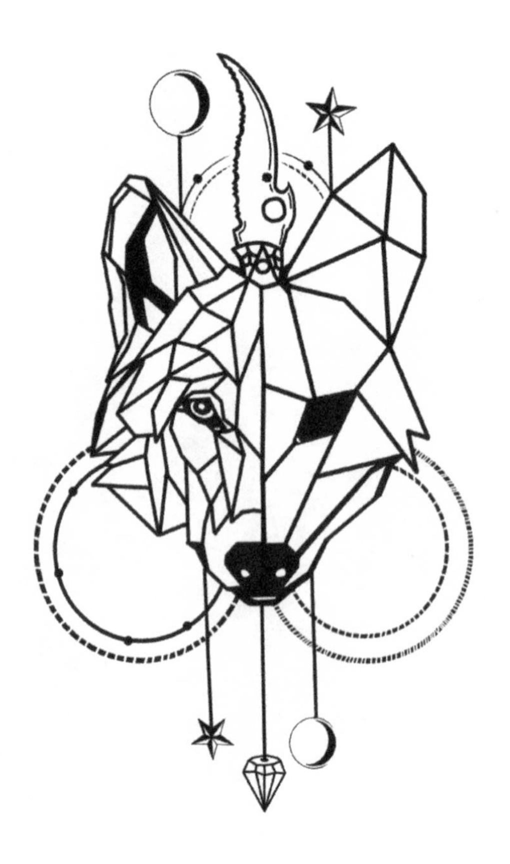

Twenty Five

Avery's room is utterly ridiculous, and I am jealous as all hell about it.

It is fitted out perfectly not only for her, but for the three guys in case they all wanted to have a big freaking sleepover there every night. There're roll-out beds under her giant Cal King and a day bed built into the window. Everything is in tasteful shades of cream and gray, pillows and throw rugs on every surface. How have I never noticed them coming and going from her room? I glance around while we wait.

The kitchen is fully stocked, I have no idea why she bothers with the overcrowded dining hall, and her closet is the size of my entire room. I only ever see her wearing her uniform. Why the hell does she need this much space? And there, in the corner, is a private bathroom. That's the thing I'm most jealous of. To be able to lock the bedroom door and shower in your own bathroom. Avery is living the dream four fucking steps from the closet I sleep in. I take some deep, deep breaths, and I tell myself I'll have this someday. Better even, because I'll have earned it myself and I'll appreciate it.

Avery paces in the kitchen area, running her hands along the surfaces like she's looking for dust, but it doesn't exist, and Ash sits stiffly on the couch. I perch on the edge on one of the armchairs and roll my eyes at Avery's dirty look.

"Is there somewhere I can sit, then? Or are you afraid I'll sully your fucking furniture?" I snap at her, and she rolls her eyes.

"That's Harley's seat. Blaise usually just camps on the floor like a three-year-old so maybe sit in his chair, the other armchair. I don't want Harley getting ideas." I open my mouth to retort 'what ideas' when Ash snaps at us both.

"She can sit wherever the fuck she wants, just tell us what's going on? How the fuck, do you know Dairmuid?"

Avery starts wiping down the kitchen counters. Huh, I did not expect her to know how to clean. I shake the thought out of my head and reply to Ash, "I'm not repeating myself; it'll only piss us all off. How far away are they? We're on a time crunch here."

"We're here." Harley opens the door, and he and Blaise stroll in. There's no tenseness to him at all, just curiosity. I sigh. Avery didn't tell him what this was all about, then.

Harley spots me on his chair, and before I can get up,

he slings himself down onto the couch so he's closest to me. Avery scoffs and scrubs harder. Blaise does exactly what she said he would and just collapses on the floor with an obscene groan. His shirt rides up, and I look away from his colorfully patterned skin before I get caught looking. I have to remember that I'm surrounded by sharks. I need to keep my head, or I'll lose it.

Harley watches Avery's manic scrubbing for a second, then says, "Fuck, Avery's cleaning. What's wrong? What's this about?"

I take a deep breath, and then just blurt out. "I have a connection to an underground criminal organization. The connection is not up for discussion. But he has a package for me. He tells me he's sending one of his hired guns to bring it here. The guy offered because he has a nephew who goes to the school. I was unaware that you're an O'Cronin."

Harley's face shuts down so fast, I'm surprised he doesn't get whiplash. Avery stops cleaning to cock her hip, and says to me with a glare, "So it's your fault he's coming here, then? You've called him in?"

Fuck. "I didn't call him in. He heard the name Hannaford and decided to come up. I am not at fault here. I could have just let him come and ambush Harley, but I chose not to. Do not make me regret that."

Harley is a blank slate. I can see the deep programming

from a mile away—I mean, I have it too. It lives in your brain, and even when you've changed your life and you're living like a civilian, all it takes is hitting that trip line and the training will fall into place. I take a deep breath and cover his hand with mine. "I will stay with you. It'll put a stop to… whatever it is you think he's going to do to you. My connection means immunity."

He doesn't react. He doesn't move at all. I have to focus on the base of his throat to see he's still breathing. I don't tell him that I'll be risking my own skin to help him. If word about Harley gets back to the Jackal… I don't think Matteo will like just how breath-taking Harley is.

I meet Ash's eyes across the room and find he's scowling at me. Their fear sends a shiver down my spine, and I tentatively ask, "What are you afraid he's going to do? I can call ahead and stop it. Believe it or not."

There's silence while they all look at one another. No one offers up an explanation.

"Do you fuck gangsters and mobsters, Mounty? Is that why you won't fuck any of the upstanding students here? Does your pussy belong to a monster?" Blaise drawls from the floor. "Do you need the violence to get wet?"

I slowly take my hand off Harley's and I stand. Blaise always knows just what to say to eviscerate me. It's his super-fucking-power.

I make it to the door when Avery calls out, "You can't

leave, we don't have a plan. I need to make a plan." I turn to ask her what the hell she's going on about and I find Harley standing behind me. He can be just as silent on his feet as I can. His eyes are blank. I hate that I can't read them, that there's none of his usual fire and wit to be found. He's a shell, the mindless soldier they have trained him to be. I hate it.

His voice is as empty as his eyes. "The plan is to keep you three out of my family's hands. That's it. I'll call when it's… done."

I take Harley into my room, and I make him face the wall as I dig out the safe hidden under my floorboards and lift the tiny box out. The diamonds all shift around and make that distinctive clinking sound.

Each of the twelve had a color assigned to them. If you were willing to pay another member in a favor, you had to have the cash to buy and hand over a diamond in the color you're assigned. I have at least three in every color except my own.

I have never given out a favor.

I can't afford to give out favors.

My color was the deep dark blue, the same color as my eyes, as close to black as blue can get. The Jackal had walked me into a ritzy jewelry store and pointed one out to me that was set in a stunning ring, just so I'd know what I needed to get if the time ever came. The last time I priced a single blue diamond out, and fuck was it hard to find, it came in just under the half-million-dollar mark.

I rummage around until I find the three little red diamonds I'd been given by the Jackal. They are the rarest diamonds, and how he found and purchased three is beyond me. These are the only favors he's ever given out and I know it's because in his mind, it's safe to give them to me. I'll just give them back to him the moment he orders me to, when he owns me.

I slip the smallest of the three into a velvet bag and then into my bra, where I can feel it against my skin. After I've hidden the safe once again, I follow Harley back downstairs and out to the front foyer. He doesn't ask me what I collected. I don't know how much time he's spent around these sorts of people, but it's enough that he doesn't ask stupid questions. I hear the roar of a motorbike and I roll my eyes.

Subtle isn't Dairmuid's specialty.

His specialty is blood.

Harley notices my exasperation and finally speaks. "You've met him before?"

I nod, then hesitate before asking, "Have you?"

Harley shakes his head, and I frown.

"Why are you so worried then?"

He chews on his bottom lip, the first sign of anxiousness I've ever seen in him. "It's a double-edged sword. He might kill me because he left the family and I'm next in line to take over. A big fuck you to my grandfather if he does that, and if anything I've heard about him is true, then I think that's how this will go. If Diarmuid doesn't kill me, it could get back to my grandfather that we're meeting up, and then the family will kill me. Either way, I'm fucked."

Fuck.

Mobster family politics.

I'm not stupid or brash, but I follow my gut, always. Ultimately, this guy took out three guys for beating me. He made Avery cut her shit out. He's made his decision not to hate me, and then he followed through with it. How can I not offer him the same loyalty? My gut tells me he's worth saving, and I'm quickly discovering we're cut from the same cloth.

"Are you going to take over the family business?" I say, curious.

He glares down at me. "I'd rather fucking die. I *will* die when my grandfather figures out I won't change my mind. I've made peace with that."

He can't die, I won't let him. I have a fairly reckless plan, and a prayer that it will work. "Do you trust me, Arbour?" I wipe my sweaty palms down my legs and meet his eyes. Something is inching back into his baby blues, and I never want to see it leave again.

“Enough to be standing here,” he rasps back.

“Then keep your mouth shut, and I’ll keep you alive. I mean it. Not a single word.”

Diarmuid is an O’Cronin through and through.

Dark, shaggy hair that falls over his green eyes as he pulls the helmet off his head. His face splits into a grin when he spots me, and he waves me over to crush my body into a hug, his legs still straddling the bike. When he speaks, it’s with a delightful Irish accent that has prevailed even though as the youngest child, he’d been born in the States.

“Jesus, Mary, and fuckin’ Joseph, you’re growin’ up, kid!” I tug away from his arms and give him a small smile. His fingers press down on the perfect circle scar I have on my shoulder, like he always does. Even fully clothed, drunk, and blind, he can find it. It is his reminder and his penance.

From the time he shot me.

The bastard.

I digress. He hands me a thick envelope, and I tuck it into the waistband of my shorts, flipping the sweater over it and concealing it perfectly. He’s still grinning like an idiot when Harley takes a step forward and silently demands his attention. The grin dries up, and he pushes me away from his body enough to swing his leg over and perch on the bike's seat. He digs around in his pocket and lights up a cigarette. I wrinkle my nose and step back until my arm brushes Harley's again.

"You're the fuckin' image of Iris. It's disturbing to see her standing there as a boy. There any of your Da in you at all, *buachaill beag*?" He takes a long drag and then blows the smoke directly up in the air, the wind catching it and letting it dance away into nothing.

Harley doesn't say a word, he just folds his arms across his chest and stares at his uncle.

Diarmuid looks back at me and says, "Can you give us a minute, kid? I need to talk some business. Family business."

I meet his eye and slowly shake my head. "I'm afraid not. It's come to my attention just how sought-after Arbour is." He quirks an eyebrow at me, and I grin, forcing the bravado I don't feel into it. "I'm a fickle sort of girl. It brings me great joy to be able to keep Harley from those who want him. I think I'll keep him."

Diarmuid blanches for a second, and then tips his head back and roars with laughter. He rubs his hands together with a vicious glint to his eye. "You bring my little nephew back to Mounts Bay and our mutual friend gets an eyeful of him? Blood and pain, little girl. Blood and pain."

I don't need to be reminded of that at all, and I certainly don't need Harley hearing it. I reach into my bra and pull out the little velvet bag. Diarmuid's eyes catch on it, and I hold it out to him. When he lets the little blood diamond fall onto his palm, he sucks in a breath. "It's a thing of beauty, this. You know what it is, *buachaill beag*?" He waits until Harley finally shakes his head. "It's a million dollars and a priceless fuckin' favor."

"Tell him I'm buying Harley's life with it, too. The envelope alone isn't worth that, and he well knows it. Tell him I've picked my first inductee, and when he has questions, he can call me."

Diarmuid sobers and looks down his nose at me. "My Da will come for you both. He'll kill him for standing here and listening in on this conversation alone."

I take a deep breath. I know the cliff I'm about to go over, and it's a scary thing to do. Harley will know more than I'd ever wanted anyone outside of Mounts Bay to know. I need this conversation over. Now. "Liam O'Cronin can't do shit to me. He knows it, I know it, and you should know it too."

Diarmuid grins at me again and tucks the diamond into his jeans. "Oh, I know it. I'm just making sure my little nephew knows it too. He looks a little green around the gills, is all." He steps forward and slaps Harley's shoulder. "I came here to have a little heart-to-heart with you about decisions you need to make, but I see you've already made them. It all comes down to this: if you don't kill the old man someday for what he did to your Ma and Da, then I will. And if I don't succeed, then your little Wolf here will do it for us both. She's got one hell of a steady hand."

He swoops down and smacks a kiss onto my cheek. As he climbs on his bike and starts the engine, he calls out to us one last time. "Call me when your tits fill in, kid, and I'll show you how real men fuck."

I roll my eyes and watch his taillights until they disappear completely. Then I turn and start to make my way back up to the dorms without looking to see if Harley is following. He's going to rat me out to his friends. He's going to hate me for interfering with his family's business. There're a hundred different things he's going to do.

I didn't bet on him pushing me through my bedroom door and then kissing me.

It's raw and dark and it's fucking perfect. He's not gentle about it at all. He pushes and sucks at my lips, but it's nothing like the one Joey had forced on me. I moan when his tongue touches mine and take fistfuls of his shirt to pull his body into mine. His hands tangle in my hair and pulls until he's got the perfect angle to deepen our kiss and steal my breath away. I feel it all the way down to my toes.

This is how my first kiss should have been.

I break away from him as my mind spins, and I try to

catch up with where he's at. He shuts his eyes and rests his forehead against mine. It's a tender moment, more intimate than even his kiss.

"Are you a member of a gang?" he croaks, and I shake my head. "Did you just tell him you recruited me to your friend's gang?" I shake my head again. I pull away so I can catch my breath because I can't breathe in his arms. When he touches me, I don't want oxygen? I just want to consume him.

"I just bought your freedom until our graduation. I'm out the second the diploma touches my hand, so you need to get a plan in place for then. I can help, but I'm letting you know this favor has an expiry date. Until then, you're… mine." It feels strange to say that to him, and I can't look at him as the words slip from my lips.

"This is seriously fucking insane, Lips. You've got to give me something. Where did you get the diamond, and how many more do you have? Why are they favors? Why is your protection greater than the O'Cronin family business? Fuck, give me anything, Lips!"

As his voice raises to a shout, I press my hands into his lips and try to calm him down. *He said my name*. I can't answer any of his questions without knowing he's all in. And why would he be all in for a scrawny little Mounty? Tears prick at my eyes, but I don't regret my hasty actions. My gut had gotten me to where I was today. It will get me through this, too.

I slip the envelope out of my shorts, and I drop it on the bed. Then I tug down the collar of the sweater until Harley can see the perfectly healed circle.

"I got that diamond by taking a bullet for the man whose favor it represented. I saved his life, and I also won him the trust of his favorite gun for hire."

Harley's fingers rub at the raised skin, pressing the same way his uncle had. My skin tingles deliciously. "Diarmuid did this?"

I nod, and then shrug. "I think… I think I have Diarmuid's trust over… the other person. I just can't afford his fees," I whisper, never having allowed myself to even think that before.

It was something else to file away for later.

Harley swallows, and then pulls away from me. His hands are shaking. I have to face the facts that the kiss was just his adrenaline needing an out.

"I won't tell the others. I don't know how the fuck I'd explain it, anyway."

And then he walks out.

Once again, I'm gutted as I close the door behind him.

I've got to stop letting him in my room.

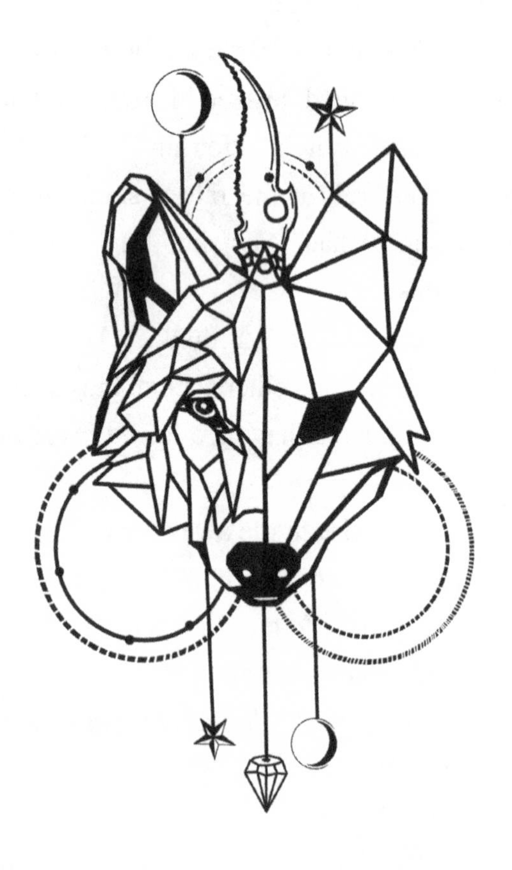

Twenty Six

I almost forget about the envelope that Diarmuid had delivered while I am wallowing over my kiss with Harley. His protection of me with Avery stays intact, but he no longer speaks to me. None of them speak to me. At first, I'm worried because I think he's told the rest of them what I did, but I can feel Avery's eyes bore holes into my back whenever she's in my proximity. It's like I'm a bomb about to go off, and she doesn't know the range of potential casualties. I make it through a few weeks of being ignored by them all and tutoring Blaise like crazy. It's only after I bump into Joey in the library punching one of his friends for not laughing at his jokes that I decide to get back to work on taking him out. I'm not sure what I was expecting to get from the envelope, but the information is brutal and sobering.

I was wrong. Joseph Campbell Fedor Beaumont, or Joey, isn't a killer *in the making*. He's already got three deaths under his belt.

Not that the file says that outright, but it's clear what's been going on. There's a nanny, a maid, and a groundsman who have all turned up dead on the property. Newspapers have declared the house haunted since the police ruled the deaths accidental. There are pages and pages of evidence that any prosecutor worth their wage would be able to convict Joey with, but it's all been swept under the rug. The autopsies are unpleasant, to say the least. The things he's done, especially to the maid, are truly horrifying. Biting, burning, stabbing. Evidence of sexual assault.

He was eleven.

It dawns on me just how lucky I was that night of the party. Had he been sober, or at a different stage of his high, if I hadn't had my knife. If, if, if. So many things had worked in my favor that I didn't know about.

At the very back of the file, there's a single page of information on the twins.

Alexander Asher William Beaumont. Born three minutes before his sister, former state swimming champion, now retired, allergic to mangoes, presented at the emergency department seventy-six times in his lifetime, which is an average of five times a year. I grimace. There's a list of the injuries too. Broken wrist, fractured skull, internal bleeding, concussions, every rib in him must have been broken at least twice. Child protection services have been contacted multiple times, but no one ever checks on the family, which tells me his parents are paying bribes. Frequent and expensive bribes.

Then, finally, there's Avery Aspen Waverley Beaumont. Only daughter, interests include ballet, violin, and the war strategy game of Go. No known allergies, though she refuses to eat mangoes thanks to Ash's allergy. One trip to the emergency department for Avery. Last year she was DOA and resuscitated. Clear signs of strangulation, another call to child protection services, but again no follow-up.

That explains the escort she gets from the guys everywhere she goes. It also explains why they're so protective. She wasn't just attacked; she was killed. My chest hurts as I think about how Ash would have felt, knowing she had stopped breathing. Knowing she was gone, even for the few minutes she was, must have destroyed him. The day Joey strangled Matthew in the library Ash didn't hesitate for a second to help me. After so much trauma, he is stronger than I would have ever thought. I've always looked at him and seen the spoiled rich brat he puts on. Even the anger and the flinches in his brother's directions didn't clue me in to how bad Joey really is.

I'm going to have to deal with Joey.

I've done a lot in life, but I've never actually planned a murder. I'm not quite sure that's what I'm doing now, but I'm going to have to start taking Joey and the warnings about him seriously. Loose cannons and unpredictable drug addicts are dangerous people to have around you, especially if you carry as many secrets as I do.

I flip the last page to make sure I haven't missed anything and there is a small, handwritten note in the back. It's not Matteo's handwriting, so it would have to be from Diarmuid.

Do not let Joseph Beaumont Sr know you're looking into his son. His hands are bloodier than mine.

Fuck. A complicated web to unravel.

Now that I'm not being whispered about or having my food spiked, I begin to use the study areas that are everywhere at Hannaford. All my assignments have been handed in for the school year, and now I'm focusing on my last-minute revision for the upcoming exams. I'm an expert at keeping well organized notes, and so I drag a giant file around with me everywhere I go, so I can read and cram at every opportunity. I'm confident I'll be the top in all my classes, but the perfectionist in me compels me to study until every second of every day until the exams are over.

I'm enjoying the quiet of one particular study nook, when Joey slips into the chair beside me. I tense and slip my hand into my blazer pocket to clutch at my knife. There is no one close by. I'm aware that has never stopped Joey in the past, but I'd prefer to never be alone with him again. The images of his maid's autopsy flash into my mind and I focus to keep my breathing even.

"It's been such a long time since we last spoke, Mounty. I've missed you," he drawls, as he flicks my colored pens so they roll around the desk.

"Is there something you want, Beaumont?" I try to keep my tone civil but uninviting. I watch him from the corners of my eyes, assessing just how high he is.

"There are so many things I want, but I've just been told I can't have one of them. Tell me, how is it you know the Jackal? I received a personal phone call from him."

I shrug and look back down at my notes. I knew this was coming. When I don't answer he continues.

"I've met quite a lot of his, shall we say, associates. I enjoy his products. They're much more pure than the crap you get out here or in the city. So, I do a pickup with my usual supplier, and he tells me his boss needs a word with me. I'm thinking I'm going to get a frequent shopper card, or a job offer, and instead I'm given an order. Stay away from one, Eclipse Anderson."

I set my pen down and turn in my chair to look at him. His eyes are clearer than they were in the library, but he is still having trouble tracking. His cheek has a little tick as he talks, and his brow is furrowed like I'm confusing him. I decide it's safe enough to speak calmly to him.

“He’s a friend of mine. It came up in conversation that you were interested in me, and he was concerned that I’m too young for such a thing, so he told me he would have a friendly chat. That’s all this is.” That is not even close to what this is.

“He told me you belong to him. He told me if even a single Hannaford boy touches your pussy, he’s going to come here and deal with it personally.”

I clench my jaw so the words I want to say don’t come flying out of my mouth. When I have myself under control, I say, “So you’re going to leave me alone, then?”

He tips his head back and laughs.

I can’t stand the manic sound of it, so I grab my books and leave.

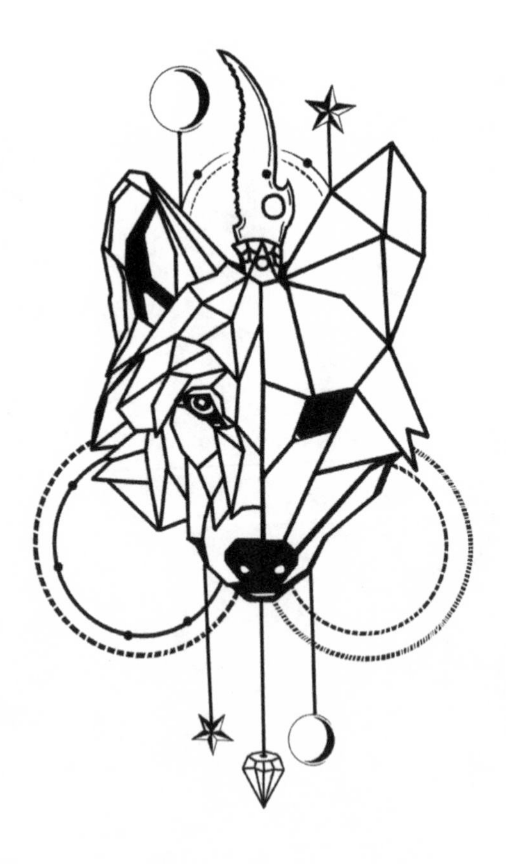

Twenty Seven

I arrived at my last tutoring session in the library early and set up the table. I've written pages and pages of notes for Blaise's final math test, and if he nails this one, he's got the B-plus. He's still being a dick to me at every opportunity, but I'm letting everything just bounce off me. He can believe whatever he wants about me; I know who I am. Plus, I'm doing all of this, so I have a new Vanth album to listen to. I want to know what he's going to write now that I've actually met him. Not that I think I'm going to affect his writing at all, I'm nothing to him, but the rock star Blaise and the Hannaford Blaise still don't completely gel together in my mind yet.

When neither of the guys arrive on time, I'm pissed. When they're both twenty minutes late, I'm starting to get worried. Ash always comes to our tutoring sessions, and he's always on time. There's a chance they had both been held up in their last class, they shared biology, but there's also a chance Joey has escalated. I'm about to pack up and leave when Ash walks in, without his bag, and sits down across the table from me.

Something is wrong.

The softness I'd once seen in Ash's eyes is gone. He's looking at me the same way he did back when I first started tutoring him and he wanted to get rid of me. I don't know what's happened. I feel like we were close to being… friends? Or friendly, at least.

"You know, the very first week we got to Hannaford, I set up a camera to watch Joey's door. We all try to keep tabs on his movements," he says without a greeting. "I've got footage of you sneaking in, and then back out again, on the day he was arrested for drugs." He's glaring at me. This is not what I was expecting at all.

I speak carefully. "So you're going to tell Joey you have proof it was me, then?"

Ash doesn't move. He doesn't lean back in his chair and cross his arms with a cocky grin. He doesn't lean forward to whisper at me. He doesn't move an inch as he says, "Joey, has told his friends you're off limits."

I close my textbook. I should have known this was coming. Matteo had told me he was going to step in now that he knows Joey wants to rape me. Not that Matteo gives a shit about rapists; he just doesn't want anyone breaking his toys. I feel sick at the thought.

"I'm going to send Trevelen the videos. I'm going to

tell him if he doesn't expel you, I'll go to my father."

I look up at him. Ash is staring at me with his face carefully blank. There's no conflict in his eyes. He's called me names and laughed at everything that's happened to me, but he's never actually tried to get me out. He's never actively campaigned against me like Avery and Joey have, but I have never doubted that he was capable of doing whatever he deemed necessary to get what he wants.

If he wants me out, then telling his father will make that happen.

Whatever the dirt Matteo has on Trevelen, I doubt it would trump the hell that billionaire Joseph Beaumont Sr could unleash. Plus, the warning from Matteo's file rings in my head. If Ash tells his father, I will have his attention. I've been very careful about the things I've done in my life, but that doesn't mean he won't be able to uncover something and destroy me. He could also just hire someone to take me out. Diarmuid comes to mind. But there is something I'm missing about the Beaumonts, a piece to this puzzle that I haven't quite placed yet—but I can feel the answer dancing just out of my grasp. Why do the twins protect him?

"So your brother finally leaves me alone, and you're just going to take his place? Is there a standard number of fucked-up Beaumonts that must bully me at any one time?" My voice is level even as my heart thuds violently in my chest.

"Joey didn't just warn them off for his own enjoyment. He told them you were permanently off limits." I nod. I already know this but it's nice to have it confirmed. I might start getting some sleep if I didn't have to worry about being killed during lunch.

"Harley told me you were dangerous, but I didn't believe him until now. You're out of this school by Friday." He moves as if to stand up and leave me. I shoot out a hand and grab him by the wrist, and he freezes. His eyes are the color of a summer storm, seething rage. It makes no sense. I've been moving the pieces on the board to get away from this sort of hatred.

"If you've chosen to take Joey's side, then I'm getting you out. I can't have you sleeping across the hall from Avery." My fingers loosen a fraction, and he rips his arm out from my grasp. I'm gaping at him; I don't even try to hide it. He shakes out his arm like he's trying to shake off the feel of my touch. I'm just Mounty trash to him.

"I would never take Joey's side. The guy is a serial killer in the making."

Ash laughs derisively and pegs me with a look.

"I wonder what it was you offered him, what someone like you could offer him, to get his protection. I know exactly what the other girls here do. I guess it was only a matter of time before you gave it up to him, too."

That final jab hurt far more than it should.

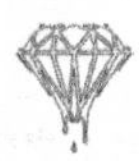

Possibly the biggest problem of being expelled is dealing with Harley.

Word will have already reached the O'Cronin family. I can't rescind my protection; he'll be killed the second he walks out of this school if I do. I could call Diarmuid and tell him the problem, but then I'll have to admit why I told him I was keeping him in the first place, and he'll have leverage over me. Leverage that the Jackal will pay him big money for.

I can't leave Harley here without some sort of warning, either. There's a whole list of people that would kill him to prove a point with me and, again, the Jackal is at the top of that list.

My only chance at stopping Ash is to talk to Harley and try to make him understand that I don't want anything to do with Joey. He's in a better position than anyone to believe me, knowing what he does about the world I'm from.

It's the weekend, so I have to search the entire school to find him. When I can't find him in the main building, I'm forced to look through the outbuildings and sports facilities. I'm about to give up and walk right into the boys' dorms when I find him.

My jaw drops, and I think I destroy my panties instantaneously.

The school has a boxing ring in the gym. I've never been down here, and I'm suddenly pissed I didn't pick gym instead of choir. In the ring, sparring, are Harley and Blaise.

Shirtless.

Teeny, tiny black shorts.

Legs, tattoos, muscles, sweat, oh my god I've fucking died and gone to the one place I know I'm not going to end up.

They don't notice me come in, thank god, so I have a minute to collect my brains from where they've spilled out onto the floor. My legs are shaking so badly, I have to give myself a stern talking-to about how serious my current situation is. I don't have time to turn into a puddle at boys' feet. Even if they are *ridiculously* attractive.

Blaise is covered in colorful tattoos. They stretch from his collarbones down both arms and his chest. One of his legs is covered, and the other has a few on his thighs, obviously a work in progress. It's shocking to see, because with his uniform on, you can't see any of them. He looks like every other polished rich kid.

Harley has a chest piece, wings and a crowned heart like a bastardized claddagh ring, all in black and white and shades of gray. It makes his chest look even wider and more impressive. I can't breathe.

I get all the way to the ropes before they notice me. Blaise's eyes flick to mine, and Harley uses the opportunity to smack him in the ribs, and then wrestle him to the ground. It's all just a writhing pile of bulging biceps, defined legs, and sweaty chests.

It's basically better than porn.

Resisting the urge to get my phone out and film this for, ahem, later and more intensive viewing, I call out to them instead. "Sorry to interrupt. Harley, can I speak to you for a minute, please?"

He releases Blaise, who stays panting on the floor, and gets up to walk over to me. He's not panting or red. The only sign of his exertion is the sheen on his chest. He unwinds the strapping on his hands and tightens it casually, like he's done it a million times before. He won't look me in the eye. Unease begins to pool in my gut.

"What do you want, Mounty? We're busy."

Yes, you are. My eyes flick over to Blaise, who's still lying on the ground, but his head has turned so he can watch us both intently. I choose my words carefully. "Are you aware of Ash's intention to get me kicked out of Hannaford?"

Harley smirks and nods, his eyes still focused over my shoulder. Not what I'm expecting. I wasn't expecting him to bitch out his cousin and best friends, but I was kind of hoping after everything I've done for him, he could at least *care* that my life was about to be ruined.

"Do you really want to discuss this with him here?" he drawls, jerking his head at Blaise.

"Will you make him leave?" I snap back.

"Nope."

I grit my teeth and smile, so it looks like I'm baring them, "I guess I have no choice then, do I? If Ash gets me kicked out, then we have some things to discuss."

"Oh yeah? Like what."

"Like the fact that you'll need to be very careful without me being here to keep an eye on you. Like there are teachers here who are on the payroll for someone other than the Beaumonts, and he's looking for an opportunity to remove you from my protection. Like you need my contact details so if something does happen, I can fix it."

Blaise's eyes have narrowed, and he has that look on his face I've seen far too much lately. The one he pulls right before he runs his mouth to try and piss me off or embarrass me. "How would you be able to protect Harley? You can't even protect yourself."

They both snigger at each other for a second, and I lose my cool. "Do you really not give a shit about whether or not your grandfather can come for you? Have you become suicidal in the last few weeks without me noticing? You should have told me that before I paid such a high price to keep you alive."

Harley's eyes turn into slits. It's the first time he's looked me in the eye since our kiss. I lift my chin and stare him down. I don't really give a shit about the favor, but I have very little to work here with them. Blaise shoots a lopsided grin at me and says, nonchalantly, "Leave, Mounty. You don't belong at this school or around people like us. You're a groupie, you fuck gangsters and serial killers, and you're playing in a world you don't belong in. No one wants you here."

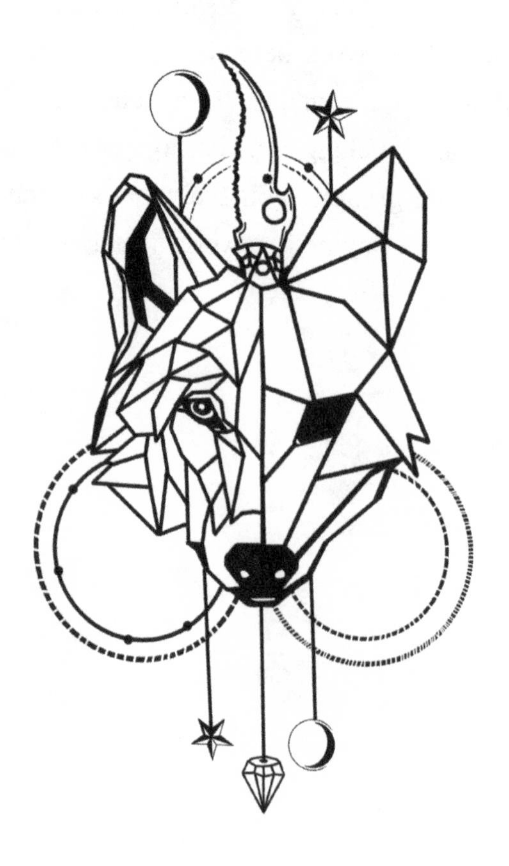

Twenty Eight

I wander through my classes on the last day of freshman year in a daze.

Ash hasn't made his move yet, but I know it'll have to be today or tomorrow. There's a closing assembly tomorrow for each school year to give out the usual awards and praises, parents are invited, so I'm sure I'm going to come face-to-face with Joseph Sr. and have to face his wrath. I think it'll happen then. Ash will tell his dad right before the awards, and I'll be dragged out of the building and thrown out of the school grounds. I'll be forced to go home to Mounts Bay and back to the Jackal.

I need a new plan.

I'm scowling so much; students are darting away from me as I walk through the school halls. Some of the guys in the upper grades flinch as I walk past, and that cheers me up a little. Punch a guy in the throat for hitting on you and they'll all learn to fall into line. When classes end, I duck into the bathroom on the lower floors to wash my hands before I have an early dinner. I'm planning on savoring the last of the good food I'll probably ever have. It's a depressing thought.

I open the bathroom door, and I can hear breathing.

A grunt. Scuffing of shoes. A slap of a hand against bare skin.

I know those sounds. Growing up in the public school system in a shitty area means I've gone into more than one bathroom to find students fucking. I think the majority of my education of what happens between two people came from these sorts of encounters, which is probably why I have avoided relationships so far. I roll my eyes and I'm about to leave when I hear a boy curse.

"Fuck you, hold still."

That doesn't sound…consensual. Without hesitation, I creep forward, just a quick peek to make sure the girl is okay, and my eyes connect with Avery Beaumont.

She's fucking terrified.

Rory has her bent over the sink awkwardly, one hand over her mouth and his body pinning her arms behind her back while he fumbles with his pants. Her panties are torn and on the floor. She's bleeding from her head, her nose looks swollen, her phone is in pieces on the floor, and that fucking dick Rory is about to rape her.

I don't even take a second to think.

I lurch forward and take Rory by surprise. As my

shoulder connects with his chest, his breath is knocked out of him and he falls backwards against the cold tiles. Avery scrambles away from him and behind me. I expect her to leave, to run away and leave me to deal with this horny rapist whose dick is just bobbing in the breeze, but she doesn't. She looks at me like she's looking at a ghost, and then she croaks, "Help."

Rory recovers and staggers at us both. He's easily twice my size and a football player, so naturally stacked with muscle. Someone you don't want to fight without a plan. He may have the advantage, but I was raised in nothing and I fought my way to where I am. I duck and kick his knee, ignoring the shooting pain from the pins holding my leg together, and then I slam my knee into his stomach until he drops. I want to kick him right in the dick, I want him to piss blood for a week, but he's hunching so I can't get to it. He manages to get a fistful of my hair on his way down and flings my head around until I smash my face into the mirror, but then Avery gives him a quick jab to his ribs, and he goes down, groaning. She swears and shakes out her hand, shifting her weight like it will help. She's obviously never had to punch someone before, and she's tucked her thumb in. Silly girl. I'm feeling a little dazed as I think to myself, *I should really teach that girl to punch properly*.

I pick up one of my textbooks, the history tome that's

a hardcover and weighs more than a brick, and then I use every ounce of strength in me to slam it into his face.

He's knocked clean out.

I'm heaving like I've run a marathon, and Avery isn't much better. Her shirt is ripped open and she looks down, clutching at the halves to hold them together. She's clearly in shock, and I know I must be as well. My brain feels like a ball in a pinball machine, like it's been shot around my skull a few dozen times. I can't think of anything to say or what to do now.

"He fractured his ribs during a football game last week. It was a lucky guess they were still sore," she says, looking down at him. He's breathing, but I'm not sure I'm happy about it.

"Fucking lucky. Piece of shit."

She hums in agreement and then steps forward to stomp on Rory's phone that's landed on the floor. I hiss at her, worried he'll come to with all the noise, but she turns a baleful look at me.

"He has photos of me."

Then we stop to look at each other.

The queen and the pauper.

There's blood dripping down her nose, her eyebrow is cut open, and I can see the fleshy muscle that lies underneath.

It will scar. I wonder for a minute if it will diminish her incredibly good looks, and then I remember that she can afford a plastic surgeon to fix it.

"Why did you help me?" she says abruptly, and I have to wipe my own bleeding nose on my sleeve.

"He's a dick and a rapist, so why wouldn't I?"

"Oh, I don't know, maybe because I've spent the whole year torturing you, turning everyone against you, helping my brother and his friends turn your whole life to shit? Give me a good reason why."

This girl is *unbelievable.* I just saved her, and she's standing there, demanding answers from me!

"The appropriate thing to say is thank you," I hiss at her instead.

I turn to walk away, and she grabs my arm. Her hand is shaking so badly I can feel the tremble up my arm. We stare at each other in silence for a minute. I can't tell what she's thinking, she's as unreadable as ever, even with the shakes. Rory starts to groan on the floor and Avery flinches, then she stomps on his phone one last time and bends over to grab the chip out of it.

"I have a guy that can get the photos out. I don't need anyone getting their hands on them; I have enough problems in my life as it is," she explains as she tucks it into her bra.

She tugs me out of the room by my elbow, and we set

a brisk pace back to the dorms. I wince as my leg begins to protest the speed we're going, but I don't slow down. When we get back, she stands and waits for me to unlock the door to my room and follows me in.

I have never been ashamed of how little I have until suddenly there's *this* girl, who has the whole world at her feet, looking around curiously. Her room is a palace in comparison. My cheeks flush, and I shake myself. What does it matter what she thinks? Three more years until I am free from all this shit. Avery turns, and I know the look on her face. It was the exact one she always used to clean up after Ash's exploits.

"I don't know what agreement you and Harley came to, but I will pay you to keep this quiet," she starts, and I snort at her. She raises a perfect eyebrow at me. "I know you need the money. Name a price and I'll pay it."

"Fuck your money. Just because I have nothing, doesn't mean I need to be paid for being a decent fucking person. That's what's wrong with you lot. You're all so busy stabbing each other in the back that you've forgotten how to be human." I start to rummage around under my bed until I find my first-aid kit. After the year I've had, it's in dire need of a top-up, but I crack two of the instant ice packs and wait until they're cold. Avery takes one gingerly, like she's never seen one, and then copies my movements to press it against her head. I'm starting to worry she has a concussion.

"Well, what do you want, then? Everyone wants something. Name your price."

"I don't want anything! You being nice to me just because I helped you means nothing to me!"

She looks at me like I've grown another head. I sigh and slump back onto my bed, glancing down at myself to take stock of the damage. My stockings have holes in them now, and I wince because they're my last pair. I'll have to get through the rest of the week with them and just deal with the taunts from the other students. There's blood on my white shirt, but I think I can get that out. I have a fair bit of practice with blood removal.

My arms and legs are starting to ache; I can feel the pins holding my leg together and the bone throbs around them. I realize how regularly I'm having to fight people and put my body on the line here. So much for this school being a better place.

Avery sighs and turns to the door to let herself out, but she hovers for a minute in the doorway. Her eyes are dry, but her mouth is turned down in a little miserable frown.

"If you're willing to do that for your enemy, then what you do for your friends must be really special."

It's… a genuinely nice thing to say, and my eyes well up despite it. I'm struck again by how much I wish I had what she has. I wish I had people who love me and watch out for me. I wish I had real friends. I wish my life wasn't empty.

"I wouldn't know, I've never really had any."

She gives a sharp nod and closes the door tightly after herself. I get up and lock it, and then I crawl under my covers and try to ignore the pain I'm in.

When I open the door the next morning, there is a brand-new uniform hanging from my door handle, stockings and all.

It fits me perfectly.

I'm not so naive to think that the universe will suddenly stop shitting on me just because of my good deed.

I make it to the chapel for the full school presentation of awards, and I find that seating is assigned. I'm between Avery and Harley, and that is when I decided that karma cannot be a real thing, because how did I deserve that torture? Avery had probably recovered well enough from the assault and would have something to say about my uniform. Would Harley tease me for taking it? Or will he just continue to ignore me for dragging him into my twisted, bullshit world? I'm still walking with a limp after using my bad leg to kick Rory.

Ugh. Rich dicks.

I take my seat, and Avery isn't there. I should feel

relieved, but my stomach drops like a stone. Is she okay? What if she did have a concussion? Fuck, I should have walked her to the nurse.

After a minute of stewing by myself, Harley takes his seat and he looks at my bandage with calculating eyes. "Who the fuck beat you up this time?" he says, frustrated and angry, which throws me. He must have not heard from Avery yet. I can't tell him, not with this many students around us. Even if we were alone, I didn't think I could tell him. Is there a girl code about this kind of thing? Did it count if the girl loathed your very existence?

Fuck.

I don't know.

"Doesn't matter. I'll survive," I reply. His eyebrows tug into a little frown, but then the lights are dimming, and the stage is lighting up. I think that will be the end of it, but he slumps down in his chair until he can whisper in my ear. "It does fucking matter. I've made it clear no one's allowed to touch you, and I'm *yours* now, aren't I?"

He says it sarcastically, and I flush. There it is; the resentment for what I did to protect him. I should feel angry at him for blaming me, but mostly I just feel guilty and miserable. Okay, I'm a little angry that he didn't care about being 'mine' when I confronted him about Ash getting me thrown out of school. Fuck, I need some time to clear my head. I need a plan for next year.

I swallow and whisper back, "That just means no one outside these walls can touch you. You don't owe me anything."

He scoffs at me. "Thank god, because I sure as hell can't afford the diamonds your favors cost."

His leg is pressed against mine, so I feel it when his phone buzzes. He ignores it until it stops. Then it buzzes again. And again. And again.

He curses under his breath and discreetly slides the phone out of his pocket. I look away because I have no interest in snooping. Okay, I do, but I'm also afraid it'll be a girl texting him and I don't need any more pain from this guy right now. He nudges me gently and turns the screen so I can read it.

Courtyard after the assembly. Bring the Mounty.

It's from Ash.

I suck in a breath. This is it; he's going to make his move and get me kicked out. He's probably already done it, but Mr. Trevelen wouldn't pause an assembly just to kick me out. I'm going to walk out there and face the humiliation of my expulsion.

I screw my eyes shut and try to fight the panic that's squeezing my chest so hard, I think my heart might explode. I start to count in French, and I miss every word Mr. Trevelen says in his speech. I clap robotically when everyone around me does, and then when Harley stands, he looks down at me with cold eyes.

I have no choice but to follow him out to face Ash.

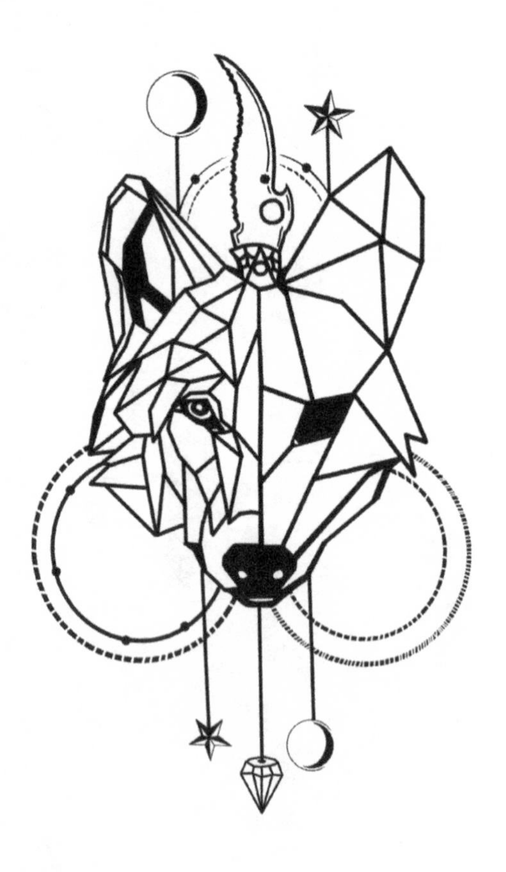

Twenty Nine

Ash is furious.

He's standing with Blaise in the middle of the courtyard, surrounded by groups of students who are all eyeing him nervously. Harley frowns when he sees him and then moves quickly to stand with him, so I'm faced with all three of them at once. I stare at Ash, refusing to even glance at the other two, and he looks at me like I'm worse than nothing.

"How the fuck did a little Mounty manage to hack my accounts and clear all of the video files? I'll have your fucking head for this. There's no way you can talk your way out of this with the principal," he snarls at me.

I have no clue what he is talking about. He's right, it is outside of my abilities, and I didn't do it. I squint up at him, and I must look like the dense Mounty they all think I am before it hits me.

Avery.

She wouldn't even need to hack in. She had all his

account details and passwords. It was the only way his data could have been wiped so thoroughly. It was a steep price she was paying for my help, and if Ash found out, he would be crushed by her betrayal.

I *could* just tell him. I could tell him every intimate detail of his sister's assault; just how close she had come to being raped. But when I open my mouth nothing comes out.

After two years in the foster care system I have seen so many kids who had been molested, and it was truly horrifying. How far away from my humanity would I fall if I use this against Avery? They may all be monsters, and I know I am too, but I don't want to be. Someday I will be a fully fledged adult out in the world, and I refuse to let this school turn me the way it has every other student.

"Get fucked, Beaumont."

Silence. The entire room holds its breath.

Ash opens his mouth to rip me to shreds, but then it snaps shut. His face shutters closed, the anger dissolving. His eyes dart to my left and narrow, but not in the same vicious way he'd been directing it at me.

Blaise crosses his arms over his broad chest, and Harley straightens. I realize Avery must have arrived, because no one else gets the boys' attention so completely. She steps up beside me, and her fingers wrap around my wrist gently, using her body as a shield so no one else can see. Her hand is cold and clammy, but her voice is firm.

"Lips didn't clear your accounts. I did."

Gasps ring out across the courtyard. I look around and see we have the attention of the entire class. The gaggle of girls that usually follow Avery around are darting quick glances between the twins, unwilling to get on Ash's bad side, and I want to snap at them. Gutless. I know in my heart she's right, none of them would have rushed in to help her. They would have let Rory rape her and then gossiped about it later.

"Avery, what—" Ash starts forward, his eyes haunted, and I glance over to see the white bandages over his sister's face. They look professionally applied, nothing like the amateur job I did with my scraps. Ash doesn't care about the accounts at all now that he's faced with his injured twin. It would be totally sweet, if he hadn't just been on the edge of ending my school career and my opportunity at a decent life.

"You would know if you had answered your phone, but you didn't, so now you can deal with the consequences. Lips, is mine."

Blaise's eyes dart between us, and my face begins to flush. Someday I will be able to handle his eyes on me, but clearly today is not that day.

"What the actual fuck?!" Harley sputters out, and I try not to laugh at the sound. I had never heard any of them sound unsure, and yet all three of the boys were gaping at us both.

"Okay, I get it. I should have answered. You don't need to take on trash just to get back at me, Floss," Ash says gently, aiming to placate her. His hands are outstretched toward her, like he wants to pull her in to him and hold her in the safety of his arms. My angry shield cracks a little at the sight.

Avery's eyes narrow when he uses her nickname, and instead of answering, she slips her arm fully into mine where everyone can see. I try not to flinch, because I know if I push her away now, it will only make things worse for me. She doesn't get the chance to destroy him, though, as the far door leading into the courtyard opens and Rory walks out.

Ash does a double take when he spots the scratches down his cheeks and the black eye. He looks back, and I watch as he takes inventory of all the marks on Avery, and then, as if an afterthought, the ones on me. I watch as everything clicks into place in his head. It's clear to everyone what has happened. Harley's face turns thunderous. Blaise's cool and unaffected mask finally drops, and his jaw clenches.

I watch as Ash's entire body begins to shake, the need to *break* and *smash* and *destroy* whoever has touched his sister so strong that the other students begin to back away slowly, and Blaise steps up to join him, his eyes dark swirling pits. Harley calls out to Rory, and when he turns fearful eyes on them, he signs his own death warrant. The guilt is written on every fiber of his being.

"Where did you get those from, dickhead?" Harley says, gesturing at the scratches. He has always hated Rory, but now his voice is dark and taunting. There is blood in the water and sharks are beginning to circle.

"We had a misunderstanding. It's not a big deal." Rory sounds arrogant, even with the quaking look on his face, and it makes me see red.

"I hope your broken ribs puncture your lungs and you drown in your own blood," I hiss at him. I would say more, but Avery starts tugging me away. She never did enjoy watching her brother mete out his physical punishments. I'm not sure if Rory will make it out alive.

"I told you, I don't want your protection," I murmur. I can't be too loud about it in case any of the students hear and it gets back to Ash.

"This isn't payment, it's a white flag. And an olive branch. I want to be your friend."

I stop dead in my tracks. I can hear screaming and yelling starting in the chapel, and I flinch. Memories of my time in the Game surface, and I shove them away. I don't have time to deal with my own issues right now.

"What?"

"I don't have friends either. I want one, and I want one

as fierce as you."

"You can't just—Blaise is your friend."

She shakes her head dismissively, and I roll my eyes at her. Had she not just seen their reactions to her injuries? I'd kill to have them defend me like that, to have my back and expect nothing but friendship in return.

"No, he's Ash's friend, and he both loves and respects me well enough, but he will always defer back to him. I want a real friend that's mine."

"You can't just claim me. I'm not property," I sputter, and my voice is louder than I intend on being. I glance around, but the halls have deserted. Everyone wants to watch Rory die. I kind of do, too. Mostly because there's something about watching justice being served that makes my dark heart sing. Plus, the boys were hot at the best of times. Watching their fists fly and beat Rory bloody? Um, yes, please. I just need a pair of earplugs to drown out the yelling, and I'm good to watch the whole damn thing.

Avery huffs and pulls me into the study den. There's a group of students packing up, and at her sharp look, they high-tail it out of there.

"I know you don't trust me, and I deserve that. I'm going to give you something as insurance, so we know we're both in this for the right reasons. That is, if you want a friend?"

I do. Desperately really, but how can I trust this girl

that looks like an angel but is really a crossroads demon, bargaining and making deals with mere mortals for their souls? She can be just as twisted as Joey; they are siblings, after all. I know in my heart she isn't a sociopath like him, but she could be just as ruthless. *She could survive the Wolf,* my mind whispers unbidden. She's probably the only girl I'd ever met who could.

"Why did Joey call a ceasefire?" she asks with a raised brow. It's a test, one last hurdle to leap before we can be friends. Could I do it? Could I take the leap?

"We have a… mutual acquaintance. Joey thought this person was under his thumb, but he was wrong. He was told that under no uncertain circumstances could he harm me again."

Avery leans forward and whispers in my ear, "The Jackal?" and I nod. A smile flits at the corners of her mouth.

She hands me an envelope. I open it and, after leafing through the papers for a second, I scrunch it up hurriedly. I'm holding the missing piece of the puzzle. I'm holding the records of the Beaumonts' mother's death. Alice Beaumont, nee Arbour, was murdered.

"Why the hell—"

"That's your insurance. It would destroy both me and my brother if that got out. I've spent years keeping that out of people's hands. Everything I do is to keep Ash and the boys safe. Everything I did to you was to keep us safe."

She doesn't look sorry at all, like my year of torture was reasonable. I don't know what to do with that, or with the envelope in my hand.

"I want a friend I can trust to have my back completely, and no girl has ever looked at me as anything other than competition or a way to get in with my brothers. You took everything I threw at you, and you're still here. Unbroken. Are you in, or not?"

God help me, but I was so in. My hands begin to shake.

"I don't want you to speak to them for me. The boys."

"Well, I don't want to speak to them at all, so you're safe there. I promise I won't tell them to be nice, but if we're friends, then I'm on your side from here out."

I bite my lip. I want this so bad, and the envelope in my hand makes me believe this is legit. I might regret it later, but I nod.

"Friends it is, then."

"*Best* friends. Now, how do you feel about helping me destroy Rory's entire existence for what he did to me? I'd love your input."

I smile and tuck the papers into my satchel. I can hear the sounds of teachers breaking up the beating, and Avery's eyes have that wicked glint in them. A shot of excitement shoots through my blood. This could be fun.

"I have a few ideas, actually."

"Let's just agree that from here on out, we only ever tell each other the truth. If we can't discuss something, then we come out and say so."

I'm sitting in Avery's room and watching while she packs. It took me three minutes to pack my entire room up, and Avery had moaned about how jealous she was I was finished. I was kind enough to point out that, she actually has the opportunity to own things, which is something I'm more than jealous of. It's utterly ridiculous how quickly we've fallen into a relaxed hang-out.

There are boxes everywhere, suitcases full of clothes, stacks of boxed-up shoes that are taller than we are, and still Avery is shoving random items into bubble wrap. I expected her to pay someone else to do this.

"I guess I can handle that," I say, shoving a fistful of popcorn into my mouth and flicking through her record collection. It's mostly classical music and scores from ballet recitals, but she also has every single Vanth Falling record, first editions and signed, and I'm trying not to tuck them under my arm and make a run for it. I put one on, and she cackles at me from the bathroom where she's trying to pack the equivalent of an entire Sephora store's worth of makeup and hair care products. Ash wasn't wrong; she has a lot of stuff.

Avery arches an eyebrow at me and grins, “I don’t expect you to tell me all of your secrets tonight. I was thinking while we’re on break, we can text each other one secret a day. When school starts again in the fall, we can do the same each morning. It’ll be a fun little bonding experience.”

I shrug in return as I tap my fingers along with the song. Some things can’t be sent digitally; texts and emails can be hacked. I’m sure I don’t have to explain this to her, and I guess it’s a way to ease into things. “I’m not sure you’ll ever know it all. There’s stuff I’ve done… I’m a dangerous person to be around. You need to know that from the get-go, so you can tap out now if you need to.”

She flops back on her bed dramatically. Her face is no longer the blank mask I’ve seen every day; it’s open, and a little vulnerable. “My cousin is a mobster’s son. My brother is a sociopathic murderer. My father is… my father is true evil. Whatever you have following you, we can sort out together, the same way I’ve worked at sorting everything out for Harley. I’m all in, Lips.”

I sigh and crawl up to sit on the bed beside her. Maybe we will get there. Maybe I’ll offer her the same protection as I’ve given Harley. Ugh, thinking about him makes my chest ache and leaves me with too many questions. Seeing as this is my first opportunity to get some answers, I ask her, “Where does Harley go during the summer break?”

It's Avery's turn to sigh. "He goes back to his grandfather's place for two weeks each year. It's part of a seedy deal the old crook cut with a dirty judge. Then he either stays with Blaise, touring or whatever, or I get him a hotel. He can't come to our house; my father would never allow it."

"Wouldn't he know you're helping him, though? Where else do you get your money?"

She laughs and pulls out a black nail polish from the box she was just packing, tugging my hand until I let her paint my nails.

"My mother and Harley's mom were twins; did you know that? Twins run pretty strongly in our family. They were heiresses themselves. If you trace our family line back far enough, you hit Russian royalty. My grandparents disowned Aunt Iris when she ran off with Éibhear O'Cronin; they were horrified their blue-blooded daughter had been seduced by the handsome degenerate." She fluttered her eyes and pretended to faint, and I giggle for probably the first time in my life. "So my mother was the sole heir. Now my father, the asshole, had a prenup to say that all finances were to stay separate, because her hundreds of millions were nothing compared to his billions. When my mother died, her will said the money was to be split and shared three ways."

"So you and your brothers each have a share of the

millions and no parental supervision on how you use it? Fuck, you are the luckiest kid in this school."

She grins and tips her head back. "My mother left her money to Ash, me… and Harley."

My jaw drops.

Avery grins and nods. "Best day of my life was seeing that murderer's face when he realized he was getting nothing."

"So then why doesn't Harley have the money?"

"His grandfather stole it. Sort of. His grandfather had custody of Harley when my mother died, so he had it put in trusts and bonds and offshore accounts, then told Harley he could have it the moment he swore in. He's using the money as leverage to get Harley to join the family business."

Liam O'Cronin is not the brightest man.

One of the very first lessons you're taught as a sponsored candidate for the Twelve is that loyalty can only be given freely. Yes, you can hire someone, but there's always the risk someone will offer them more money. You can torture and break someone, bend them to only serve you, but there are limits to what a broken person can do. Blackmailing Harley into the family would only succeed in letting a bomb tick in your organization.

Fucking dumb.

"Harley can't go to his grandfather's house anymore."

Avery looks up from where she's blowing on my nails

to dry them. "Oh? Is this part of your little agreement? His grandfather will kill him if he doesn't."

I don't want to talk about the mess I've made to protect Harley. I need some time and space to figure it out before I discuss it with her. Now that I know a little more about the situation, I can make a plan. So, instead I say, "He can't kill him. I've tied the old fuck's hands for the moment. Now that I have a little more information, I'll see what I can do about getting Harley out of there permanently."

Avery swallows, and her eyes grow glassy. "I started to come around to the idea of being friends when you started messing with Joey. No one, has even been brave enough to take him on. When Harley showed up with his mom's necklace and told me we were done messing with you, I knew you would fit in with us."

"I think Ash would disagree with you strongly there," I mumble. I'm still smarting over his dismissal of me and how easily he believed I was sleeping with Joey.

"Ash will get over his issues. He's angry with himself more than anything. He thinks he's responsible for taking care of me, and he's pissed that he failed."

I cock my head at her. "Are you pissed?"

She shakes her head with a little frown. "I'm only upset that he doesn't trust my judgement of you. He's hellbent on you being in league with Joey, and it's clouding his decisions."

I don't think he's upset. I think he's decided I'm evil, and I'm going to spend the rest of my time at Hannaford fielding both of Avery's brothers and their desires to get rid of me. At least Ash doesn't want to kill me. I groan, and Avery smiles ruefully.

I shake my head to clear it. "Back to Harley, I'll pay for a hotel for him for the entire summer break. He's my responsibility."

She raises her eyebrows at me with the shadow of a smile on her face. "The bill for the hotel he stays at comes in at seventy thousand dollars if he stays for the entire break. Then I give him a credit card with a fifty-thousand-dollar limit, and he uses that to cover food and boy stuff. He usually uses about ten grand of it. Do you have a spare eighty grand lying around to fund his summer holiday?"

"Fucking rich people. Who spends *seventy thousand dollars* on a hotel?!" I sputter.

Avery throws herself back on the bed and laughs so hard tears, stream down her face. I'm laughing too, but it's more of an angry sound. "I'd pay ten times that if he'd let me pick where he stays. The hotel is on the coast, right on a cliff, so he can be moody and watch the waves and mope. That's all these boys are good for, really."

I groan and grab my phone. This is my mess; I need to be the one to clean it up. "Does he have a bank account? Give me the details, and I'll transfer the cash across. I'll do eighty-five so he has a buffer. Fucking boys."

Avery's head snaps around so she's scowling at me. "You have money? You have enough money to pay for that?"

I let a smug little grin creep onto my face. "I do. I'm going to be working over summer break, so I'll just take an extra job to cover his break."

"Take an extra—*what the hell is happening right now*?"

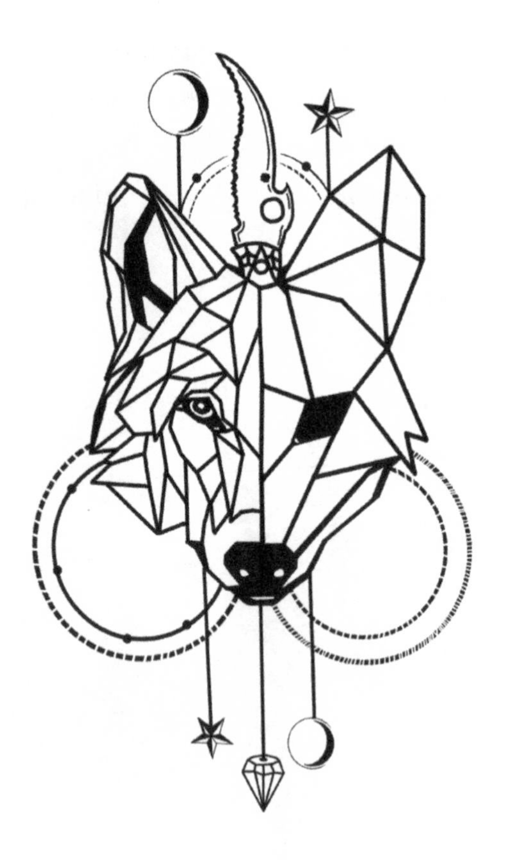

Thirty

I call a taxi to pick me up from Hannaford by 8 a.m. the next morning.

I'm the only student who doesn't have a car of their own or parents who send a chauffeur to collect them, but it's not at all surprising to me. What is surprising is that Avery helps to carry my pathetically small amount of belongings down to the school entrance. I carry the bag with the safe tucked in it.

We had spent two hours in her room last night getting to know each other. The switch from bully to best friend had flipped so suddenly and completely that I felt like I had whiplash. She is actually really funny, and smart too. Before I went to my own room for bed, she had put her number in my phone and made sure I could text her.

Now, standing together by the gate, we laugh about the shocked looks from the other students. "They should know by now that I do what I say I will. You should find next year much easier to tolerate."

I laugh, and she grins at me.

"Avery." Ash steps up beside us, and I flinch. I can't hear his voice without thinking of how he wanted to destroy my life. Avery stiffens, and then turns to him with sharp eyes.

"Please stop ignoring me. Whatever happened, I can help you fix it."

She laughs, and it sounds like the one she had always used with me; cruel and lacking in humor. "Lips fixed it and wanted nothing in return, so don't concern yourself."

"Floss—"

"Don't you *dare*."

She had told me last night about how much she loved Ash and how she had spent years fixing his entire life. She wouldn't be angry at him forever, but it would be a while before she got over him ignoring her call.

"I beat him for you. I'll fucking kill him, if that's what it takes to get you to stop looking at me like that."

My taxi rolls in. She shakes her head at Ash and walks up to drop my bags in the trunk. I move to follow her, and his hand shoots out to grab me.

"Whatever you've done to get her on your side, I will fucking end you for it. You think my brother is bad? You have no idea what I will do to you next year."

"Why don't you want her to have friends?"

The glare he leveled at me was so dark, a shiver ran up

my spine.

"She can have friends, just not Mounty trash," he sneers at me, his eyes icy blue.

And in that moment, I don't care if I am signing up for another year of hell. I give him my own dark glare.

"Fuck you." I pull my arm out of his grip, and I give Avery a quick hug before I drop into the taxi. Ash glares at me as Avery waves cheerfully, and then the taxi takes off down the driveway and out of the huge, ornate school gates. My grin is plastered to my face. I survived Hannaford, and I made a friend.

The ride back to Mounts Bay is over an hour, and I enjoy watching the scenery as it changes from the lush, sprawling, reticulated green to the urban coastal wasteland. It feels like coming home. I'm going back to where I belong, and where I'm running from, even if I do feel nostalgic looking at it all.

I'm lost in thought when my phone buzzes in my pocket.

Club party next week. Be there.

I roll my eyes, as the taxi stops outside the dingy apartment I rented for summer break. It's an absolute hole, but it was cheap and wouldn't be too much of a drain on my dwindling stash of cash. Originally, I'd planned to rent a tiny townhouse in a gated community that cost four times what this place does, but now that I have a pampered rich guy I have to fund, I am on a budget. I didn't tell Avery, but part of why I have to pay for Harley is to make my protection legitimate. If Matteo starts to look into his life and his financials, and he sees Harley being supported by someone else, he will kill him and tell me he was a snitch. I am just going to have to go to the Club party next week, like Matteo wants me to, and pick up some extra jobs.

My phone pings again. I smile down at Avery's text.

Ash is a nightmare, Harley is pouting, and Blaise is pleading with me to seek therapy. I'm going to enjoy taking these boys down a notch or two. I'll text you tomorrow x

I went against my better judgment to trust this girl, but I do not regret it.

And I can't wait for school to start back.

SIGN UP FOR MY NEWSLETTER TO HEAR ABOUT UPCOMING RELEASES

ALSO BY J BREE

The Bonds That Tie Series

Broken Bonds

Savage Bonds

Blood Bonds

Forced Bonds

Tragic Bonds

Unbroken Bonds

The Mortal Fates Series

Novellas

The Scepter

The Sword

The Helm

The Trilogy

The Crown of Oaths and Curses

The Throne of Blood and Honor

The Mounts Bay Saga

The Butcher Duet

The Butcher of the Bay: Part I

The Butcher of the Bay: Part II

Hannaford Prep

Just Drop Out: Hannaford Prep Year One

Make Your Move: Hannaford Prep Year Two

Play the Game: Hannaford Prep Year Three

To the End: Hannaford Prep Year Four

Make My Move: Alternate POV of Year Two

The Queen Crow Trilogy

All Hail

The Ruthless

Queen Crow

The Unseen MC

Angel Unseen

ABOUT J BREE

J Bree is a dreamer, writer, mother, and cat-wrangler. The order of priorities changes daily.

She lives on the coast of Western Australia in a city where it rains too much. She spends her days dreaming about all of her book boyfriends, listening to her partner moan about how the lawns are looking, and being a snack bitch to her three kids.

Visit her website at http://www.jbreeauthor.com to sign up for the newsletter or find her on social media through the links below.

Printed in the USA
CPSIA information can be obtained
at www.ICGtesting.com
LVHW091519011023
759827LV00043B/494